His Lovely Wife

His Lovely Wife

ELIZABETH DEWBERRY

Harcourt, Inc.

ORLANDO   AUSTIN   NEW YORK   SAN DIEGO   TORONTO   LONDON

With gratitude and affection for Emma Sweeney and Ann Patty.

www.HarcourtBooks.com

Library of Congress Cataloging-in-Publication Data
Dewberry, Elizabeth.
His lovely wife/Elizabeth Dewberry.—1st ed.
p.   cm.
1. Diana, Princess of Wales, 1961—Death and burial—Fiction.
2. Americans—France—Fiction.   3. Beauty, Personal—Fiction.
4. Paris (France)—Fiction.   5. Married women—Fiction.
6. Photographers—Fiction.   I. Title.
PS3572.A936H57   2006
813'.54—dc22   2005020985
ISBN-13: 978-0-15-101221-3   ISBN-10: 0-15-101221-0

Text set in Garamond MT
Designed by Cathy Riggs

Printed in the United States of America
First edition

A C E G I K J H F D B

*This is a work of fiction. Names, characters, places, organizations, and events are
the products of the author's imagination or are used fictitiously for verisimilitude.*

FOR ROBERT OLEN BUTLER

*P*RINCESS DIANA WAS DECLARED DEAD AT FOUR A.M., about an hour ago, but I don't know that yet. I can't sleep, so I've just put on my jogging clothes and slipped out of my room at the Paris Ritz, where I'm staying with my husband. He's attending a meeting of physicists about black holes and the chaotic order of the universe, and I'm here mostly to shop. Or so I think.

I also think Diana's staying here with her boyfriend and I'm passing their suite. Actually, I'm stopped in front of it. The bodyguard is gone — off duty, I assume — and I don't want to warm up outside the hotel where I'm expecting two or three hundred paparazzi to be waiting for her as they were yesterday, so I'm standing in front of her double doors, but discreetly separated from them by several feet, and I'm pulling first one arm across my chest, then the other, when I notice there's no newspaper hanging in a little white plastic bag from her gilded door handles, as there is on ours.

I tell myself, —She must be up already, reading her paper.

I clasp my hands behind my back, slowly bend forward, and wait, perfectly still, stretching my arms and my legs and straining my sense of hearing. The walls are surprisingly thin here, but there's not a sound coming from the room, not the turning of a newspaper page, the murmur of a television newscast, no early-morning lovemaking. So I assume one of them woke up, got out of bed, grabbed the paper, read the headlines, then went back to sleep.

I straighten up, feeling slightly ashamed of myself. Wanting to hear them watch TV was borderline all right, but hoping to listen to them make love is going too far. So I leave.

Just before I get to the revolving door in the lobby, I slip on a pair of sunglasses and put on a baseball cap, pulling my ponytail through the hole in the back. I'm thinking that maybe in the dark, with the cap and the sunglasses and photographers who've waited up all night to see Diana, I have a shot at being briefly mistaken for her. It happened yesterday, but at the time, I didn't understand what was going on—I felt like I was under attack—so I want to do it again. It's a fantasy, a harmless fantasy for a Buckhead housewife on vacation in Paris.

But I walk out into silence—not a single photographer is here—and I feel as if I'm the one who's being stood up.

I shrug it off, though, and go down to the rue de Rivoli and cross the place de la Concorde. I turn right at the river, where I run along the cours de la Reine, which I'm trying to remember how to translate: —The heart of the queen? Hearts of the queen? The queen's corpse?

—Surely not.

After a mile or two, I come to a street that's closed to motor traffic, though people are stepping over the barricades, walking down the middle of the road toward the entrance to a tunnel, where a small crowd is gathered. The sun isn't up yet, but the tunnel—the pont de l'Alma underpass, actually—is brightly, almost blindingly lit, and so many cameras are pointed at it that the thought crosses my mind that I've wandered onto a movie set. But there's no director, nobody yelling, Action! or,

Quiet. There's no noise to quiet—no traffic or bustle, no human voices. And the sadness in the people I might have taken to be extras feels all too real.

I cross the barricade and move closer to find out what they're looking at: a huge black Mercedes that's been crumpled like a wad of paper.

I stand for several minutes with a group of strangers, watching the car being hoisted onto the back of a truck. There are no bodies, no ambulances, but it's obvious that someone has died. Some people are taking pictures, but none of us is saying a word. Everybody's barely breathing except for one woman in a sari who starts weeping and can't stop.

The flashes from the cameras keep hitting the car and screaming off, and the air is full of a scent that's not exactly oil or smoke or wet pavement or muddy water or human sweat or the smell of your own skin after you've wept, but some combination of all that and something else, something earthy and otherworldly and sorrowful, and I hear a distant sound like musical voices echoing inside a metallic cave, and I feel a tearing in me, a memory starting to rip open: my mother's gold station wagon with the fake wood paneling on the sides and sleek chrome luggage rack on top, and the last time I saw my father, he was tying my little blue and white vinyl suitcase to the roof with a rope, and the last time I saw the car, in the dark, through the cracks between my mother's fingers, it looked black, not gold, and it was not a car. I thought it should have been making a noise, a hiss, a steely scream—somebody should have been screaming—but the only sound I could hear was crickets, crying in the night. I didn't know what had happened—I still don't remember the crash—and I tried to tell myself the car had exploded like in a cartoon and my father had been ejected and he'd gone for help, he would come back with a little X-shaped bandage on his forehead and save the day. Though another part of me knew he was still in the car, and he was dying, or dead.

My mother, a former Miss Alabama with a singing ventriloquist act, had been performing at a church in Mobile, after which we'd gone to the beach for a day, and on our way home, late on a starless, moonless night, we'd hit a black bull in the middle of a black country road, and I found myself sitting in the dirt next to the car, hearing my mother call my name. The stuff in my suitcase—books and bathing suits and sundresses—was scattered over the road like so much garbage. My mother held Katie, her dummy, under one arm, and when she found me, she took my hand in her other hand, and I stood up. I didn't ask about my father and she didn't say anything about him, and we left our footprints on my things as we walked away from the car and into the black of the night. We never spoke directly of the accident again.

And thirty years later, in Paris, I'm trying to put my father's violent death out of my mind—I don't think of him that often—as I linger a few more minutes in front of the remains of someone else's crash. Part of me wishes I could call my mother now, but what would we say?

—Hi, Mother, how are you?

—Fine.

—Good . . . I'm fine, too.

And then what?

I can't get myself to imagine her saying, Ellen! or, How nice to hear from you!

But she'd have to say something. She wouldn't hang up on me.

Maybe, —I thought you'd dropped off the face of the planet.

I wouldn't point out that I could have come to the same conclusion about her. I'd just say, —No, I'm still hanging on.

A man in a bright blue jumpsuit quietly sweeps up the last of the broken glass. Then a few other men in jumpsuits turn off the floodlights and take them away while another, almost imperceptible odor begins to fade — a combination of sulfur and silver and the way paper smells after whatever was written on it has been erased. I think we would stand here longer, gazing at the empty space where the car was, but men in uniforms are quietly asking people to move off the street.

The woman in the sari is moving in the general direction of the drift of people toward the huge fake flame on the plaza above the underpass, a life-sized replica of the flame on the Statue of Liberty, and I'm following her. I'm debating whether to try to comfort her or give her some privacy when she crosses a side street ahead of me while the WALK signal — a green man with one foot extended in front of him — blinks. Then he changes to red, feet together, and I stop at the curb and she disappears into the crowd.

So I'm just waiting to cross the same side street, not headed anywhere in particular, when I hear a cell phone ring and turn to see whose it is and I look at the man standing next to me and he looks at me. He seems familiar, though I can't place him instantly. He sort of nods at me, though whether it's because he recognizes me or he's apologizing for the loud ring, which seems disrespectful under the circumstances, I can't say. Then he pulls back from the curb and speaks softly into the phone: "Oui?" His voice is familiar, too. He's standing behind me now, so I can't see his face, but I listen.

He says, "Yes, I'm here," in English, and his accent is American and I think I remember where I've seen him before, and he says with some irritation in his voice, "No, there's nothing left for me to photograph now, anyway, just a bunch of rubbernecks," and I know where I saw him. Then he says, quietly but with some disgust in his voice, "Right," and then, even more quietly, almost a whisper, "Go fuck yourself."

And the WALK signal comes on again and we cross the street and I move slowly until he catches up with me and now we're walking side by side toward the flame. Maybe somewhere in my unconscious, I'm already starting to put things together—the missing newspaper, the silence in Diana's room, the lack of paparazzi at the hotel and the abundance of them here—and I don't want to know it. But for whatever reason, I'm not going to ask him who died. I tell myself that's because I think he's assumed I already know and I'm grieving, as he is, or at least paying my respects, when what I was actually doing there at the tunnel, I have to admit, was more like rubbernecking. I tell myself I probably won't recognize the name when I do hear it, assuming the person is French. I try to convince myself that this odd feeling I've got in my stomach is about him, an intuition that being Americans in Paris in this particular spot at this particular time of this particular day means we have something important in common. Which will turn out to be true, though not in any way I'm imagining right now.

I'm trying to decide whether to say anything at all to him.

—Hey, remember me? You took my picture yesterday in front of the Ritz?

—Oh. Yeah.

—So . . . how're you doing?

—Fine.

Probably not.

Yesterday morning, Lawrence and I hired a car through the concierge — a huge black Mercedes, as it turned out — and when we left the hotel, the whole place Vendôme, the granite-paved square in front of the Ritz, sat quiet, almost deserted in the sun. But by the time we came back that afternoon, it looked like a street fair: hundreds of cameramen, some of them on little scooters that were practically toys, some on motorcycles, revving their engines, some in cars so small they could have been driven by clowns, but most of them on foot, and they'd been forced, squirming, onto the sidewalk by Ritz security guards, a long line two- and three-cameramen deep with the ones in front crouching so the ones in back could get a shot. They were waiting there the way people wait for parades in New Orleans during Mardi Gras, everybody wanting something, wanting it with their bodies the way it feels to want sex, and everybody feeling generous and pink and just a little giddy because they think they're about to get what they want. But as soon as our car with its slightly tinted windows slowed down near the hotel entrance, something shifted to red, like when sex play goes too far and desire becomes demand and your heart races on in front of you while your head says, Stop. Only there *is* no stopping. They spilled into the street and closed in a circle around us, aiming their cameras at our faces and flashing their lights before they knew who we were — or, weren't — and yelling, "Lay Dee Dee Lay Dee Dee Lay Dee Dee."

I had no idea who that was. As far as I knew, Princess Diana was still in the South of France. I'd seen pictures of her vacationing there in the British tabloids earlier that day. So I assumed Lay Dee Dee was a French celebrity, a rock star, maybe.

We didn't get out of the car right away—we couldn't—and they kept yelling, "Lay Dee Dee Lay Dee Dee," almost like a chant, chanting and growing louder.

I said, "What's going on?"

I had to scream to be heard, and Lawrence screamed back, "I don't know," and the driver rolled down his window and the noise from outside grew louder and our driver yelled at them all, louder still, and the camera lights kept flashing, pulsing, the lenses moving in closer, closing in.

Lawrence was trying to figure out how much to tip the driver, which gave them time to crush in closer—two hundred desperate men with cameras, jostling each other and pressing so tight I couldn't open the door of the car.

"Qu'est-ce que c'est?" Lawrence said to the driver as the cameras kept clicking, the men kept yelling, "Lay Dee Dee."

"Ai yi yi," the driver said. "C'est fou."

Then one of them tripped or was pushed and he fell and he lunged so hard into the window next to my face, I was afraid the glass would shatter, I covered my eyes, and the car lurched under his weight.

"It's *what?*" I said.

"C'est *fou,*" the driver said again, louder. "C'est . . ." He pointed to his ear and made three little circles with his finger.

"Crazy?" I said. I was starting to feel dizzy.

"Yes, crazy. My English is not so good. I do not know what happens."

"Well, thank you," I said at the top of my voice. "This is crazy. That's very helpful."

Lawrence touched my hand, patted it.

A camera hit the car with a loud crack, and our driver yelled, really mad now, and stuck his hand out of the window and half shoved, half punched a photographer and opened his door hard, knocking another cameraman off balance, and the security guards were ordering the men out of our way, everyone talking too loud and too fast, and the cameras kept clicking and flashing.

"We're trapped," I said. I could feel my heart flashing.

"No we're not," Lawrence said. "Don't panic." He was rubbing my arm to calm me down, which just irritated me.

"We can't get out of the car, Larry. That's the definition of trapped." I was sweating.

"Take a deep breath, Ellen. Wait."

And before I had time to tell him it wasn't going to work to try to calm me down by telling me that we weren't trapped when a blind man could see that we were, we weren't.

My door opened and a uniformed bellman offered me his arm and I grabbed on to it and let him pull me out of the car as if into a raging current, though as soon as I stepped into the crowd, the roiling stopped.

It was that sudden, like when you put whatever you're trying to cook into a pot of boiling water and the boiling stops. They saw I wasn't who they'd expected, or most of them did—some in the back couldn't see at all, they were still holding their cameras up over their heads, clicking away—but as soon as the ones in front saw me, they stopped. They stopped yelling, they stopped shoving, crushing. Their cameras stopped clicking. Then they lowered their cameras from their faces, as if they were taking off masks.

I took a breath.

The little piece of street theater where they'd played cyclopses with pulsing black lenses for eyes was over, as quickly and unexpectedly as it had begun, but my heart was still racing.

My face was so hot it was throbbing. I wanted to move past them into the hotel, away from the heat and the press and the old-sweat smell of them, and I was trying to think how to excuse myself in French, a language I studied for two and a half years in college and which I hadn't understood one word of in all the yelling, but I was still so rattled, I couldn't even think of excusez-moi.

"I'm sorry," I said, feeling embarrassed, which I always do after an attack of claustrophobia—and this was not a full-blown attack, but the symptoms were there, the angry light-headedness, the certainty that I'm making things worse than they are by panicking but that I can't stop, which just makes me panic more.

One of them—the dark-haired photographer standing beside me, the same man I would see the next morning at the crash—offered his hand and said, "No, *we're* sorry," and a hush fell over the crowd and landed on me.

I'd been in France less than twelve hours—we'd flown all night and arrived that morning—and I was already homesick for the English language, and he spoke English with an American accent. I liked him for that. And I believed him, that he was sorry, and I liked him for that, too.

He had a fresh cut over his left eyebrow, a small one, as if his camera had been knocked into his forehead during the scuffle.

"It's okay," I said, and he offered his hand and I took it. I was starting to calm down. The thought crossed my mind that he might kiss my fingers, which I didn't want him to do, and he didn't, and I liked him for that as well. He did hold on to me for just a second longer than absolutely necessary, and to my surprise, I liked that, too.

I said, "Your head," and I slid my hand out of his and touched my right eyebrow, as if I were his mirror image, and he touched his right brow, and I said, "No," and I took his hand and moved it to the other side of his face, and then he had a drop of blood on his finger, and I pulled my hand away. He looked at the blood and shrugged.

And then, feeling awkward—awkward for having apologized for no reason, awkward for the cut on his face, which was not my fault but which wouldn't have happened if I hadn't been there, and awkward for being the center of attention for reasons that had nothing to do with me—and trying to come up with an explanation for why I'd said I was sorry in the first place, I said, "I'm sorry I'm not Lay Dee Dee."

The American photographer—his name was Max Kafka, though at the time I thought of him simply as the American— was wiping his hand on his pants. Another photographer said in a French accent, "You will do in a pinch, beautiful lady," and took my picture again. They all laughed. All the tension had vanished now, at least all of theirs, and I tried to smile. Several more of them took my picture, their cameras clicking like applause. They'd already begun to move back, a parting sea, leaving a red-carpeted path between me and the hotel entrance, and as I walked up the stairs on the arm of my bellman, every move we made was accompanied by the clicks and slides of the camera shutters.

I turned to shake Max's hand again, to tell him good-bye, but the security men weren't letting the photographers that close to the door, so I waved and said, "Thank you"—I did feel grateful to him, though I couldn't have said exactly what for—and he smiled and took my picture.

Several of them were still taking my picture. Maybe they

were just bored, or maybe every man who was photographing me—and they were all men—was doing it because he figured the other photographers knew who I was and that I was worth photographing. But the attention felt different now, like the difference between being elbowed by a stranger and being bumped accidentally by a man you know, but not well, and you say, I'm sorry, as if you didn't mean for it to happen, which you didn't, and he touches your arm and says, Are you okay? as if he did. You're fine, you tell him, looking him in the eye. And he smiles as if he's thinking that yes, you *are* fine, and you re-alize he's still touching your arm, and you don't pull away.

Later, when you look back on the moment, you smile to yourself and think, —Nothing happened.

Which is only partly true.

When I got to the revolving door, before I went in, I turned around and waited for Lawrence, who was a few steps behind me. He was carrying my packages—I'd bought a new dress and a pair of shoes to wear to dinner—and I'd forgot-ten all about the clothes, not to mention him.

Lawrence could light up a room full of physicists, turn every head just by walking in the door, but anywhere else, he was not a man people noticed—thinning brown hair, brown eyes, slightly tall, average weight for his height—and the pho-tographers were completely ignoring him.

I thought, —This is crazy. He's the Nobel laureate. If they had any idea who either of us was, they'd be photographing him. Or neither of us.

I waved at them, and they waved and cried out good-byes in English, and I said, "Au revoir," and smiled for the cameras. Then we went into the lobby, the click-slides still ringing in my ears.

When I got inside, away from the paparazzi, I asked my bellman, "Why are they out there?"

He said, very quietly, sort of patiently, as if it should have been obvious to me by now, "Lay Dee Dee." He said it in the same cadence that we say lah de dah.

I said, "Who's Lay Dee Dee?"

He said, even more quietly, "The princess."

"Lady *Di?*" I said, now finding myself whispering with him and suddenly aware of how American my accent was. "Princess Diana is here?" I said, pointing at the floor, my voice barely audible.

"No. She is coming."

"Wow."

"Yes," he said, with a little smile. And then, in an American accent, either agreeing with me or slightly mocking me or both, "Wow."

AND THE NEXT MORNING, I FIND MYSELF WALKING ACROSS the place de l'Alma with the same photographer from yesterday, only he doesn't have his camera with him, and he looks like he hasn't slept or showered or changed clothes.

"Are you all right?" I say.

He looks at me as if he's not sure I'm talking to him.

I say, "You okay?"

"It's so sad and so . . . I can't think of the word," he says, shaking his head. His voice is softer than it was yesterday. Softer and heavier at the same time. He hasn't shaved, and he still hasn't put a bandage on his forehead. He's developed just a little bit of a bruise there. He says, "It shouldn't have happened." Then he whispers something in French I don't understand, something angry.

I want to talk to him, comfort him, but I don't know what to say. He's obviously deeply moved by this death, but there's something about the way he's reacting to it—alone but in public, saying it shouldn't have happened instead of asking why it did—that gives me a feeling he hasn't lost someone he knew intimately and loved, which would have its own set of, granted, inane condolences—I'm sorry for your loss—but I can't think of anything to say about a famous dead person without knowing who it is, and asking where his camera is, why he didn't film the towing like all the other photographers, which I am curious about, feels like the Ugly American way of looking at death—why weren't you trying to profit?—though again, I wouldn't mean it that way. I'd only mean, What's wrong?

I say, "Yes, it's sad."

"And my colleagues—my *friends*—have been arrested," he says. "I can't find out anything. This country . . ." He shakes his head again, almost as if he's trying to erase a memory. "It's all screwed up. It's chaos."

We seem to have moved from the crash to another sort of chaos: His friends have been arrested, but they couldn't have been in the car. To put it bluntly, I'm pretty certain that whoever was in that Mercedes hasn't been arrested because they're dead. And even if another car was involved and was towed already, surely the people in it, if they survived, would have been hurt and hospitalized, and that's what he'd be worried about.

I think, —But you never know. I walked away from the crash that killed my father.

—You walked away and left him there to die.

A therapist once called the voice in my head that criticizes everything I do my internalized mother, a different thing from my real mother and my memory mother. We worked for a few

months on building an imaginary soundproof vault to lock
them all up in and on my fear of getting locked in there with
them, all of us screaming our hearts out and nobody being able
to hear us, but then my insurance ran out.

I say to the voice in my head, —Don't do this.

—He wouldn't have been on the trip in the first place . . .

—That is not how it was.

— . . . if it hadn't been for you.

—It was not my fault.

—It wasn't *his* fault.

—Okay, it was my mother's fault.

—Right, take the easy way out. Blame it on Mom.

—Fine, it wasn't anybody's fault. It was an accident—
that's the definition of accident.

—There are no accidents.

—Stop this. Stop it, stop it, stop it.

I feel an old sadness creeping up in me, clawing inside my
chest, which I try to ignore.

I make myself stop and focus on what's here and now: a
totaled car, cops and photographers everywhere, a distraught
American whose friends have been arrested.

I'd like to ask him how he and all the other photographers
knew to be here at five o'clock in the morning—I want to
have a long conversation with him where he tells me all kinds
of things I don't know—but I have a feeling he's a very private person, used to hiding behind a camera, and I'm afraid
anything I might say at this point would make him realize he's
already revealed more than he meant to and leave.

We pass a small, slightly nerdy-looking man with wire-
rimmed glasses, receding dark blond hair, and a large camera
bag who nods almost imperceptibly at us—at him—and he

doesn't nod back. Then the American says, under his breath, "Good morning, you son of a bitch," and a flash from somewhere else goes off in our eyes, and he says, louder, "These photographers, they're all vultures."

I feel a stopping in me: A white space opens up in my chest like what happens in front of your eyes after a flash goes off.

—Pull yourself together, Ellen. He's upset because his friends are in trouble and he can't do anything to help them and he wishes the photographers would be more respectful because he's a decent human being and somebody is dead.

We walk a few steps without saying anything.

I'm thinking about touching him—his arm, or maybe his shoulder. I want to—I've always been attracted to sadness in men—but I don't.

He has thick, messy brown hair with just a touch of gray in it and dark brown eyes. He's just under six feet tall, maybe a little thin, a pleasant face. Something's pulling me to him, but it's not his looks. He reminds me, in a way, of a stray cat. I want to rescue him, stroke his back, but I'm afraid if I try, he'll run away.

Except there's more to it than that: I don't just want to touch him. I want him to touch me. And call it pheromones or intuition or wishful thinking, but I think he wants to.

We keep walking, and his shoulder brushes against mine once and then twice, and now I know he wants to.

—This is not, I assure myself, about sex. It's simpler and stronger and sweeter than that. It's about two people wanting to connect, two strangers in a foreign country, each having been reminded of their own mortality, yearning to feel safe in a dangerous world, and wanting not to feel so completely alone in the universe.

—In other words, it's about sex.

I put my hands in my pockets.

When we get to the flame, we stop. Six or eight bouquets have been placed around it, roses and wildflowers mostly, apparently from people's own gardens—it's too early for flower shops to be open—and somebody's left a playing card, the Queen of Hearts, which doesn't instantly translate for me.

He kneels and places a small picture at the base of the flame.

I'm standing and the sun isn't up yet and I'm not wearing my contacts and it's a full-length shot: I can't make out who it is. I could bend over to see the picture, but I don't. I'm still more interested in not letting him think I'm a voyeur than in finding out right away who the dead person is.

After a minute, he stands up and looks at me as if he wants to say something, so I wait, listening. I'm looking at his face, which is more than pleasant. He has a sharply defined jawline and high cheekbones and clear, tanned skin. He's about my age, maybe a little older. He's not macho-looking. He has a very gentle quality to him, especially through the eyes, which are big and clear and the color of Godiva Chocolate liqueur. They're full of old sorrow but framed by deep laugh lines. Something about his build and the muscle-tone of his neck makes me wonder if he likes to run long distance, or sail.

I think, —I'll ask him about that, later.

I think we have all the time in the world. I think eventually, I'll ask him about that and what he's doing in France, whether he's on vacation or working here temporarily or living here as an expatriate and whether he's a professional photographer—a journalist or maybe an artist—or something that has nothing to do with photography. And I'll ask why he was at the Ritz yesterday—on a lark or as a favor for a friend or maybe he's researching a book about fame or the media or a biography of Diana. I'm pretty sure he isn't really a paparazzo.

But then he would say, —And what do you do?

And I don't know how I would answer. I could say charity work—I'm in charge of the silent auction at an annual gala that benefits the Atlanta Symphony Orchestra, I sit on the board of a local theater called Horizon, I volunteer at a coalition to eradicate world hunger—but I don't put that many hours into any of them, and the idea of telling anybody that what I do with my life is work to support the arts and end hunger strikes me as desperate and sort of former-beauty-queenish, though I never even won a local pageant. I could say I'm raising my husband's son, but I don't want to talk about Alec, who's more or less grown up now, anyway, or our relationship, which has devolved into a mutual suspicion society. He's in college, and when he comes home, I try to stay out of the way of his moods and mind my own business when he and Lawrence discuss money. So no, I won't mention Alec.

I think about laughing and saying, —Oh, I don't do anything, I'm a trophy wife.

Then watch how he reacts.

Or not. For that matter, I'm in France, and I'll never see him again: I could tell him I'm a caterer, a horticulturist, a therapist, a decorator, a painter, a children's-book author—all careers I considered at some point or another, if only briefly.

I'm pretty sure I don't want to have that conversation, though I'm vaguely curious to find out what I'd say if we did.

But then he averts his eyes, whispers, "Au revoir," and turns to leave.

I watch him walk halfway across the bridge over the river

and stop. I think I'm waiting for him. I really think we've connected in some meaningful way, and I'm certain he's going to
come back.

Then he lights a cigarette while looking out over the water
and keeps going.

Part of me wants to follow him, catch up with him, but I
don't know his name, so how would I get his attention without sprinting across the bridge, yelling, Wait! or Hey! But we
didn't even say hello before we said good-bye—I didn't even
say good-bye—and I feel like I have to fix that. I want to talk
to him, despite the fact that he didn't really seem to want to
talk, but I could ask him to have coffee. I don't have any
money with me, though, and I don't want to ask him to buy,
although I could use some coffee and it wouldn't cost him that
much. I also don't want to look like a flirt, even though two
adults having coffee together after just having seen the place
where somebody died is hardly flirting. Mostly, I don't want to
miss my chance, though I also don't want to look like the
pushy American.

—And miss your chance for what? What are you thinking,
anyway?

—Nothing. This is not a thing I do, go off alone with a
man I don't know. I don't even do it with men I know well.

—And obviously, you didn't do it now, either.

—No, but I didn't make the whole thing up. Something
happened.

—Nothing happened.

I'm arguing with myself when he disappears.

I look around. Nobody's looking at me. I could be invisible. Nobody's looking at anybody.

Then I kneel to look at the picture he left. It is, of course,

Diana, but that's not the thought that goes through my head. Nothing goes through my head: My mind completely shuts down. I stare at the picture for I don't know how long, and not one thought moves through me, not one feeling.

After a while, a few seconds, a few minutes, maybe, I think, very slowly, —No.

Then nothing.

Then, —Princess Diana?

Pause.

—No.

Long, gaping pause.

Then, —That's Princess Diana.

Her arm is lifted as if in a wave.

My brain seems to have taken a break, given itself one more moment of status quo before it has to process the next piece of information: I am looking at a photograph of Princess Diana, which was placed on this makeshift memorial near the site of a fatal crash.

Then I notice the Queen of Hearts again, and it suddenly makes its own terrible sense.

And then, in a rush, —Is all this about Princess Diana, is Princess Diana the person who's dead?

—No, she can't be, she's back in the hotel, sleeping, I passed her suite.

—Wait. So there was no bodyguard, no newspaper, no noise, and no paparazzi because she's dead?

—This is not right. That is not logical.

—When did she even have time to die?

We saw the bodyguard sitting outside her suite last night when we went to our room around midnight, and I have no idea how long it takes to clear an accident in France, but this is five o'clock in the morning and I didn't see an ambulance or even hear a fading siren on my way here.

I feel something shift: The tunnel underneath me opens to traffic, and several cars speed through and out the other side. Everything is suddenly louder and brighter, crasser. The air starts moving—the early-morning fog is beginning to dissipate. It feels somehow emptier, thinner, dirtier.

Nothing feels true.

I saw her, in person, at dinner last night—just a few hours ago. Very much alive. I could describe what she was wearing. I had imagined telling my friends, who would have wanted to know: skinny white jeans, a tailored black linen jacket over a simple black top, gold earrings, pearl bracelet, black pointy-toed stiletto-heeled slingbacks. And after dinner, after a nightcap in the bar, Lawrence and I passed her suite on our way back to our room, nodded to the bodyguard—we recognized him from dinner—sitting outside it, and when we got out of voice range of the bodyguard, we wondered aloud to each other whether she and her boyfriend were in there making love, joked about it and a play we'd once seen in London called *No Sex, Please, We're British,* except we changed it to *More Sex, Please, We're Royal*—when somehow, all along, they'd been out here crashing their Mercedes into a tunnel?

—No. I saw that car. I looked carefully at it, and I didn't see a single drop of blood.

—My God, if that car is from the Ritz, I probably rode in it yesterday.

—This is all wrong.

—Except it's not. Something about it already feels inevitable. Of course she died young and violently. How else could the fairy-tale-gone-bad have ended? You either live happily ever after or ... What is it that happens to the other people, the stepmothers and stepsisters and wolves and witches? They get pushed into ovens or hacked up by hunters or cast into fiery pits. Once you find yourself in a fairy tale, you either live happily ever after or you die.

—Which is why—part of why—it's such a shock: It's not a story. She was real.

I put my hand flat on the concrete ground, press my fingers there, then my palm, then look away.

In the distance, the Eiffel Tower is lit up against the early-morning sky. Halfway up, they're counting down in lights the days left in the century. It reminds me of the millennium clock that hangs on the front wall of the post office in Buckhead— home—counting down the seconds and tenths of seconds and hundredths of seconds, which are passing in a blur, faster than you can see, and I feel the same way now that I do every time I go in to buy stamps: slightly panicky, as if there's something important I'm supposed to do before the time runs out, but I'm not ready, I don't even know what it is, though if I don't start doing it soon, there won't be enough time left to finish it when I do think of it.

I think, —Everything is rushing to an end: the summer, the century, the millennium, the stars Lawrence studies, Diana. Something in me I can't articulate. My marriage.

I hear traffic noises: whooshing, rushing on every side of me, even underneath me.

It's not hot, but I'm sweating. I suddenly feel deathly calm.

Then I think, —No, not my marriage. Lawrence is a good man. I'm proud of him. I'm not a trophy wife—that's not how he sees me—and if other people sometimes treat me that way, which they do and which I'm hypersensitive about, as

Lawrence reminds me every time it happens, it's only because I'm younger than he is and he's successful, neither of which I would change if I could.

—Don't get carried away, Ellen. Your marriage is fine. This is not about Lawrence. It's just you.

I pick up the picture for a closer look: It *is* Diana, but she isn't waving. She's giving the photographer the finger.

My heart jumps in my chest, and I almost burst out laughing, but I stop myself, and what comes out sounds more like a sob, and I hear, *My mother couldn't understand how frustrating it was.*

I hear the words, very clearly, in my head, but the voice doesn't feel like my internalized mother or my memory mother, like objectified parts of myself, articulating my own suppressed thoughts and fears. And it's not whatever crazy people hear when they hear voices. I'm not crazy.

Just smile for the bloody camera, she'd say, and that's what I did for years.

It's more like the way you hear a song playing in your mind, where you know it's coming from inside you—you know nobody else can hear it—but it also has its own reality. You didn't choose it, you're not making it up, and sometimes, you can't get it to stop even if you want to. It feels like it has that kind of life and identity of its own. Though of course, it isn't a song, isn't a reconstituted memory of something I've heard before.

Look at me in the papers. I'm always smiling.

It's Princess Diana, complete with British accent.

I have no idea what her voice is doing in my head.

But they made my life hell.

I think I'd heard her say that—the last part—at some point.

Chasing me down the street, yelling, "Why don't you act like a fucking princess?" and I'd think, "Why don't you treat *me like one?"*

I look at the picture of her again, closer. She's standing on a sidewalk in her workout clothes—gray biker shorts, a black sweatshirt, a baseball cap, slouchy socks, running shoes—giving the photographer the finger. Giving anybody who looks at the photograph the finger. Giving *me* the finger.

And she's back: *People were always taking pictures of me, but every photo was taken because I was the Princess of Wales, not because I was Diana. Everywhere I went, I went because I was married to Prince Charles, people reacted to me because of that. But I knew I'd taken on a role, and I didn't want to let anyone down, so every morning I'd go through the papers and study the pictures, trying to figure out who this Princess of Wales was. When the media praised her for being something I wasn't, I tried to become that, and when they criticized her for not being what I thought I was: self-doubt all over the place.*

So your whole life became a pose because you're always being photographed. I got to where I barely knew the difference anymore between feeling a moment of real joy and doing a happy snap for the camera. I was the most photographed woman in the world, but ninety-nine percent of those images are lies.

Except the one in your hand: That was true. I quite like that photo, actually, because I wasn't posing in the sense of trying to look however I thought I was meant to look. I was doing and looking exactly what I felt. I even like that photographer. I was fed up, but it wasn't him I was fed up with. He just happened to be there. So I gestured to one photographer in particular, very aware I was being unprincesslike, and he stopped snapping because he knew he couldn't sell this, it was not the picture people wanted to see. But I stood there by the car for a whole minute, maybe two, and there was one photographer—this one—who hadn't been yelling at me before, and then he smiled as if he got the joke, and

he snapped me in that pose, kept doing pictures until he was out of film.
It was as if he'd let me say my piece, which is a big part of finding your
peace.

To the extent that things are beginning to sort themselves out at all,
it's along those lines. Not what was good or bad, acceptable or unaccept-
able. Just what was true.

Then she stops, and I feel several quick, dull thuds in my
chest and then another and another and another, footsteps
running, then walking, slowing down. Then they stop.

I wait, listening.

I'm just a little dizzy, the kind of dark-cloud dizziness that
makes you feel like you could disappear.

I think, —That was Princess Diana.

I make myself take a deep breath.

I think, —Diana?

I'm questioning myself, but also calling out to her, and
though I can't identify anything other than the voice in my
head that made me feel like she was there, before, I suddenly
feel quite sure she's gone now.

It's warm, but I feel a slight chill.

Still, I wait for more.

I look around. I don't believe in ghosts. Or, to the extent
that I believe in them, I certainly don't believe that of all the
people she could haunt, Princess Diana would choose me. I
couldn't get my own father to haunt me, and I tried. For three
years while I was in college, I did ouija boards and séances and
spent several hundred dollars I couldn't afford to waste on
mediums and psychics. Never heard a word from him. Though
apparently I do have an aunt named Helen or possibly Helene
or Helga who died as a baby in the nineteenth century, and
now, for whatever reason, she watches over me. I gave that

psychic a ten-dollar tip for originality. Then I stopped going to psychics.

There's a wall behind the flame, a ledge about waist high, and I stand up and walk over to it and press the small of my back against it. I look at my knees, my shins, my socks, my running shoes, at the concrete under my feet, a weed growing out of a crack.

I think, —There's a logical explanation for this. It's just how I am. I'm not a person with a quiet head—half the time, I can't sleep, and I've never been able to listen to a whole symphony because I've always got words tumbling through me. This is nothing new. Sometimes I'll work through a problem, but usually, it's grocery lists, errands I need to run, conversations I've had or overheard or wished I'd had, clever replies to passive-aggressive insults that at the time I received them I just smiled through. Arguments with my mother.

—So now I'm hearing Princess Diana, but it's the same thing.

—Okay, not the same, but similar: Whatever just happened to make you believe you heard Princess Diana's voice in your head was some kind of empathetic response to having just learned you were standing over the spot where she crashed to her death less than five hours ago, the content of which was inspired by the picture you were holding and the knowledge that she'd never been able to tell the paparazzi to fuck off and now she never can when clearly she wanted to, needed to.

I think, —Breathe in.

I can hear my yoga teacher: —Breathe in through your nose. Inspire. Literally, inspire yourself. Connect to your own life force. Now breathe out. Exhale through your mouth. Let all the negative energy you hold inside you leave your body with the air you exhale.

I exhale. I'm trying to let go of something.

—Inspire. Exhale.

I think, —Why not, Inspire, expire?

I turn the words over in my head: inspire, expire. The story of Diana's life. The world's shortest eulogy. It's the story of anybody's life, if they're lucky. Otherwise, it's just inhale, expire. Live, die.

I'm not dizzy anymore, but I'm not exactly back to normal. I take another deep breath. I feel strangely detached from the moment, as if the sounds and the colors and smells around me are muted and I'm observing everything from inside an invisible glass bubble and the world outside is full of sometimes cruel but mostly insignificant ironies, Diana's death being just the latest. Which, it occurs to me, is probably something like how it feels to be a ghost.

I suddenly feel drained of energy, and I exhale, replaying in my head a conversation I once had with Lawrence—I don't remember when or where—but he said, "All we are is energy. All *anything* is, ultimately, is energy."

I said, "But what's energy?"

He looked at me like I'd asked what was two plus two and said, "Mass times the speed of light, squared."

I think, —Release your negative mass times the speed of light, squared.

I'm still holding the picture of Diana in my hand. It's a real photograph, not a postcard or a cutout from a magazine. I turn it over. There's a copyright sticker on the back. There's his name, Max Kafka. And there, in black and white, are his address and phone number. He lives in Paris.

I say his name to myself. —Max Kafka.

I look at his phone number—it's a long sequence of numbers, and too many things are happening at once: I can't focus well enough right now to memorize it.

—He has to be in the phone book. Just memorize his name: Max Kafka. Max Kafka. Max Kafka.

I try to imagine a big picture of Franz Kafka, but I can't remember what he looked like so I make him up, a cross between F. Scott Fitzgerald and Faulkner, plus a little mustache, blown up to poster size: Max Kafka.

I stand up.

I think to put the photograph of Diana back down where Max Kafka left it.

I know I should.

It isn't mine.

Then I put it in my pocket, go back to the pathway along the river, and head toward the hotel.

ALL THE WAY BACK, THE WHOLE CITY FEELS EERILY QUIET. I'm walking slowly, not jogging, but I'm very conscious of the thuds my feet make when they hit the ground, the shock from the impact moving up my legs, the sound of my breath: —In: Huff. Out: Puff. Huff. Puff. I'll huff and I'll puff and I'll blow your house down.

I think of a conversation I once had with my boss at the children's bookstore where I worked about whether we should read fairy tales to kids during Story Hour.

I said, "Of course we should."

She said, "What's the moral of 'The Three Little Pigs'? If you don't have a good enough house, you die. What's the moral of 'Snow White'? Taking care of other people—little people—is not enough. If you don't have a man, you live a completely worthless life, in a box, and you may as well be dead. What's the moral of 'Rapunzel'? Without a man to rescue you, your life is just . . . hair. And the message behind Cinderella's godmother? The greatest gift God and your mother can give you is some natural beauty and a makeover so you can attract a husband who's rich enough to give you a castle, or at least a house that won't fall down."

I said, "I was raised on fairy tales, and I turned out okay." She shrugged.

I thought I was being tactful not to point out that the three little pigs didn't actually die.

—Why did that seem like a good idea to me, teaching little girls that if only they married well, and only if, they would live happily ever after?

I feel full of dread, and what I'm dreading, as best I can identify it, is all the mistakes I've made, some I'm not even aware of, catching up with me, my life falling down around me like a house made of straw.

And then, without warning, I'm full of Diana again, of her voice: *I loved fairy stories, too. I remember my father reading "Cinderella" to me in bed, smelling like hot milk, and it's drafty in the house but I'm snug under the covers and Cinderella's on her way to the ball and I know how that's going to end and I go to sleep dreaming about Prince Charming and I wake up knowing somehow that something important is coming my way in the marriage department. Despite my clodhopper feet, which I loathed. I'd have been one of those stepsisters who had to break her toes to get her foot into the glass slipper.*

So many memories: a trip to an amusement park with my brother and both my parents, a year or so before Mummy bolted. I remember the House of Mirrors where you could be tall or short or thin or fat, depending on which mirror you looked in. Loved that. Laughed our heads off. Then it became a hall of mirrors, and you couldn't tell what was real space and what was a mirror. Everywhere you looked, there you were, hundreds of copies of you, you kept bumping into yourself. You had to make your way to the other end, but so many of the mirrors were fake doors that you thought you might be stuck there and never get out.

That—not "Cinderella"—turned out to be the story of my life. I had no idea what was in store. No earthly idea.

Then I feel a lifting inside me, a lightness, and she's gone.

I'm trying to understand what's happening. It's more than empathy. It's real. The words aren't coming from the photograph, but I have a feeling I can't explain—even to myself—that what I'm hearing is connected to having stolen it, almost as if she chose me to talk to because I chose to keep that image of her, made myself its caretaker.

I know that doesn't make sense. But none of it makes sense. I just know the words aren't my own thoughts, and maybe skeptics would call them auditory hallucinations—they're that clear—and maybe kinder skeptics would call them wishes, but I think they're more like gifts.

I try to imagine how I might discuss this with Lawrence.

I'd say, —Where do you think Diana is now? What do you think she knows that we don't?

—She doesn't know anything. She's just entered back into the nitrogen cycle.

I'd say, —I can't believe there's not more to it than that. I think we're somehow deeply connected to the past and to the future, even after we die.

He'd say, —Well, on a molecular level, yes, we *are* our past and our future. Every molecule in our bodies used to be part of a star and will be again. If you want to insist on an afterlife, that's some sort of argument for one.

—Not much of one: your atoms flying into outer space to be stars.

—Returning from whence they came. We're all just aliens on this planet.

—We're all aliens everywhere in the universe, by that standard.

—Yes, we are.

—Then we're not aliens at all, I'd say. We're as much natives of this planet as we are of any other galaxy.

—Right. Life goes on.

—Atoms aren't life. What about consciousness? What about . . . *life?*

—Well, energy goes on, he'd say.

—Something goes on.

I don't have to understand what's happening with Diana in Lawrence's terms.

—However I end up explaining this to myself, I decide, I won't even try to talk about it with Lawrence.

WHEN I GET BACK TO THE ROOM, LAWRENCE ISN'T THERE, though he's left an addendum on the bottom of the note I left him: "At breakfast. L."

It's a little after seven o'clock. I don't know what time they start serving breakfast here, but I probably just missed him. I'm sweaty, and my hair's dirty, and my mind is roiling with things I don't want to talk about, at least not with him, so I don't go down to join him.

I open the desk drawer, looking for someplace to hide the

picture. There's no Gideon Bible, just stationery, so I put it in a Ritz envelope to protect it, then I go into the closet and put it in the outside zippered pocket of my suitcase.

I'm not sure why I don't want Lawrence to know about the picture. He wouldn't care.

I take off my shoes, get back in bed in my running clothes and sock feet, pull the covers up to my chin, and turn on the TV with the remote to a photomontage on CNN of Diana transforming from a sad-looking little girl to a shy teenager with her head lowered to a pretty but sedate bride to a loving mother and, finally, a sexy divorced woman. She was thirty-six. My age.

I'm vaguely aware of something pressing on me, very gently, on my skin and inside my chest at the same time, sort of like the feeling you get on the back of your neck when you're being stared at, only it's all over my body. I'm not paying much attention to it, though. I'm thinking about how what I'm seeing on TV reminds me of the way I used to imagine Judgment Day as a child: You die — or if you're lucky, you get raptured up into the clouds — and you find yourself lifted out of your everyday existence and placed in this elegant though slightly over-the-top room with gold furniture and silk-tasseled curtains and gilt-and-crystal chandeliers, watching a fast-forwarded movie of your childhood, your wedding, every good deed you ever committed, every bad one, while somebody tallies up your score, when Diana says, *But it's not that way at all. It's not sequential, and it's not the big moments, and it's not as if you're watching something in front of you. It's a kind of remembering that's so vivid, you're almost living it again, as if it's a dream that you're in but you do also watch, only it's very real. I remember feeling I'd just made a choice, albeit an inevitable one, and then I was waking up, or I knew I'd recently woken up, and it was yesterday on the boat and I thought for a moment I was back in my body, in that morning, and the strangeness I felt when I moved was the boat rocking. I went through the whole day, the flight to Paris, the tour of that awful house, every little thought and conversation I had, but with no sense of being judged. Just, this is what happened to bring you here.*

I can't say when I knew I was dead. Maybe once you die, your definition of death changes, not to mention your definition of life. They change before you even know what's happened, along with your definitions of past and present. The distinctions simply aren't as clear as they used to be, certainly not as important.

It's a bit like becoming the Princess of Wales. People were suddenly acting differently towards me, curtsying and calling me "Ma'am," but more than that, very much like, "Oh, there she is," treating me like glass, or sometimes, as if I wasn't there. "Does the Princess want this? Does the Princess think that?" I wasn't any different, essentially. Inside, I was exactly the same person — I was still treating everybody the same — but for all anyone else knew, Diana Spencer was dead. Eventually, I came to the same conclusion, tried to do myself in four or five times. And still later, tried to bring myself — my former self — back to life.

But now, of course, I have changed, in a certain way. I am dead, except I'm not. I'm not here, except I am. So I'm not fully aware of what this means, haven't had time to process it. Maybe that's why I've got all these memories swimming through me. Or I'm swimming through them, it's hard to say which.

I used to love to swim. Loved that moment your dry body enters the water and your boundaries disappear. Never was a tiptoe-in type. I liked to dive right in, over my head from the beginning, and swim and swim and swim until I was too exhausted to feel anything. It's like that, dying — your center of gravity shifts, all the rules change, instantly, only at first you don't realize it. But it's like you've gone from air to water — you're in a different element now — and you've got to do everything differently than you would have, you've got to live in your body differently, move differently, breathe differently. So it's an adjustment, but it's nothing to fear. I knew that when I was alive. I felt so comfortable around the dying. Those who had accepted that they were dying radiated calm. I hated being taken away from them, felt such a kinship there.

Then she's quiet, and I feel something in the room, a sort of movement, but nothing I can see, which could be, in fact, nothing, or the air-conditioning or my imagination. It could be *me,* scaring myself, though it isn't.

I sit up.

It was *her,* and now she's gone, and I'm alone in my body in front of the TV, where people who never met her are expressing their opinions about her:

"She was a natural with children."

"Quite the shopper, you know."

"Her heart was in the right place, most of the time."

"Tried to fit in at first, but became a bit of a rebel."

"Terrible taste in men, but kept looking for true love."

"It can't be said that she didn't make mistakes, to put it kindly."

"She was raised with very traditional values, but she tried to make a place for herself in the modern world."

I think, —The things these people are saying sound more like me than Diana. Me and my friends and my mother and all her friends.

A picture of Diana wearing a pearl-and-diamond crown like a halo comes on the screen while a man's voice describes her as "a natural beauty whose heart was an alloy of gold and steel."

—My mother, right down to the crown.

Diana touching the face of a young land-mine victim: my mother again.

My mother must have posed with at least a hundred children, looking sad but loving and beautiful in her rhinestone Miss Alabama tiara, the uglier or sicker the child, the better. She's got a whole scrapbook full of them.

I start flipping channels. Every station is doing All-Diana-All-the-Time: Diana is dead, her boyfriend is dead, their driver is dead. They show the driver's picture, and I feel greatly relieved to see he isn't the driver we had yesterday, though slightly guilty that it didn't occur to me to wonder about him until now. The bodyguard—the same one we nodded to outside her room last night—is in the hospital in critical condition. And seven members of the paparazzi—Max's friends—have been arrested for chasing her to her death. They're still looking for at least two others.

—No, I tell myself before I even let the question form in me. They're not looking for Max.

—So it's a good thing I stole the picture. Because there's no need for the police to find it and take him in for questioning when he already feels bad enough because surely he wasn't there, at the scene of the crash. There were probably three hundred of them here yesterday afternoon waiting for her, and the police are only looking for two, so even if you just play the odds. But beyond that, if he was there, at the crash, and ran from the police, he wouldn't have come back just a few hours later, and he certainly wouldn't have left a picture of her with his name, address, and phone number on the back.

—Unless he felt guilty and part of him wanted to be caught and leaving the picture was a kind of passive way of turning himself in, which would explain why he hadn't changed clothes from the day before: He'd been up all night wrestling with his conscience. Murderers often go to their victims'

funerals and can't resist eventually returning to the scene of the
crime. I think I got that from a TV show. Which shows what
this whole line of thinking is worth.

— He's not a murderer. He was just there to pay his respects. He was grieving.

I want to talk to him. I want to tell him I took the photograph, in case he goes back to get it himself and assumes the
police picked it up and are on their way to question him, and
I want to ask him if he ever talked to Diana, and if so, what
she said. I won't ask him directly if he's hearing her voice now,
but I want to know because surely I'm not the only one. But
either way, I have a feeling he put the photograph of her on
the memorial because he believes in some sort of afterlife
where people who have just died still have a sense of what's
going on here, and I think he was trying to say something to
her by doing that. I also think he'd be able to articulate why
he believes what he does, and it would be a way of looking at
death and therefore at life that I've never thought of before,
something to do with photographs and the fact that most
people who are genuinely grieving for Diana only knew her
through photographs, something about photography as a way
of knowing and something about time moving on and the impulse in all of us to stop it even though we know we can't, so
we're all constantly grieving for the moment that just passed,
which is, paradoxically, why people used to photograph dead
bodies, because the photograph itself is also acknowledg-
ment—proof—that the moment the photograph preserves is
gone, so a photograph is a moment's afterlife and therefore offers us at least a metaphorical hope of an afterlife for ourselves
and the people we love.

I think, —I have his phone number. I could just call him

up and we could have that conversation: Hi, you don't know me, but I was wondering if you have any thoughts on Diana and the afterlife that you'd like to share and whether you've heard anything from her since she died.

—You have to stop thinking about this man.

I change the channel to a BBC story about Diana's difficult relationships with her mother and stepmother and mother-in-law and several of her friendships with older women who functioned as surrogate mothers, and I keep thinking, of course, of my own mother. Diana hadn't communicated with her mother for several months, and TV commentators on both sides of the Atlantic are in general agreement that this is a small part of what makes her death, or its timing, so tragic. I haven't spoken to my mother since Christmas.

I look at the phone. I can feel a fistful of dread tighten in the center of my chest.

If I called her, what would we say?

—I saw Princess Diana's car this morning.

—Where are you?

—I'm in Paris.

—You sound like you're next door.

—No, I'm in France.

—Well, good for you. I just hope you're holding on to your purse. France is chock-full of pickpockets, and they all hate Americans. If anybody asks, tell them you're Canadian.

—Okay.

—A part of Canada that doesn't speak French, obviously. Say you're from Toronto.

—Okay. Anyway, I saw Princess Diana's car this morning.

—So you said. They've only shown it on TV here about a thousand times.

Then a long silence.

Not speaking is much less painful when you don't call.

Since Christmas, eight months, I've had at least eighty imaginary conversations with her, some of them monologues on my part where she just listened sympathetically and finally understood everything I've ever wanted to tell her, some of them monologues on her part where she gave me advice in the form of criticism and I held my tongue, but most of them arguments, which are more like our real lives.

And now here I am, staring at the phone, imagining hearing her real-live voice instead of the one in my head, and I say to myself, —Don't do this.

I look away from the phone toward the TV just as Diana's car—what's left of it, a chrome and black-metal tangle—appears on the screen, looking small and sanitary and shockingly ordinary.

I change the channel to a grainy picture of Diana and Dodi kissing.

A week or two ago, when I first saw a copy of it on the cover of a tabloid, I asked Lawrence if he thought it was really them. We were in the checkout line at the grocery store, having stopped for a bottle of chardonnay on our way to some friends' house for dinner.

"It could be anybody," he said.

"Why is it so blurry?"

He looked closer. "It was taken with a telephoto lens."

"Yeah, but if they can take clear pictures of stars—*star* stars, not movie stars—why can't they get a better picture of her?"

"The same thing happens when they photograph space, except that there, you get cosmic rays in addition to dust and reflections and other noise, but they clean up the pictures on the computer. The film just sees too much, including some things that don't exist."

I'd meant it as more of a rhetorical question.

I change the channel one more time. A small but growing carpet of flowers in front of the gates at Kensington Palace, with close-ups of some of the notes people have left: "We love you, Diana." "I'll miss you, Di."

I take another deep breath.

I say to myself, —I miss you, Mother.

I'm trying on the thought to see if it sounds true, and that's not exactly it.

I don't miss her sadly, the way you miss someone you love who's dead. I don't miss her sweetly, the way you miss some-one you love when you're apart but you know you'll be to-gether again. I feel about her the way you feel about something important like a set of keys that's missing—anxious, even though you're pretty sure they'll turn up eventually. They have to. But nothing is going to be right until you find them, so your only choices are to pretend they're not lost and keep ignoring your growing anxiety until they show up on their own, or tear the house apart until you find them.

—All right, all right.

I turn off the TV and crawl over the bed toward the phone. What am I going to say?

—Hi, Mother, guess what? This morning I stole a picture of Princess Diana off her memorial.

—That might be the tackiest thing you've ever done, Ellen. Right.

—Hi, Mom, guess what? I saw Princess Diana twice yes-terday before she died.

My mother—who I never call Mom, always Mama or Mother—would want to hear about that.

—I was having my hair done in the hotel salon yesterday afternoon when she came in to get hers done, and the same guy who was doing my hair did hers.

No, that's pathetic, calling your mother from France after not having spoken to her for eight months to tell her about having your hair done.

The fist in my chest clenches.

The hairdressing story is pathetic, maybe, but it isn't controversial. And of everything I could tell her that's happened to me in the last eight months, it's probably the thing she'd be the most interested in. Plus, there's nothing in it she could possibly criticize me for, out loud or in her head.

—You had your hair done in a hotel? Ellen!

—I had it done at the *Ritz,* Mother.

—Nobody gets a job in a hotel when they could work at a real salon. They know they'll never see any of their customers again.

—Princess Diana had hers done there.

—And now she's dead.

—Well, yeah, but not because she had her hair done.

—In a way.

—In a way what?

—She wasn't wearing a seat belt. It's all part of a pattern of reckless behavior: Date a playboy, let a stranger do your hair, don't wear a seat belt. Die. So did you have yours cut?

—Yeah, but . . .

—You let a stranger cut your hair. A complete stranger who doesn't even speak English?

—He spoke English.

—What were you thinking?

What I can't say to my mother, my beautiful, beauty-queen mother, is that I was thinking I wanted to look beautiful, and wanting that the way I did had something to do with her and something to do with having been mistaken for Diana earlier that day and something to do with the conversation Lawrence and I'd had on the way back to our room afterward.

As we walked up the stairs, I said, "Can you imagine dealing with that every day?"

"She loves it," he said. "She creates it."

I said, "I'm not sure she loves it as much as she *needs* it. Anybody that pretty whose husband preferred a woman so horsey—imagine what that would do to your sense of yourself."

Lawrence didn't say anything. We walked down a wide hall, passing a row of double-doored suites with their names engraved on brass plaques: the Imperial Suite, the Chopin Suite, the César Ritz, the Windsor. Then we turned the corner.

I said, "I think it's why she keeps choosing the wrong men. She has a bad self-image, so she dooms all her relationships from the beginning. I mean, what do you think she sees in this boyfriend?"

"Billions and billions," he said, imitating Carl Sagan.

"Ha ha. But he's not even handsome. He's dumpy. He's being hounded by creditors. And he's got this girlfriend who claims he was sleeping with her on one boat while supposedly falling in love with Diana on the other one. I don't get it."

Lawrence shook his head. "Rich, dumpy, unfaithful, and dominated by a powerful parent must be her type."

We came to our door, and Lawrence opened it. I had a feeling he was finished with the conversation, but I didn't want to stop there.

I walked into the room and put the bag with my shoes in it on the bed and hung my new dress in the closet. Then I said, "I think she just wants to feel loved, and she won't settle for anything less than that, even being the Queen of England, which you have to give her credit for, because a lot of people would trade being loved for being a queen. A lot of people *do* trade being loved for a lot less than that—for being comfortable, financially stable, for having a warm body next to them in bed, for not having to go to the trouble of starting over. But once you give up being the Queen of England to get out of a marriage . . ." Then my voice trailed off. I didn't know how to finish the sentence. "I mean, what's *enough* after that?"

"Nothing," Lawrence said. "That's her problem. She'll never be happy. She's just going to wish her life away."

He'd accused me of that before—wishing my life away—and I didn't defend myself at the time because I was afraid it was true.

I said, "No. After all that, how could *any* amount of love from just one man be enough?"

Lawrence made a sound full of Ms, as if he was agreeing with me without listening to me. He was in the bathroom, washing his hands. He had a thing about washing his hands. I'd followed him to the doorway. I was standing on the marble threshold, talking to his back.

"Don't you think?" I said.

I almost felt like screaming, though I couldn't have said why.

He picked up a towel to dry his hands and turned around to face me. "She wants to be adored."

He walked past me into the sitting room and sat down in a chair.

"Well, yeah," I said.

—Who doesn't?

"She wants to be adored by a billionaire," he said, picking up the newspaper.

"Okay. True enough."

"Wanting to be loved and wanting to be adored are not really the same thing," he said.

I didn't want to argue about nuance.

I said, "Okay, but in her mind they're the same thing."

"Well, then that's her problem."

"No, it's not. That's not what I'm saying. Maybe part of her feels unworthy of that adoration because who could ever be worthy of having every time she changes her hairdo be international news, especially when she wouldn't be famous at all if a prince hadn't married her and everybody projected a fairy tale onto her? So then, when it turned out that Prince Charles didn't really love her, so the thing that got her all the adoration, which wasn't anything she'd earned in the first place, and then *that* turned out to be fake, then maybe unconsciously, she started choosing men who give her what she thinks she really deserves instead of the love she wants, and then she does all her charity work and land-mine work and stuff to compensate for that because she still *wants* to deserve it. You think?"

I was talking about Diana, but somewhere in me, I was also trying to figure out myself.

"Maybe," Lawrence said, though his voice implied, Or maybe not.

"What?" I said.

"Maybe she's just a publicity-hungry gold digger who's incapable of sustained intimacy."

I took a deep breath.

If I told him he was being cynical, we'd have an argument—I was already mad, though he didn't seem to know it—and I didn't want to argue. I didn't even want to be mad. I didn't care what he thought about Diana. I didn't care what anybody thought about her. I just wanted to be happy and pretty and lovable and I wanted to feel loved.

I thought, —I wouldn't mind being adored, either.

I sat down on the bed. I slipped off my shoes, took the new pair out of their box, and put them on. They were silver satin Christian Louboutin pumps with pointed toes and three-inch heels. I crossed my legs and looked in the mirror at their red soles.

I said, "I love these shoes."

I was waiting for my heart to slow down.

Lawrence said, "Good."

"I adore them."

Lawrence either didn't get my little joke or chose to ignore it.

Then I stood up, took off my top, and said, "I want to take a shower before I get my hair done."

He looked at his watch and said, "What time is your appointment?"

I said, "Four thirty," and he opened his newspaper.

"What time is it?" I said.

"Ten after four," he said, settling the paper in front of him.

I took off my shoes and went into the bathroom, closed the door.

In the shower, this thought crossed my mind: —If I married again, what would my second husband have in common with Lawrence?

AND TWENTY MINUTES LATER, I WAS SITTING IN FRONT OF a long burled-wood table in the hotel salon wearing a thin white robe with a blue Ritz crest embroidered onto the right breast pocket, waiting for the hairdresser. I was thinking about Diana, feeling like I hadn't said what I meant about her to Lawrence, but I didn't know what I meant, much less how to say it, so it was still gnawing at me, but I was trying to let it go.

A woman came in and said something to me in a thick French accent, and it took me a second to figure out that she wanted to know if I'd like some water.

I said, "Yes, water, thank you."

She said, "Avec gaz?"

I said, "Yes. Merci."

She nodded and said, "Gaz," as if she approved, and I smiled, and she left.

Then I felt irritated at myself that the salon employee's approval of my choice of water had made me feel as good as it had: —This desperate need you have to be liked.

I was suddenly very thirsty.

When the hairdresser came in, he introduced himself and said, "What do you want?"

I'd just spent the day in the most beautiful city in the world, reading its violent history in the guidebook in between shopping for beautiful clothes in a month when most of the better boutiques were closed. I was full of yearnings for things I didn't know how to name.

I said, "I don't know."

We were having dinner that night with an old colleague of Lawrence's, Eric Mandelstrom, as we did every year on the Saturday night before the annual physics conference. The summer before, in Madrid, Eric brought a tiny Norwegian graduate student with skin the color of snow and straight white hair and whitish-blue eyes like an albino cat's and lipstick so dark a shade of red it was almost black. She was drop-dead gorgeous, if a little scary. I felt invisible next to her.

I thought, —I want Lawrence to look at Eric's date at dinner tonight and think I'm prettier than she is, and I want Eric to look at his date and think the same thing.

I did and didn't want that: It wasn't about Eric's date, and it wasn't about Eric. It wasn't even really about Lawrence. It was something in me that had been there since before I even knew Lawrence.

At some point before you're thirty-six years old, you have to stop blaming your mother and take responsibility for how you see yourself—I knew that—but you also have to know what you're dealing with, and when I was six months old, I lost my first beauty contest. My mother kept a picture of the winner in my baby book, along with my birth announcement and a cutting of my hair, tied with a pink satin ribbon. I came in second in the same contest when I was one, lost again when I was two, came in fourth when I was three. Then my mother retired me until I was thirteen, when she took me to Houston for a makeover by the guys who'd done four out of the last five Miss Texases, head shots by the official Miss Texas photographer, voice lessons by a soloist in the Houston Opera. I lost, after which I informed my mother that if she ever entered me in another beauty contest, I would kill myself.

I'd gotten the message that I was pretty-but-not-pretty-enough in a world where being pretty was the most important thing there was to be since before I could remember being anything.

The hairdresser took off his black jacket and said, "You want color?"

"Yes." I'd told them that much when I made the appointment. "I just don't know what color. Or style. I was thinking something . . . different."

He started picking up my hair in sections, examining it. He parted my hair down the back of my head and looked at my roots. There was, for me, something intimate about it—him seeing this secret part of me—and I looked at him in the mirror, at the completely blank expression on his face. I had to fight feeling rejected.

"Your hair is very long," he said. "Your skin is very light."

"Yes."

"Is not possible."

"What's not possible?"

"Big change in color."

I thought, —Movie stars do it all the time. It can't be that hard. But then again, if he doesn't think it can be done, he's probably not the right person to do it.

I said, "How about strawberry blonde?"

He picked up a notebook like a photo album, and he opened it to show me several hair-color samples—a page of blonds, a page of reds, pages of browns and blacks and grays. The samples were curled and tied, like cuttings of baby hair.

He held up the page of reds next to my ear and said, "You see? Not with your face. You are too pink. Red, pink, orange. Not pretty."

"Okay," I said.

Then he turned the page to show me the blonds. He pointed to one that was just barely lighter than the shade I already had and said, "This is for you."

"Okay," I said.

"With these highlights," he said, pointing to another, even lighter cutting. It was almost the color of my baby hair.

"Good."

"Very pretty."

"Good."

"Okay," he said. "I go mix."

Then he left, and I was alone.

I looked around the room. I liked the gold-gilt-and-crystal chandeliers, the marble floor, the cheery baroque music that was being piped in. I told myself I liked the buttery leather sofa with armrests like movie-theater seats and the retro helmet-style hair dryer on wheels that was parked next to it. I tried to like the heavy gilt mirrors, the slightly fruity, slightly formalde-hydish smell of the air—all of it over the top but somehow, and I thought unintentionally, whimsically so.

I had picked that salon out of all the salons in Paris because I'd read in the book about the Ritz in our room that they would consult with you and give you a "coiffure that flatters and complements your personality," which I suddenly realized was pathetic.

—How did this happen? How did I become a woman who's willing to pay a lot of money for the promise of empty flattery from a complete stranger?

I glanced at a stack of magazines, trying to distract myself, but I didn't feel like leafing through hundreds of pictures of perfect women. I thought about Princess Diana, who was just beginning to get wrinkles around her eyes when she smiled but who still looked good. I wondered if she'd arrived at the hotel yet, wondered if the next day, the pictures the paparazzi took of her when she drove up would be in the papers. Then I thought about the American photographer I'd met outside the hotel and the feeling I got from him when he shook my hand. He took my picture even after it was clear I wasn't a celebrity. I liked him for that. I wished I could redo that whole encounter.

That was when I decided to go jogging early the next morning wearing sunglasses and a cap.

And makeup. I figured even if every picture that got taken of me ended up in the trash, or, better yet, in some cameraman's photo file in case he needed it later, I'd rather be the Unidentified Woman Outside the Paris Ritz with lipstick than without it.

WHEN MY HAIRDRESSER CAME BACK, HE STARTED APPLYING the dye, painting it on with a paintbrush.

He said, "You are having a nice time in Paris?"

"Yes," I said. "Very."

"You like the Ritz?"

"Yes. It's a wonderful hotel."

"First time?"

"No, I've been here before. My honeymoon, actually. Fifteen years ago, now."

"So this is your second honeymoon?"

"Yeah," I said. Lied. It was easier than trying to explain to him or, for that matter, myself, how this was different from a second honeymoon, what had happened to our marriage to make it just a trip to Paris. Nothing had happened. Lawrence had had a mild heart attack. I'd had a breast-cancer scare. Lawrence's sweet little boy had turned into an angry twenty-year-old with a driver's license. But that's life. Basically, we'd just been married for fifteen years, gotten fifteen years older. And Lawrence's main reason for being there had more to do with what holds the universe together than with our marriage. Why should every trip to Paris be a honeymoon?

The hairdresser said, "Paris is very romantic place." He was still painting my hair.

"Yes," I said, feeling an ache through my shoulders.

When he finished painting, he started wrapping my head in Saran Wrap and we heard some commotion in another room—people talking excitedly, furniture being moved. He looked toward the room and said something under his breath in French. He was clearly irritated.

Then a woman I hadn't seen before rushed through the room, carrying a stack of folded white towels, and another woman called for my hairdresser. As best I could follow their conversation, he told her to wait until he was finished wrapping me and she told him it was urgent. He didn't believe her, she convinced him it was, and he hurriedly finished my Saran Wrap and said to me, "You wait here, okay?"

I said, "Sure."

—What choice do I have?

He practically ran out of the room.

Another woman rushed in and rolled the hair dryer to the opposite wall, and then the receptionist came in, and the two of them were excited, talking so fast in French that I couldn't pick up even a hint of what they were saying. After less than a minute, the receptionist moved the dryer back to where it had been before. Then my guy came back in and put on his jacket, and after a slightly heated discussion between the three of them, the first woman took the dryer out of the room altogether, and my guy and the other woman walked out the front door into the hall, and I was alone again.

I wasn't particularly interested in whatever beauty-parlor politics were bothering them. I was thinking about the dinner we would have that night, wondering whether the pressure to compete with Eric's women came from Lawrence or from me or from somewhere else—magazines and movie stars and my mother and human nature—when Princess Diana walked into the room.

My hairdresser was with her—he'd greeted her in the hall—and the staff were putting a robe like mine on her, treating it like it was a fur, and the same woman who had offered me water appeared and offered her wine or coffee or tea or water, and Diana thanked her, but she didn't want anything, and the woman insisted, in much better English than she'd used with me, that she must have something, so Diana asked for a spot of tea if it wasn't too much trouble.

"With milk or lemon?"

"No, thank you, just tea."

She ran to get it. Then my hairdresser sat her down in the chair directly across from me, but there was a big double-sided mirror on the table between us, so we were facing each other, each looking at our own reflection, and I couldn't see her.

—There's Princess Diana, almost close enough to touch, and I'm wearing a bathrobe and no makeup and no earrings and I have Saran Wrap on my head!

The hairdresser asked her what she wanted, and she asked for a wash and blow-dry.

He said, "Would you like a little color, highlights?"

"No, thank you," she said.

I imagined him picking up her hair between his fingers, letting it fall back onto her head.

He said, "A little trim?"

"Not today, thank you," she said.

She sounded shy, sweet, but also sad, I thought. Maybe just tired.

Then the woman came back in with a cup of tea, which was either very weak or had brewed miraculously fast, and set it on the counter between us.

"Madame."

"Thank you."

"It's good?"

I was looking at the mirror, though not at myself. I was trying to imagine what she looked like behind it without looking like I was trying to look at her when I saw her hand come out from behind it and lift the cup. She had long, slender fingers. Short, unpainted fingernails. No rings.

She said, "Yes, it's lovely." Her voice was small, full of air. She put the cup back down.

Tea Lady left, and nobody said anything for a minute. I imagined the hairdresser combing her hair.

I was trying to think of something to say to her if I got a chance, not coming up with much.

Then the hairdresser said, "Okay, come with me," and she stood up and moved out from behind the mirror and I looked straight at her, at her hair, which was already perfect, at her eyes, which were bright blue, at her skin, which was tan, slightly pink.

She was pretty, but in a regular-person kind of way. And she was Princess Diana. She was both stunning and stunningly ordinary, and as she walked past me, looking at the floor, I adjusted my Saran Wrap. Our hairdresser was just barely touching her back with his fingertips as he took her into the next room. I breathed in her perfume — musk and narcissus and lilies — and the smell of my own hair dye, and she didn't seem to notice me, she was vaguely preoccupied, but I opened my mouth to say hello, and nothing came out.

While she was having her hair washed, I looked at myself in the mirror: —What is wrong with you? You could have said, Hi, Princess Diana. You could have said, How are you? You could have at least smiled at her, nodded, but instead you just opened your mouth like a complete starstruck moron.

When she came back in, she was towel-drying her own hair—I liked that about her—and our hairdresser escorted her back to her seat and I still didn't say anything.

The woman who had carried the towels came in and asked our guy something in French. He looked at his watch and answered her, and she asked me to follow her into the sink room, where she washed my hair. Then she pumped some conditioner into her hand, showed it to me, and said, "Is to make you shine like star." She worked it into my hair and massaged my scalp, and we waited for what seemed to me like a very long time before she rinsed it out.

When I went back into the main salon, Diana was gone, though her cup of tea was still there, full, and the hairdresser just barely trimmed my hair and blew it dry. Then he plastered it with hair spray, though it wasn't clear to me what he thought he'd done to it that needed spraying. I left looking pretty much exactly the way I had when I walked in.

I grabbed a mint out of a bowl on my way out, and as I walked down the hall, I unwrapped the mint and put it in my mouth. I never did get my water.

On my way back to my room, I thought of a long list of things I wished I'd said to Diana, beginning with, —Hello.

I imagined our hairdresser leaving to mix her color and she and I were alone in the room, side by side, looking at each other's reflections in the mirrors, and I'd say, —Hi, I'm Ellen Baxter.

She'd say, —I'm Diana.

We'd turn to face each other and shake hands and I'd say, —I know!

We'd both giggle.

And maybe I'd say, —Did you have a nice vacation?

Or I'd tell her how much I admired the work she was doing with land-mine victims. Or I'd ask how her sons were, and she'd say they were fine, but she missed them—I would read in the paper the next day that she hadn't seen them for a month—and maybe she'd ask if I had children.

—One, I'd say, a stepson, Alec, who's in college.

And maybe she'd say something like, —You must be so proud.

Which is a thing people say to me often, and I just smile and say yes, but maybe with Diana I'd confide in her that I didn't meet him until he was five and his mother had recently died, and though I quit my job to be a full-time mother, raised him and loved him as if he were my own, he never really bonded with me. Now he calls me Ellen.

No, too much information. Way too much.

So maybe I'd just say, —Yes, very proud, as I'm sure you are.

And maybe she'd have said she was, but she worried about her sons, too, so much pressure on them—the next day, the papers said she talked to William on the phone that afternoon, probably just before I saw her, and he asked her to intervene with the royal family about a back-to-school photo call he didn't want to do, which may have been what she was thinking about when she passed me on her way to the sink, how to tell the Queen of England to let her son have some privacy.

So maybe I'd have said, —I think *I* have an intrusive mother-in-law. I can't imagine what it's like for you.

And maybe she'd have sensed a sympathetic ear and said, —I have to fight for my children to get what everybody else takes for granted—freedom, independence, some small bit of self-determination.

And I'd have said, —But you *do* fight, you go up against the whole establishment, and so many people admire you for that. They feel like you're fighting for them.

And she'd have said, —Thank you.

Maybe I'd have told her she was a good mother. She loaned glamour to an otherwise-thankless job.

I wouldn't have mentioned her wedding, wouldn't have said I thought even then that she looked like something was wrong, but my mother said no, she just had perfect composure, you don't want to be grinning like a Cheshire cat. She was planning my wedding, though I wasn't engaged. She took notes about Diana's flowers, her music, the length of her train.

Maybe I'd have said something about her divorce, how it inspired a lot of women I knew.

I could have said, —I think almost everybody whose marriage turns out to be a mistake tries to hang on long after it's clear that nobody involved is going to live happily ever after, but a lot of women looked at you and thought, If she can't do it, I don't have to feel so bad about myself. So, thank you.

AND THE NEXT MORNING, I'M BACK IN OUR ROOM FROM THE site of her fatal crash, lying in bed watching TV and thinking about calling my mother, and I'm still wishing I'd thanked Diana for that.

I think, —Maybe that—all of it, some of it—would have meant something to her. Maybe if I'd told her she gave a lot of women who felt like failures the courage to hold their heads up high, she would have taken it with her to her grave a few hours later.

And she says, *Thank you, Ellen.*

I sit up. It hasn't occurred to me that she could hear my thoughts.

I think, —You're welcome.

That's not how it felt, though, she says.

Then she's quiet.

I think to myself, —Wow.

And then to her, —What did it feel like?

As if I'd let everybody down. It was a fairy story that everybody wanted to work, most of all me, and when it didn't, my mother told me I was an embarrassment to the family. Her mother took my father's side in their divorce, so she lost custody, and you'd think she'd have learned from that, your mother's got to stick by you, but no.

—No.

I remember once, she's talking to me on the phone and I'm in my robe at the palace on the floor, on all fours on the floor just weeping like a baby, but I can't take the phone away from my ear. I should hang up on her, telling me what a disgrace I am—I don't need that—but I can't. I'm howling to the four walls, feeling as if my voice is echoing inside a cave, nobody listens to me, and at the same time, I'm worried that someone is going to hear me and call the media, tell them Diana's finally having her nervous breakdown, somebody call the men in white coats to drag her away.

I had to put some distance there, build a wall around her. Otherwise, she had such capacity to shatter me.

I feel an enormous sadness hovering over me. I feel it in the silence of the room, and I want to comfort her, but I'm at a total loss for words. I want to ask her if she's all right now, if she regrets not having spoken to her mother before she died, if she's spoken to her since, and I want to ask her if we'd talked yesterday in the salon, would it have made any difference at all in how she feels now, but the sadness suddenly wraps itself around me so cold and tight that it's almost suffocating, and then, just as suddenly, the pressure on my skin and in my chest lifts, and I take a breath, and I think I smell something like narcissus—a whiff of her perfume—and she's gone.

What would I have said?

—Your mother always loved you. I'm sure she's proud of you.

As if I had any way of knowing that.

I look at the clock. It's seven thirty, which means it's the middle of the night in Louisiana.

I think, —I can't call my mother now. I'll call her this afternoon. Maybe I'll tell her I talked to Diana in the salon before she died. I'll say I had a nice, vapid conversation, but I'll also put something funny in it that she can tell her friends.

—Maybe I'll tell her I didn't talk to Diana, but I keep thinking that maybe if I had, she'd still be alive.

Like maybe what she was thinking about when she walked past me was that she knew Dodi was going to propose to her that night, and maybe when I saw her, she was arguing with herself about what she was going to say to him, and maybe something I could have said would have brought her to her senses because surely somewhere in herself she knew what a terrible idea marrying him would have been. So maybe she'd have gone back upstairs after she'd had her hair done and said, Dodi, we have to talk. Then she'd have told him she didn't want to marry him, she'd just wanted a summer fling, and he'd have been hurt but he'd have understood, and he'd have gone back to his apartment alone, called his other girlfriend in America, who would have taken him back if he'd offered her enough money, and Diana would have stayed at the Ritz, just down the hall from us, ordered room service for dinner, and woken up the next morning and gone back to London, alone but alive.

I think of saying to my mother, —Have you ever heard of the butterfly effect, the idea that nothing about the future is certain because of the way one tiny act can make a huge difference down the road, the flap of a butterfly wing in New York could set off a chain reaction that ultimately causes a tsunami in Japan?

—Wasn't that in *Jurassic Park?* she'd say.

—Yeah, but it's also real, and I can't stop wondering if a quick hi-how-are-you-I'm-fine-thank-you-so-nice-to-meet-you would have somehow changed the rhythm of her evening just barely enough that they still would have done everything they did, only everything would have been pushed back a minute

or two—even a second or two, the flap of a butterfly wing—
and somehow they didn't crash, and they didn't die. They went
through the tunnel seconds later than they otherwise would
have and came out the other side and went on with their lives.
Or they crashed, but somehow, because they'd gotten into the
car two seconds later, when she'd finished whatever thought
had been distracting her, she'd remembered to put on her seat
belt, and Dodi and the driver died, but she survived.

I can hear my mother saying, —I'm not sure I buy that
butterfly-flap idea. I think when it's your time, it's your time.

If I call her, I won't tell her any of this.

I could tell her about Diana's ten minutes in the hotel
restaurant last night, which is at least slightly entertaining and
doesn't really involve me.

—Lawrence and I were eating dinner with Eric Mandelstrom. Remember him from the wedding?

—No.

—Lawrence's co–Nobel laureate? From California?

—Oh, right.

She hadn't much liked Eric.

—And Eric's date, a German woman named Mart Something, who was also a physicist . . .

—Very scientific dinner.

—Yeah, so . . .

—Did you have anything to say? Or did you just sit there?
I would have just sat there.

—I mostly listened.

—Right.

—So anyway, two hours into our dinner, a couple of men
came into the restaurant, and they started walking around the
room staring at all of us.

—That is so rude. The French are the rudest people on earth.

—They weren't French, and it was their job.

—That's no excuse.

—So then they asked one couple to let them look in their shopping bags under their table, and once they asked, everybody there wanted to know what was in there, and it was in today's papers that they were bodyguards looking for cameras, but as it turned out, the bags just held cigars. But we didn't know that, so everybody turned their heads to see what was going on, and I was thinking it might have been a bomb scare, except the men weren't dressed like police, just like regular people, but I thought they could have been plainclothes detectives. So everybody was sort of edgy before Diana even showed up, and then she stepped into the doorway and stood there on the threshold for a minute, and every single head in the room turned her way, nobody could stop themselves, and it's not just that she's dead now, because I thought even at the time that she was so much prettier than she looked in pictures, and taller, and the way the light was bouncing off her hair, I'm serious, she almost glowed.

—Well, I'm sure they have flattering lighting there.

—Yeah, but nobody else glowed.

—You probably did.

—No, I didn't. But she did, and it was a quiet restaurant, but the whole room fell almost silent for ten or fifteen seconds—the harpist and the violinist kept playing, but nobody said a word above a whisper—and by the way, even though everybody did look at her, we didn't all stare at her like one of the papers said we did.

—Thank heavens.

—I mean, for one thing, it's a one-room, fifteen-table restaurant with mirrored walls on three sides and floor-to-ceiling windows on the other that you can see people's reflections in, so see-and-be-seen is built into the architecture: You don't have to stare. It's like having dinner on the alterations pedestal in the dressing room at Saks.

—With better lighting.

—Right. And a ceiling that's painted like a sunny sky with puffy clouds, like a perpetually beautiful day.

—Oh, how nice.

—It *was* nice. So the bodyguards okayed a corner table that an older couple had just left, and Diana and Dodi came in and sat down and the waiters brought them the same chanterelle mushroom and foie gras mousse in little wineglasses that they'd brought us when we first got there at eight o'clock, and the bodyguards took the table next to theirs where a middle-aged woman and a young boy had been sitting and had also just left, after which the waiters had pounced on the table to clear and reset it. So for a few minutes, it looked like Diana and Dodi were going to have dinner not fifteen feet from our table. They were reading the menu—or, she was—but Dodi kept getting up to talk to the bodyguards, and every time he did, people noticed. It was obvious something was wrong—he was very agitated—and then they got up and walked out of the room, which looked more like it was Dodi's decision than hers. He took her hand and led her out and she was just looking at the floor like she was embarrassed. I felt bad for her. The restaurant had built to a quiet roar—every person at every table there had stopped whatever conversation they were having to say, "Don't look now, but there's Princess Diana!"—and when they rushed out not fifteen minutes after they'd come in, it turned quiet again, like we'd all been suspended in air from a helium balloon, and you could feel it deflating above us as we fell back to earth.

My mother would ask at this point what Diana was wearing, and I'd tell her.

Then I'd say, —So then the waiters were clearing our cheese course, and the harpist and the violinist stopped to take a break, and surely the lights didn't go up, but they felt like they did, it seemed brighter in there. And people started laughing, and maybe it was partly because the music wasn't playing, but even though the room got quieter, the laughter seemed louder. The whole room turned a little giddy, like we'd all gotten the joke. We'd all just seen the most famous woman in the world, thought she was having dinner there, with us, and then we'd all been dumped. And of course it wasn't just what it seemed at the time. It was also what she was doing less than three hours before her fatal crash, her last night on earth, her last meal. And leaving the restaurant before they'd eaten their dinner was the first in a series of actions that would lead directly to her death—leave the restaurant, leave the hotel, try to outrun the paparazzi. You can't help but think, —If only she'd just stayed there and eaten dinner and then gone upstairs to bed.

If I tell my mother about last night, I'll stop there. Then I'll say, Anyway, how are you?

I won't tell her that right after Diana left, I looked at Lawrence and said, "Wasn't she pretty? Prettier than in pictures?"

Mart, Eric's date, said in a thick German accent that made me think of a Nazi in a movie, "You are a member of the Princess Diana fan club?"

"No," I said.

"But figuratively," she said, making things worse.

I could have asked her if she thought I thought she meant a literal fan club and whether mentioning seeing Diana, which everybody else in the restaurant with a beating heart did, too, made me a member of her fan club.

I thought about telling her that if I'd eaten dinner in the same room with Hitler, I would have thought that was worth commenting on, and I personally was no fan of Hitler.

But I said, "No. I just think she's interesting."

"Everybody thinks she is interesting," Mart said. "But why? Because she is rich and beautiful and stupid, what everybody else either is or wants to be."

When Mart said why, she pronounced it vie.

"I wouldn't want to be her," I said, realizing a second too late which category that left me in.

Eric and Lawrence had retreated into their own conversation.

"Did you read her interview in *Le Monde*? What was it, Eric?" she said, touching his arm.

"Yes?" he said.

"When did *Le Monde* run the interview with Diana?"

"Last week? Two or three days ago?" he said. "I don't know."

But she didn't wait for his answer before she turned back to me and said, "*Le Monde* is not a tabloid, it's a highly respected French newspaper."

"I know," I said. I'd read excerpts of that interview in translation. Or retranslation.

"And she said anybody who needs her, anywhere in the world, she will be there for them. Oh yes, anybody with a camera. She spends her life posing, and then she complains about the paparazzi."

I had a feeling I knew something about Diana—something about anybody who'd ever had their heart broken—that Mart would never understand. I thought of my college boyfriend, my first love, and how when that relationship went bad, most of me just wanted him to go away and never come back, but then he did, and part of me thought, —How could you?

I had a feeling Diana felt something like that about the paparazzi. And about Prince Charles.

I said, "I know she likes to be photographed, but I think she's also sincere about wanting to help people. Wasn't *Le Monde* the interview where she said if she could give love to somebody who was suffering for a minute, five minutes, half an hour, that's what she wanted to do? Maybe it's not much, but it's more than most people do for complete strangers."

"She sits for one minute with an AIDS victim, touches them, poses for a photograph in full makeup and professionally done hair, and she calls that love? She has no idea what love is."

I couldn't think of a comeback.

I didn't think to say, —Okay, don't call it love, call it something else, but it's still worth something to the people she does it for, so what do you care?

It didn't occur to me to say, —If she thinks she's loving those people, and by the way, they think they love her back, who are you to say you know better?

I didn't have the nerve to say, —If Diana doesn't know what love is, how are you, who work in a field that can't even agree on a definition of consciousness, suddenly some sort of expert on love?

Mart said, "And what does she call it when she's sleeping with another woman's husband? Is that love, too?"

I didn't want to defend Diana's sex life, didn't want to say I thought that somehow, in the big picture, it was part of her same—okay, misguided—attempt to give love. And get it. Which was probably just as well. I realized I was on the verge of sounding like a country song: Looking for love in all the wrong places.

I smiled as if I found Mart's cynicism vaguely amusing, and the waiters started bringing out the first of two desserts—chocolate and Earl Grey tea mousse topped with slivered almonds, matchstick-cut green apples, and green apple sorbet—which I told myself to remember so I could try to replicate it at home. Mart took the interruption in our conversation as an opportunity to join Eric and Lawrence in theirs, and I ate.

Lawrence was bothered because somebody—"some idiot," to be precise—named Joseph Something was on the program to give a paper about the relationship between wormholes and alternate universes, despite the fact that there was no scientific evidence that alternate universes even existed.

"I've read the paper," Mart said to him. "It's brilliant." And for a fraction of a second, I liked her for disagreeing with Lawrence, sticking up for her friend, but then she said to me, "Wormholes are the places where this universe and the next have their little trysts, so of course they cover up the evidence."

And I said, "Of course."

I didn't say, —I know what wormholes are. I've seen *Star Trek*.

So I also didn't mention that I thought wormholes just

provided shortcuts within this universe, and I thought they were fictional.

And I didn't say, —Trysts?

Lawrence said, "Are you serious?" and ate a spoonful of sorbet.

"No, she's not," Eric said. "She's joking."

"I'm dead serious," she said. "String theory accounts for wormholes, alternate universes, *and* our lack of evidence for them in ways no other theory has been able to do. It's very exciting."

According to string theory as I understand it, the fundamental elements of the universe—this one, anyway—aren't waves or particles, but strands of vibrating energy, most of which are shaped like impossibly tiny strings or rubber bands, but some of which stretch themselves in all directions until they become gigantic membranes, or branes, in the language of scientists.

She said to me, "String theory posits that when a wormhole is created, it rips open the fabric of spacetime and connects this universe to another universe that's only millimeters away," then to Lawrence, "closer than I am to you," and to me again, "and when they're . . . finished, the hole disappears, and a brane like a liquid Band-Aid repairs the rip." Then to Lawrence, "So no one's the wiser." With no one's the wiser, she winked at him. She actually winked.

I felt a quivering inside me, a stretching.

Eric said to Mart, "Do you really believe there's a universe right next door to ours?"

"Or right under us," she said. Then to Lawrence, "And right above us. We could be in a cosmic three-way right now."

Lawrence and Eric laughed. I kept eating.

Mart said, "All right. But the fact that we don't have the math for it doesn't mean it isn't true."

Lawrence said, "I'm simply asking for proof, and there's no way to prove that wormholes lead to other universes this far away." He held up his thumb and index finger, about a half inch apart. "Is this what physics has come to," he said, "that you expect people to accept your view as an act of *faith*?"

For a scientist—or for Lawrence, at least—faith isn't a last resort. It's not an option.

She said, "I believe the proof will come. Wait until you hear the paper, my friend," and he smiled at her, as if to say, Okay, my friend, I will wait before I take a position on cosmic three-ways.

I felt like screaming, —Lawrence, you know there's no universe next door, you know there's no other universe any-where, no afterlife, no nothing. This is all there is.

He was more certain of that than I was.

Still, I knew it wasn't the possibility of other universes that was upsetting me. I was irritated with Mart, irritated with my-self, and I'd felt a little strand of irritation with Lawrence about something he said before dinner, which I thought I'd gotten over, but now it was back.

We'd been having drinks in the Bar Vendôme there in the hotel with Eric and Mart, and I was nervous to start with, and Lawrence and I had gone to the Hemingway Bar in the back of the hotel first, which was closed for August, but we waited for them outside it for twenty minutes before we decided to try the other bar, and I can't stand to be late, so I was both-ered about that, too. But finally we found them, and Eric stood to kiss me on both cheeks even though he's American, and I didn't realize what he was doing until too late, and I bumped my forehead into his teeth.

Then Mart, who was over six feet tall, stood up, and Lawrence said, "And you must be Mart."

She held out her hand. "Yes."

How do you say yes condescendingly? It's one syllable. I don't know, but she managed it.

She's a real physicist at a university in Germany, and she just published a paper with Eric in a prestigious journal, which Lawrence complimented her on lavishly.

Then Eric introduced me to her and we shook hands. She had a firm handshake like a politician, and I disliked her instantly. Her fingers were large and ungraceful, and she had straight brown hair about an inch long that stood up like fur and so many studs in her ears that I had to figure she had more piercings, elsewhere, that I didn't want to think about. She was wearing a mannish black pantsuit with a scarf at her neck that almost looked like a tie, no makeup, severely plucked eyebrows. I tried not to imagine her wearing a studded leather dog collar, holding a whip.

I was wearing a low-cut clingy silk sheath the color of a thunderstorm with beads on the straps and neckline. My hair was long and stiff with hair spray and very blond, and I was wishing I'd worn boots and a power suit with a tight bun.

Then we all sat down and Eric asked me how I'd been, but before I could answer, our waiter came over and asked if he could get us anything, and I thought, —Yes, get me out of here.

Eric and Mart were halfway through their martinis with twists—I can't stand it when couples drink the same drink, it's too cute—and then Lawrence ordered one for himself and looked at me like didn't I want one, too? I couldn't do it. I scanned the little menu quickly and chose something I'd never had before. I'd never even heard of it.

When the waiter left, Eric said, "So, where were we?"

Mart said, "You were asking Ellen how she is," which was harmless enough, but there was something about her tone that made it sound like she thought asking me how I am was the most idiotic, American thing Eric had ever done.

I said, "Yes. I'm fine."

Eric said, "Say that again. Say 'fine' in your Alabama drawl."

"Fine," I said.

"Sexiest accent in the world," he said.

"Are you from Alabama?" Mart said.

"Originally."

"Isn't that where Zelda Fitzgerald was born?" Mart said.

"She grew up in Montgomery. I'm from Birmingham."

"I just read a biography of her," she said. "What a waste of a life."

Then a tiny silence opened up over us and I fought the urge to explain the differences between Zelda and me, how she was from a different generation, a different part of Alabama, different family, completely different situation, not to mention that she married a very different kind of husband and she was mentally ill, because for one thing, Mart could have said she didn't mean to imply any comparison at all, I was just being paranoid.

So I should have just left the silence alone, but it made me uncomfortable, and I rushed to fill it with the first change of subject I could think of.

I said, "Did you see the paparazzi outside when you came in?"

Mart said, "Yes, someone said Princess Diana is here."

"Yes," I said, not slowing down to read her tone. "I saw her this afternoon. I was in the hair salon, and she came in and sat down this close to me, no entourage, no bodyguard. Just her. We said hello. She was really nice, very sweet."

Mart looked at me as if I'd just confirmed her earlier suspicions about me and pushed her lips into a little closed-mouth smile, and I realized, an instant too late, that of course she was one of those people who had nothing but disdain for Princess Diana. Fine, I wasn't trying to prove anything other than that I wasn't pathetic—I had no more invested in Diana than I had in Zelda—so I said, "Lawrence says you and Eric were just in Greece? I love Greece."

"Yes," she said, and she looked at me almost suspiciously, as if to say, What of it?

"Did you have a nice time there? Isn't it beautiful?"

"It was hot," she said and turned back to Lawrence and Eric. She didn't want the conversation to divide along gender lines—she wanted it to divide along physicist/nonphysicist lines—and I couldn't really blame her. This was what she'd come to Paris for, not to talk Greek weather with an American housewife. Fine again.

—Where's that drink?

She said to Lawrence, "Have you read what Greene and Dyekman are working on, with spatial velocity?"

"Yes, I saw Dyekman in New York last month," Lawrence said. "We talked about it at length. Fascinating."

"How is Edward?" Mart said, and I got a feeling from the way she said his name, holding the W in her mouth just a fraction of a second longer than necessary, that she'd slept with him.

"He seemed fine," Lawrence said.

"Did you know his wife left him?" Mart said.

"No, he didn't mention that. He had lost some weight," Lawrence said. "But he looked good."

"She's with a musician now," Mart said.

"A musician?" Eric said. "She left him for a musician?"

"A very famous one."

"A fucking rock star?" Eric said.

"No," Mart said, laughing, "a concert violinist. I can't think of his name."

"My God," said Eric.

Lawrence turned to me. "Promise me if you ever leave me, it won't be for a violinist."

Eric and Mart laughed.

I said, "Okay. I'll never leave you for anything less than a cellist."

"A cellist?" Lawrence said. "That's worse than a violinist."

We were all laughing.

"Okay," I said, "no musicians."

"Thank you."

"Could I leave you for a mathematician who plays in a country-western band on weekends?" I said.

"Do you have one in mind?"

"No. I just want to know all my options."

"No. If he's a mathematician—no matter what he is—he *cannot* be in a country-western band."

"You're not making this easy," I said, and we all kept laughing.

Eric took my hand and said, "Mathematicians are intellectual masturbators. If you ever want to leave him, you just come to me."

"Would that be okay?" I asked Lawrence. "Could I leave you for Eric?"

"Well, you could," Lawrence said, "but why?"

We laughed again, though not as loudly as before.

I looked at Eric, who kissed my hand.

Mart said to Lawrence, seductively, "And where would that leave me?"

We were all still laughing, sort of.

Lawrence said, "Only time will tell."

"Unless, of course, time is moving at light speed," Eric said to them, and Lawrence and K-Mart laughed.

I didn't get it.

Eric said to me, "There is no passage of time at light speed. Anything traveling at the speed of light doesn't have, well, time, to travel through time."

"Thank you," I said. I knew about there being no passage of time at light speed—that's Physics 101. It just hadn't struck me as funny.

"I prefer my time to travel very slowly," Mart said to Lawrence, who said, "I bet you do," while Eric said to me, "So light doesn't age, it's timeless."

"It doesn't age, but can it die?" Mart said. Then to me, "And of course it can't, nothing dies, except . . . metaphorically." And to Lawrence, "But what happens to it when it goes into a black hole?"

With "hole," she shaped her lips into an O, like a kiss.

I looked at Lawrence, too, and he threw up his hands, and Eric said, "Chaos."

The three of them laughed out loud.

Some French call black holes hidden stars because the literal translation of black hole—trou noir—sounds too much like their slang for vagina. I didn't know where Germans stood on the issue. Was she discussing vaginas and what happens inside them with Lawrence? In front of Eric? In front of me?

Eric said to me, "So tell me, my future paramour, what you've been up to?"

I glanced at Lawrence and said, pleasantly, that it had been a slow summer.

I didn't mean anything seductive —I didn't mean anything, it *was* a slow summer—but Eric raised his eyebrows as if I did and said, "You're bored?"

I tried to laugh. "No," I said. I'd had enough.

Then Lawrence volunteered that I'd been writing poetry. "No I haven't," I said.

"Yes you have. She's a wonderful poet. She's being modest."

"I have not," I said.

Mart looked past the shiny black grand piano and the tuxedoed piano player, through the French doors, one of which was open to the fountain on the terrace. We'd been there less than five minutes, and she was tired of us all.

Eric wasn't pressing for more information about the poetry, either, which was fine with me, as I didn't want to discuss it.

Our table already had a little white dish full of salted almonds and another full of dried fruit, which Eric and Mart hadn't touched, and our waiter brought some potato chips and phyllo pastry triangles, which, he explained, were stuffed with minced lamb.

Lawrence said, "Keeps a whole stack of poems locked away in a drawer."

I smiled, trying to cover how irritated I felt, and shook my head to get him to stop. I was trying to think of something to say to change the subject when our drinks arrived, doing it for me.

　—Thank you, God.

I'd ordered something called an Iron Lion Zion—chocolate and banana liqueurs with rum—and it came in a sugared martini glass with a little piece of fudge stuck on the rim.

Lawrence lifted his martini and said, "Cheers," and Eric said, "To old friends," and I said, "Yes," and Mart kept her mouth shut and we all drank.

I put the fudge in my mouth and let it start to melt on my tongue.

Mart said in her Nazi accent, "You are having dessert first?" She didn't approve.

I said, "Life is short," sounding like a bumper sticker.

I looked around. There was a beautiful harp next to the piano—inlaid wood, with gold gilt trim—though no one was playing it. I wondered if it was just for show. The piano's trophy harp.

I swallowed the fudge—I eat when I'm nervous—and took a bite of a lamb pastry.

I was thinking about Mart's bizarre sexiness and how there's something in physics called a strange attractor, a mathematical shape that looks sort of like multilayered butterfly wings and that explains turbulence by showing how it follows its own set of rules, creating a pattern, just not one that we can see. According to the theory behind it, much of nature's apparent chaos is actually just invisible order. It was a comforting idea. Sort of.

　—But then again, I thought, much of nature's apparent order—everything we can see—is, on a subatomic level, a great big mess.

"I'll Be Seeing You" segued into "The Last Time I Saw Paris" on the piano, and our table's conversation had come to an awkward halt when I heard a man's voice, a Texan, judging from his accent, say, "A big plate of spareribs!" as if it was a punch line. Then he said, "Do they have spareribs in Vienna?" I wanted to turn around and look at him, but I didn't.

Nobody else at my table seemed to have heard him, but Eric said "Oh!" as if to say, Speaking of punch lines. Then he touched my hand and said, "You'll love this," and I took another sip of my drink to keep him from holding my hand. He acted like he didn't notice and said, "A poet, a priest, and a physicist walk into a bar, order a round of drinks. The bartender says, 'You're all storytellers. You're all trying to figure out the meaning of life. Tell me a story.' So the priest says, 'Well, first God created an orderly universe, then man fucked it up, then God sent Jesus to fix things, and two thousand years later, here we are.' Then the physicist says, 'No, first there was chaos, then a big explosion, then the universe started evolving, and billions and billions of years later, here we are.' Then the poet looks around, finishes his drink, and shoots himself in the head."

We all laughed.

I could hear the bartender mixing a martini in a shaker, ice beating rhythmically against metal, like a headache.

Lawrence said, "But seriously, chaos before the Big Bang?"

Eric said, "Yeah, that's why this physicist hangs out with priests and poets. He didn't get tenure."

Big laughs all around. Jokes about people who don't have tenure never fail to get huge laughs from people who do.

I thought about pointing out yet again that I was not a poet, but decided against it.

Mart said, "I think before the Big Bang, there was another universe that had expanded and contracted, and before that, another, and before that, another and another and another, an infinite number."

"How can you possibly say such a thing?" Eric said. Then, looking at Lawrence. "I sleep with her, but it's like I don't even know her."

They laughed, and then they were off on a friendly but passionate argument about what came before the beginning of time, and the piano player started into "Stars Fell on Alabama," and I thought, —This is my favorite rendering of the Big Bang.

When we got back to the room, I said, "Why did you say that, about me being a poet?"

"Because it's true," Lawrence said, taking off his jacket. "I was trying to rescue you."

"But I'm not a poet. I've written half a dozen poems in the past year."

I'd written seven, but I wasn't sure one of them was really a poem. I was also working on a children's book, though I hadn't told Lawrence.

It was a young adult novel about a girl whose mother was Miss Alabama, 1957. The mother's talents were ventriloquism and operatic singing, which she performed at the same time and which, after the pageant, she dedicated to God. That was the deal she'd made: Give me this crown, and I will use it to spread Your word. So for the first ten years of my narrator's life, she rides with her mother all over Alabama and parts of Mississippi to church youth groups, children's hospitals, and prisons, where her tiara-clad mother and Katie, the dummy, lead untold numbers of girls, boys, and felons to Christ.

My narrator can't stand Katie, who siphons the hate off her love-hate relationship with her mother, and she has mixed feelings about Jesus, but she adores her mother. The mother is beautiful, manipulative, self-absorbed, and utterly charming, and the daughter thinks she's good and famous and as close to being a real queen as anyone outside a fairy tale can get. She tries hard to be exactly like her.

But the summer she turns eleven, her father dies in a car accident, and the mother sends the daughter to live with her grandmother in Bovary, Alabama, for six months while she's looking for her next husband. Then she marries a car dealer and moves the daughter with her to a big house in Hammond, Louisiana. The daughter, of course, resents the new husband and all the time her mother has spent away from her, so the mother enters her into a beauty pageant, which she thinks will be a thing for them to bond over, and at first it is. For about a day, it's a kind of Cinderella story where the mother is the fairy godmother, and she buys the girl the most beautiful dress the girl has ever seen, her first pair of high heels, drives her to Houston to get her hair and nails and makeup done and they get head shots taken by a photographer who has pictures of beauty queens all over the walls of the studio, including one of her mother when she was Miss Alabama, and the girl feels awkward in front of the camera until the mother teaches her a way of looking at the camera, a thirteen-year-old version of making love to the camera, and the girl has a little bit of a sexual awakening, and she gets into it and starts imagining her own picture up on that wall someday, she starts wanting it.

So on the drive home, they're trying to decide what she can do for a talent, and she realizes she doesn't have a talent even though she's taken ballet and piano and voice lessons since she was three but she knows she's not very good at any of them, she's no good at anything. So the mother gets off the highway, pulls into a gas station, takes her by the shoulders and says, "Look, you need a talent for this contest, so you'll sing. Anybody can sing a song. And if you're not the best singer in the world, you know what? It's okay." For about a second and a half, the girl feels a tremendous weight lifted off her shoulders, a weight she didn't even know she'd been carrying, though as soon as it's gone, she realizes it's pretty much always been there, but then the mother says, "But what you need to understand, now that you're becoming a woman, is that life is a pageant. It's one big, long beauty contest, and the girl who gets the best husband, wins. Ultimately, being Miss Anything is just a step on the way to being a better Mrs. Everything, and you don't need to know how to sing to do that. You just need to look your best at all times and know in your heart that you can have any man you want, and you will do anything you have to get him."

The girl tries to take this in. The weight is back, only now it's heavier, and it's moved from her shoulders to her gut.

Finally, she says, "How is being Miss Crawfish going to get me a better husband?"

"Because men can't think for themselves. Oh, it opens doors, you get to meet the governor, you meet a better class of men. But the main thing is, every man wants the most beautiful girl he can get, and eventually, when you're Miss Louisiana, you'll officially be the most beautiful girl in the whole state. Meanwhile, if you're Miss Crawfish, or Miss Junior Crawfish, technically, you're the most beautiful thirteen- to fifteen-year-old in whatever—in the parish, I guess. This is practice."

Then they go get cherry Icees, and the cold red sugar sliding down the girl's throat makes her feel better.

When they get home, the mother takes the daughter into Katie's bedroom, which is also a shrine to the mother's Miss Alabama days. The evening gown that she wore when she was crowned is on one mannequin in one corner of the room, the one she wore in the Miss America pageant is on another, and the bathing suit and sash are on another. The tiara is in a glass case. There's a little bed with a white eyelet canopy where Katie sleeps, though most of the time she sits in a miniature wicker chair by the window. The closet is full of Katie's clothes—Katie has twice as many clothes as the main character, which is a source of tension between the main character and the mother, who says the dummy needs more clothes because she and the mother have a singing act together and that daughter has to be nice to the dummy, who isn't as pretty as she is and therefore whose marriage prospects aren't as bright as the main character's, who, if she marries well, can have all the clothes she wants when she grows up.

There's a little bit of a reverse Pinocchio thing happening, where the girl wishes she could be a doll, at least in the mother's eyes, but she can't figure out what to do, what lies to tell, to make that happen.

Anyway, they go into the room, where the main character is not usually allowed, and the mother gets the tiara out of its case and puts it on the girl's head and has her look in the three-way mirror and says, "Now look in the mirror and imagine yourself as the Crawfish Queen."

She can't, of course. She just sees herself—three different views of her.

The mother says, "You have to believe that crown is yours from the minute you step onto the stage. The crown loves you, the camera loves you, the judges, everybody loves you. The talent, the interview, the swimsuit, the evening gown, all that's just hoops you have to jump through to get what's coming to you."

The girl looks in the mirror again. The crown is starting to slip off her head, and she's reaching up to adjust it when she hears the dummy's squeaky voice say to the mother, "You'd never have won yours without me. She doesn't stand a chance."

The narrator agrees with her, though not out loud. She turns around to see that her mother has picked up the dummy, who is talking to the mother. The mother says to the dummy, "What a terrible thing to say!" sounding like she's trying to seem shocked.

And the dummy squeaks, "I'm just trying to help!" Her voice sounds like a combination of Mickey Mouse and fingernails on a chalkboard.

"How so?" the mother says in her own voice.

"It's what the other girls are going to try to make her feel," the dummy says. "She may as well figure out how to deal with the pressure now."

Then the mother says to the main character, "She has a point."

"Don't take her side," the girl says.

"I'm not!" the mother says.

"You always do," the girl says.

"No I don't. I'm being impartial. *You* tell your sister how wrong she is if you really believe that. You tell her why you know you're the next Crawfish Queen."

The main character doesn't answer. One, she doesn't *have* an answer, but two, she refuses to have a conversation with a piece of wood. A piece of wood who is capable of reducing her to tears. A piece of wood who's not even pretty and who has won more beauty pageants than she'll ever enter. A piece of wood she hates like a sister. The favorite.

The dummy says, "You're going up against girls who've been doing this since they were babies, titles out the wazoo. You've got to learn not to be intimidated."

"I'm not intimidated," the girl says, "I don't *care* who was Miss Crawfish or Miss Crab or Miss Shrimp or Miss Lobster, all the Crustacean Queens can keep their damn crowns. I don't want to do this," and she throws the crown on the floor, where it breaks.

That was where the novel was falling apart.

In real life, most of that happened, except that I was six when my father died, not eleven. I did live with my grandmother in South Alabama for most of first grade, but I'd been living in Louisiana with my mother and her husband, Big John, for several years when she entered me in the pageant. I was, like my narrator, thirteen when I entered the pageant, but I didn't say I didn't want to do it, certainly didn't curse at my mother, and couldn't bring myself to do anything to the crown other than carefully take it off my head and hand it over to my mother. Then I burst into tears.

Two weeks later, I found myself on the stage of the local high school gym, my hair up in a bun with little ringlets coming down everywhere, so much hair spray I could barely move my neck, wearing a pink dotted-swiss prom dress held up by spaghetti straps. The interview had gone exactly as we'd rehearsed it. When they asked me what I wanted to be when I grew up, I said, "I would like to be a helpmeet for my husband, support him, be there for him in any way I can. I want to have lots of children." When they asked me what woman I admired most in the world, I said, "My mother." But this was the talent portion, and I was singing "All You Need Is Love," and playing the guitar, using the three chords I had mastered only a few days before, when we decided we needed something to punch up my singing. So I made it as far as "Nothing you can sing that can't be sung," which is about the second line, and I thought, What a stupid thing to say, how *could* there be something you could sing that couldn't be sung? And then I was lost. I sang that line again, and then I completely blanked out, couldn't even think of the tune. So after the five or ten longest seconds of my life, I just ran off the stage. Or, I tried to, but I tripped on the microphone cord, dropped the guitar, and the sound of a guitar crashing onto the floor is one of the all-time worst sounds there is. The wood cracking, which sounded to me at that moment like somebody's heart breaking, and all the dissonance from the strings vibrating, and the complete, horrified silence from the audience.

It was a long drive home in the car. After the first several minutes, my mother said, "Well, we'll just have to be better prepared next time."

I told her there wasn't going to be a next time.

She stiffened. I could feel the air between us stiffen with her. I could barely breathe it.

She said, brightly, "That's how you feel right now, but you'll get over this. There'll be other pageants."

"You don't love me," I said.

She didn't answer.

A few minutes later, she said, "How about Miss Peanut in June? Peanut is huge."

I didn't answer her.

She kept driving through the night.

A few miles later, I said, very calmly, "I don't love you either."

I wasn't crying. I hadn't shed one tear.

"You don't mean that," she said, and what I heard was, You *do* love me, and to prove it, you will enter Miss Peanut and you will win, and then I will love you, too.

That was when I told her that if she ever entered me in another pageant, I would kill myself.

She pulled to the side of the road and turned off the car. Then she put her hands back on the steering wheel and took a deep breath, and one second passed, the flap of a wing, where the rest of our relationship, the rest of my life, could have turned in another direction.

Then, without looking at me, she said, "My God, Ellen. After all I've done for you. Driving you everywhere you ever wanted to go like I was your personal chauffeur, all the money I spent on lessons and photographs and clothes, all the time I spent coaching you. All I ever wanted was for you to have a better life than I did, and this is the thanks I get."

"You were Miss Alabama. How could I do better than that?"

She turned toward me, though it felt more like she was turning *on* me, and said, "You could have been Miss America. You could have had it all. When I entered my first pageant, I didn't know a soul in the pageant world. I had to figure it all out for myself. But you had every advantage there was, and you're throwing it down the drain. The level of ingratitude here is incomprehensible to me."

"Mother, look at me. Please. I'm never going to be Miss America."

And she sat there looking at me, and part of me wanted her to tell me no, I was wrong, I was prettier than I felt, or I was only thirteen and I had good bones underneath my baby fat, so it was only a matter of time, like the Ugly Duckling. But she looked me over, and I watched the fire in her eyes go out as she realized it was true. Her expression didn't change, her face remained perfectly still, not one muscle twitched, but I could see that she was forcing herself not to show what she felt. She finally saw the truth about me, but she couldn't accept it, so she said nothing.

I started screaming. "So I'm supposed to be grateful to you for trying to turn me into somebody I'm not? I'm not your dummy. You can't pull my strings and make me say anything you want me to say and want everything you want me to want and be everything you want me to be. I'm a *person*."

My mother whispered, "You think I don't know you're a person? My God, Ellen, I could not be any more painfully aware that you are a person than I am at this moment. It's *what kind* of person you are that's breaking my heart."

I thought about saying, What kind of person is that? Ugly? Awkward? Untalented? Inarticulate? Hateful? Doomed to end up an old maid?

But I didn't want to hear her answer. Plus, I was suddenly crying too hard to talk.

She started the car, merged back into traffic, and we drove the rest of the way home without speaking.

Later, in the middle of the night, I got up to run away and

walked into the kitchen, headed for the door, and there in the dark was my mother.

I stopped. I had a pillowcase full of clothes, and I set them down on the floor.

She had her back to me. Her hair was pulled up off her neck, and she was wearing her long white cotton nightgown, her thin body silhouetted by the cold light coming from the open refrigerator door, which cast ghostly shadows into the kitchen. She was standing there looking into the refrigerator, though something about the way she held on to the door, leaning on it, made me think she'd been standing there for a long time, doing something other than trying to decide on a snack. Her feet were bare.

I was trying not to breathe.

She turned around slowly and said, "You hungry?"

She was wearing her tiara. She had a cut-crystal glass of Scotch in her hand.

I said, "Yes, ma'am."

And she set down the Scotch and got a box of butter pecan ice cream out of the freezer and opened it. Then she took two spoons from the drawer and put the ice cream in the middle of the breakfast table.

I sat down across from her and looked at it. It was a new box. The surface of the ice cream hadn't been broken. I didn't know where to start.

She put her spoon right in the center and scooped up a big bite, and I did the same. It was cold and it tasted so sweet it hurt my jaw. Sometimes Mama would say things were sweet as memory or sweet as angel's breath—those were the words that went through my head—but neither of us said anything out loud.

Mama didn't put down her spoon, though she didn't take another bite, but I kept eating and eating, devouring that ice cream until I could feel the sugar melting in my brain like kisses.

There were no lights on, but the moon was bright outside, shining in through the patio doors and the window over the sink. We could see well enough.

The thought occurred to me that if somebody were to look in on us, they might believe the lie we were trying to convince ourselves of, that this whole night and everything leading up to it had never happened. We had never said the cruel things we'd said, hadn't meant them, and nothing but my pageant career had ended.

I was stuck on the novel—afraid to write it the way it happened and unable to write it any other way.

I WAS GLAD LAWRENCE DIDN'T KNOW ABOUT THE BOOK— glad, and sad that I was glad.

He went into the walk-in closet to hang up his jacket and I sat down on the edge of the bed.

"How many poems do you have to write to be a poet?" he said from the closet.

"More than six," I said, ready to drop the whole argument but not willing to say it didn't matter.

"How many?" he said, coming back out and facing me. Then, slightly sarcastically, "Ten? Fifteen?"

I swallowed. I was not drunk, but I'd had several glasses of wine—with dinner, over several hours. This was the kind of thing I usually let slide—I hadn't been stewing on it all through dinner—but I was pretty sure it wasn't because of the wine that I was saying something this time. I thought it was connected to having seen Diana, though I couldn't have begun to explain how.

Lawrence said, "I just want to understand the rules here."

I said, "Sixty-four."

He put up his hands in mock surrender, then started taking off his tie.

"Okay, I won't call you a poet."

"Thank you."

I sat in the chair and slipped off my shoes, which had been pinching my feet. I spread my toes as if they were strange little wings. I thought we were done. I wanted to be done. Or, part of me did. Part of me wanted to walk into the bathroom and close the door and not come out until I was ready to act like the whole poetry conversation—the whole evening— had never happened. But I just sat there, looking at my feet.

"But I didn't call you a poet," Lawrence said. "I said you write poetry. And that's true."

I looked at him.

I said, "But why? Why did you have to say that? Especially after you'd just told Mart, one minute after meeting her, that the way her paper on string theory connected the movement of quarks with the orbits of binary stars was a stunningly elegant marriage of science and poetry."

"Are you jealous of her?"

"Should I be?"

"Please. It was Eric's work. He supposedly cowrote it with her, but it was clearly his work, his fingerprints were all over it."

"So why did you say it?"

"Ellen, that's what people do. You get a paper published, you expect your colleagues to tell you they read it and liked it, whether they actually give a shit or not."

"No, why did you say I wrote poetry? Do you have some sort of Emily Dickinson fantasy about me?"

Lawrence was neatly folding his tie. He liked expensive ties, and he always took special care with them, which suddenly bothered me. He always wore Brooks Brothers all-cotton oxford button-down shirts, medium starch, white or light blue, and he always kept his shoes—black Italian leather wingtips—perfectly shined. I had liked this about him in the beginning—most scientists have no fashion sense at all—but now it struck me as both arrogant and boring at the same time. Diana's boyfriend had been wearing a brown suede jacket and brown suede cowboy boots. In August. I couldn't imagine being with a man who wore brown suede.

"I promise you," Lawrence said, "I have never had any kind of Emily Dickinson fantasy. If I had to have an Emily Dickinson fantasy, I wouldn't know where to start. Wasn't she a virgin spinster?"

I stood up and took off my pantyhose, draped them over the back of a chair.

"Don't," I said. "I'm asking you, do you have a fantasy that I'm a great poet, a great intellect—a great *anything*—but nobody knows?"

Lawrence's first wife, who died of breast cancer, was a great chemist. Ironically, she spent most of her career working on a drug to treat breast cancer.

—Do you wish I were a scientist?

Lawrence said, "No."

I wanted him to put his arms around me. I wanted him to say he loved me, he wasn't ashamed of me, didn't secretly wish I was anything other than what I was. I wanted him to say, You *are* great. You're a great friend, a great lover, a great wife, a great mother to my son, and those things mean more to me than if you were the greatest poet in the world.

But he just said no, and something shifted in me, something so deep inside me that it almost felt like it was underneath me, the ground moving under my feet, and all I could think about was keeping my balance, and all I could say was, "No?"

He said, "I can't say anything right, can I?"

I said, "You can."

And I waited one, two, three, long, silent seconds.

Then I said, "But you don't."

He said, "What do you want me to say?"

"Nothing."

—If I have to tell you to say it before you say it, then it wouldn't count when you did.

He sat on the edge of the bed, setting his tie on the nightstand, and bent over to untie his shoes.

I wanted to let it go — part of me did — but I couldn't.

So I tried again. I was trying to redo the moment, better, and to undo it, to make it disappear by replacing it with another. I made my voice sound calm: "You wanted Eric to think I had whole manuscripts hidden away in the attic, that I have everything it takes to be famous except the fame."

"God, Ellen. One, I don't care if you write poetry. I said that because I thought you cared. Two, if I did have a fantasy about you being secretly famous, I wouldn't . . . I mean, name one famous poet."

"Emily Dickinson!" I said.

I stood up and unzipped my dress, let it fall to the floor.

I wasn't wearing a bra. I hadn't thought out what I wanted to get from him by doing that, but when he carried his shoes into the closet without even glancing at me, I realized I hadn't gotten it.

I looked at the closet door. I knew without seeing that he was placing his shoes carefully on the floor, side by side, exactly parallel to one another, not touching.

"So why did you say it?" I said, raising my voice just a little to compensate for his being out of sight. I picked my dress up off the floor, draped it over the back of the chair with my pantyhose. When he didn't answer, I said, "I don't care that much about poetry to begin with, but to the extent that I do, I certainly don't care whether Eric thinks I'm a poet. But wouldn't it be perfect for you if I was? Because I could be as famous in my field as you are in yours, or better yet, almost as famous, but it would be a totally esoteric kind of fame that would never for one second eclipse yours."

He came out. "There is no such thing as esoteric fame," he said, unbuttoning his shirt. He was in his sock feet.

I hadn't meant fame. I'd meant respect. I'd meant accomplishment. I knew he didn't care if I was famous. I'd fucked up my own argument.

—Idiot.

While he unbuttoned his cuffs, he said in a pseudo-calm, "My point is, if I had some absurd fantasy that you were famous, or semi-famous, or not-famous, or whatever it is we're talking about, which I don't, I wouldn't fantasize that you were a poet. Give me a little credit."

Then he went back into the closet to hang up his shirt.

I said, "Is that your whole response to what I just said?"

He walked out and stopped. Stopped talking, stopped un-dressing. Looked at me.

"Okay," he said. "I know you sometimes feel insecure around Eric, and I was just trying . . ."

I was standing in front of him, naked except for some see-through panties.

I said, "Trying what?" and sat down on the bed. I folded my arms across my stomach.

"I don't know," he said.

"Yes you do. Say it. You were trying to make it look like I had a reason to feel good about myself, like I'd accomplished something. But you had to make something up to do that. Jesus, Lawrence, do you have any idea how that makes me feel?"

"Obviously not."

He sat down next to me on the bed, and I stood up.

"I meant well," he said, and I believed him. Which just made it worse.

"It's okay," I said, lying. "Forget it."

I went into the bathroom. I looked at my makeup spread out all over the counter and stuffed it back into its case. I slipped on a robe, brushed my teeth, rubbed moisturizer onto my legs, flossed, peed, washed my hands, washed my face, ap-plied wrinkle treatment.

When I came out again, he was in bed, in his pajamas, reading. He looked up.

I took a bottle of water out of the minibar, poured some into a glass.

I said, "Do you want some of this?"

"Only if you're not going to drink it all."

I poured some into another glass and brought it to him.

I sat down on the edge of the bed, my back to him. I was thinking about what it would be like to get divorced and start over.

—What are my chances of falling in love at this age?

—I don't even know any single men, and I don't want to raise somebody else's child again, but I'm no good at being alone. I've been wanting a dog because I don't like being by myself so much during the day.

—Plus, Lawrence would get the house, since it was paid for before he even knew me, and most of our income is generated by royalties from two inventions involving superconductivity that he and Eric patented in the early eighties and investments from Nobel money. So there's always alimony based on his salary from the university, but if I wanted to live the way I do now, I'd have to work, and I don't have a single marketable skill. I'm good with people, but I would rather slit my wrists than sell real estate. I love my charities, but eventually, I'd be rotated off the boards of the theater and the symphony because those positions are invariably held by people who can be expected to donate large amounts of money to the causes. I could still volunteer for Feed the Hungry, though I'm not sure I'd have the time or energy for it if I was working a real job I didn't even like. So I couldn't live the way I do now without the money a real job would bring in, but doing that work would make it impossible for me to keep the kind of life I have.

My hands felt heavy. I looked at them in my lap, turned them over. Either way, they looked like they'd been put on backwards.

—Maybe I am a little drunk. Probably I should have kept my mouth shut.

I heard him pick up his glass, take a sip of water, put the glass back down.

I got up to put on my nightgown.

As soon as we turned out the lights, Lawrence fell asleep, and my mind started racing. I replayed the entire dinner conversation, only this time I said witty things and Eric laughed and Mart said nothing and Lawrence didn't claim I wrote poetry. I replayed our argument. Then I started wondering if Lawrence's first wife, Angela, had felt the way I did around Eric, if Lawrence had told him she was about to cure cancer, and she'd thought, No I'm not, I'm not even close.

— Go to sleep, I said to myself. Stop thinking, and go to sleep.

AND THE NEXT MORNING, AFTER MY RUN, AFTER MY EN-counters with Diana's car and Max and his photograph, not to mention Diana, I'm sitting, alone, on the same edge of the same bed, feeling the same heaviness in my hands that I did the night before but for a different reason.

I take a shower and get dressed, and Lawrence is still not back from breakfast.

I look at myself in the full-length mirror. I'm wearing black linen pants and a white crewneck T-shirt over a sporty white bra that you can just make out under the shirt, walking shoes that look only slightly less ugly than most walking shoes. I may as well have my hair in a ponytail.

I think, —If I were sitting in a café and saw myself pass by on the sidewalk, I would think, That woman, that American woman, is recently divorced, and she's traveling alone, determined to enjoy her independence. She has a map and a small leather-bound notebook in her purse, and she's got every minute she'll be in Paris scheduled out and written down. Every night she goes back to her room in a little hotel near the Luxembourg Gardens and checks off the things on the list. Louvre, done. Eiffel Tower, done. Notre Dame, done. Now, on to Italy.

I think, —This is not who I am.

I take off my top, my bra. I turn so my left breast is in three-quarter profile, stand up straight, and suck in my stomach, but not too far, not so it looks sucked in, just so it's slightly flatter. I don't have the world's greatest stomach and I'm just glad my butt is in a place where I don't have to look at it, but I have good breasts. Not too droopy. Not too small. I cup them in my hands. I press my fingers in concentric circles around each nipple, checking for lumps. All clear.

I think, —I'm not dying.

I put on my shirt without a bra. I can see my nipples through it.

—No.

I go back into the bedroom and get out a black bra and put it on with a black plunge V-neck Calvin Klein T-shirt with three-quarter-length sleeves. It's a plain cotton top, not evening wear, nothing overtly revealing, but it shows a little cleavage. I slip out of my walking shoes and put on my black Prada sandals.

Then I sit on the edge of the bed and watch Diana on TV.

When Lawrence comes back from breakfast, I kiss him and say, "Did you hear about Princess Diana?"

"Yeah," he says. He doesn't look at the TV, at the endless stream of pictures of her, smiling, and he doesn't seem to have anything else to say about her.

"Isn't it sad?" I say.

"Yeah, it's too bad," he says, without emotion.

He sits down at the desk and takes off his shoes. He's wearing old khakis, not how he'll dress for the conference. He hasn't shaved, which means he hasn't showered. Which means that as soon as he woke up, he threw on some clothes and went down to eat, rather than shower and dress for the day while he waited for me to get back and go downstairs with him.

I turn off the sound with the remote.

"How was breakfast?" I say. It's after eight now, so he spent over an hour in the restaurant, though he usually just grabs a piece of whole-wheat toast and a cup of coffee in the morning on his way out the door.

"It was good. It was great. I ran into Eric and Mart, and we had the most interesting conversation I've had in *months*."

I open a bottle of water from the minibar and take a sip.

"Great," I say.

He goes into the bathroom without closing the door. I don't know what he's doing in there.

I sit down on the end of the bed and drink some more water.

He says, "We started talking about the hole."

The hole is a three-thousand-light-years-wide black hole at the center of the Milky Way, pulling matter toward it and into it as it swirls. He's part of a team of scientists who discovered it and is on the verge of proving it exists, though he's less interested in the proof now—he's certain it's there, so let the mathematicians do the math, he says. What he's obsessed with—one of the things he's obsessed with—is that this black hole spews antimatter, the atomic opposite of matter, and when antimatter particles collide with their corresponding matter particles, as they inevitably do, they annihilate each other.

So he's trying to figure out what that implies about why the universe exists in the first place, because if at the time of the Big Bang, the universe contained equal amounts of matter and antimatter, as most scientists believe it did, why didn't they annihilate each other then?

I say, "What about it?"

"We were talking about not only *this* hole, but the idea that there's a black hole at the center of every galaxy, and Mart, who's just a real freethinker, started speculating about whether there's some sort of superhole at the center of the universe, and on reflex, I said, 'There *is* no center,' but . . ."

Then he stops, and there's a stopping in me, as if I've just taken a mental snapshot of this moment. I'm not a jealous person—when other faculty wives flirt with Lawrence at parties, it doesn't bother me—but I find myself bizarrely irritated by his admiration for Mart's mind, which I try to tell myself is ridiculous. I'm also feeling left out, that the three of them had breakfast without me, but of course they did. For one thing, I wasn't even in the hotel, I was at Diana's crash site. For another thing, I don't eat breakfast, though I could have sat there and drunk coffee with them. But this is why people go to conferences—it happens every year and I never think a thing of it—so I don't know what's gotten into me.

—Yes you do. It's the implicit criticism of every single conversation you and Lawrence have had for months: None of them was as interesting to him as this one. Not one.

—That's not what he meant.

—It's what he said. It's exactly what he said. It's also true. We don't have interesting conversations. We talk about what's for dinner, we talk about painting the house, remodeling the kitchen, getting a dog. We talk about bills, schedules, doctors' appointments. And I read his manuscript—he's writing a book about the cosmos for laypeople—and I tell him what I don't understand, which could lead to interesting conversations, but it doesn't. We never discuss it because the few times we have, he tried to explain the thing I didn't understand to me and I still didn't get it and we both got irritated, so now I just read it and put either exclamation points or question marks in the margins, and he says thanks, and I say you're welcome. And today, he had the most interesting conversation he's had in months.

He comes out of the bathroom with his socks in his hand and the same distracted look on his face that he gets when he can't find his glasses, and I say, "What's wrong?" and a tiny part of me, one cell, thinks maybe he realizes what was happening to us—there's a black hole at the center of our marriage—but then he sits back down at the desk and picks up a pen, and that cell dies off.

"A note I need to make," he says. "I just thought of something, for the book."

I say, "What? Now you think there *is* a center, and it's a superhole?"

I really want to know. Some physicists think that what we call black holes are really more like tunnels—not wormholes, which appear and disappear, if they exist at all, where black holes never appear because they're invisible, but they never go away, either—and whatever goes into our black holes comes out transformed at the other ends in alternate universes. Lawrence thinks they're all quacks, but it makes sense to me, because otherwise, where does the gravitational pull in a black hole come from? Doesn't there have to be something huge in there? So what if they're right? Would a superhole posit some sort of superalternateuniverse?

I want to ask him all that. I want to have a conversation with him that he thinks is more interesting than the one he had at breakfast with Mart, but for one thing, I'm not sure what's the difference in Lawrence's mind between a freethinker and a quack.

He's tapping his pen on the notepad, frowning in concentration.

I say, "Is that what you're saying?"

He shakes his head to say, Don't interrupt me. I'm thinking. So I wait.

Some conservative physicists still think that the density at the center of our galaxy is a clump of stars that are too dark to be seen, but I know in my body that it's a black hole. The whole Milky Way is in the process of destroying itself from the inside out, literally consuming itself. So a superhole at the center of the universe, at the place where the Big Bang occurred, wherever that is, wouldn't surprise me at all. I think we're all intimately connected to the universe in ways we can't explain, and sometimes I feel it, that infinite yearning for light, in my own center, plain as desire.

And there it is, in my opinion, the force at the center of the universe: desire.

It's muddled science, I know, pseudoscience, which is what Lawrence calls the alternate-universe theory—he says they're going to be able to create microscopic black holes in a lab someday, and they certainly won't create microscopic alternate universes when they do—so I don't say anything even when he finishes writing.

He says, "I'm sorry. I can't talk about it right now. I don't even want to think about it too much. I need to let it ferment. Sorry."

I say, "It's okay."

He makes another note.

And I feel my own black hole, spinning around itself at the center of me, reminding me that I have the capacity to hurl my quiet life into utter chaos.

He's emptying his pockets, putting his wallet and a few pieces of paper on the desk, while he says, "I need a fast shower, and then I've got to get going. I'll meet you back here tonight between seven and seven-fifteen at the absolute latest, okay?"

"Okay."

"Eric's already made dinner plans for him and Mart, and she asked him to change them so the four of us could eat together, and he refused like the asshole he can be, but she recommended a restaurant for us, her favorite restaurant in France, and she's something of a restaurant aficionada, so I asked the concierge to make reservations, gave him a huge tip, and they're not open yet, but he says he thinks he can get us in tonight because it's Sunday and it's August if we're willing to get there by seven-thirty, and it's a fifteen-to-twenty minute cab ride away, so really, ten after seven."

He's talking in run-on sentences. Usually, this early in the day, he's not ready to talk at all, and it's petty of me, I know, but I don't like it that what's revitalized him in a way that being with me doesn't is a conversation with Mart. And now Mart's telling us where to eat. She's probably told us what to order, too. Everything but what to wear.

"Great," I say. "I'll be ready."

Lawrence is unbuttoning his shirt.

I look at the things he's left on the desk. On one scrap, in what I assume is Mart's writing—it's angular and messy and hard to read, like an arrogant man's—but I can make out the words, "Alain Ducasse, btw r de Longchamps & pl Victor Hugo."

I read a rave about this restaurant not too long ago, either in *Gourmet* or *Condé Nast Traveler,* I think. Alain Ducasse — the person, not the restaurant—has six Michelin stars, three each at two restaurants, and he's only three years older than I am. I didn't suggest eating there for this trip, though, because the article said you had to make reservations at least two months in advance, and Lawrence won't do that at this conference. You never know when you're going to run into an old colleague you want to have dinner with, he says. So I'm wondering why we're going to Mart's favorite restaurant without Mart, trying not to work myself up about it.

Lawrence drapes his shirt over the back of the desk chair, then goes to the closet, undoing his belt and unzipping his pants as he walks.

He goes into the closet and—I know this without look-ing—carefully hangs up his khakis, double-checking to make sure they're folded right on the creases.

Then he goes into the bathroom, still wearing his boxers, and closes the door behind him. I hear the shower turn on. This is his routine: He turns the water on to let it heat up, goes to the bathroom, then takes off his underwear at the last second before getting into the shower.

I take another sip of water. And another. I'm not about to cry, not anywhere near, but I feel that kind of tightness in my throat, as if I'm stuck on a pill, and I try to swallow it.

I hear the toilet flush.

I look at the note Lawrence made on the desk:

EH of SH >> end of time???

p-brane (SB?) morphs >> Ω pt

Check with BG re branes &—then there's something illegible.

I'm pretty sure SH is the superhole, and I'm guessing that EH means event horizon, the boundary of a black hole from which it's impossible to escape, so I figure he's thinking maybe that's how the universe will end: It reaches the super-hole's event horizon, gets sucked in, and all of space and time collapse.

Dust to dust.

I take off my sandals.

It makes sense. It makes horrific sense, but it makes sense. If I understand black holes correctly, anything that's spinning around one is ultimately going to fall into it, like water spinning around a drain, because the fact of the spin means there's no counterforce acting on the spinning thing that's stronger than the hole's gravity.

I take off my top.

On the other hand, if something traveling through the universe on its own momentum—light, for example—comes near a black hole, it might be thrown off course a little, but as long as it avoids the event horizon, it can just pass on by.

I sit on the edge of the bed and take off my slacks.

I'm missing some science here, I think. Some light does get trapped in black holes, which is why they're black, but other light doesn't, which is how they first realized black holes existed, by watching light bend as it passed by them. I'm just not sure why sometimes it happens and sometimes it doesn't.

I stand up and unhook my bra and let the straps fall off my shoulders onto the floor.

I do know it's possible to feel the effect of a black hole's gravity and not fall in. Somehow. It's a matter of avoiding the event horizon, but that begs the question, it seems to me, because if you don't fall in, you have, by definition, avoided the event horizon, and if you do fall in, you haven't.

I take off my watch, my earrings, my rings and put them in an ashtray on the desk.

If you did fall in, say, feet first, the difference at the event horizon between the gravitational pull at your feet and that at your head would cause you to be stretched into a long, thin thread, a process some physicists call spaghettification—I don't know why you wouldn't just break, but everywhere I've ever heard this phenomenon described, they say you'd be stretched so long that your feet would be too far away for your eyes to see them—but eventually, once your whole body passed the event horizon, you'd presumably snap back to your old size on your way to being crushed to nothing.

I step out of my panties.

Nobody knows for sure what goes on inside black holes.

I wrap my hair around itself into a little bun and hold it with a rubber band and go into the bathroom.

He's in the shower, facing the wall, lathering up, so he doesn't see me come in.

I stand at the shower door and say, "Knock knock," and he opens it and says, "What's this?" and I step in—it's a huge shower—and put my arms around his neck.

"I have to go to the conference," he says.

"So you'll be ten minutes late," I say. "What are you going to miss? Coffee and doughnuts? Café au lait and croissants?"

I pick up a box of soap and start to open it. I'm going to wash his back, starting with his neck and shoulders and moving down slowly until I get to the heels of his feet, then I'll wash his feet, talking as I go about the whole universe collapsing inside the superhole, then move to his front and work my way up, talking about the possibility that the amount of energy concentrated there—all the energy in the universe—would cause another Big Bang and start the whole process over, the universe expanding and contracting and expanding, again and again, an eternal cosmic orgasm.

I tilt my head. I'm still smiling as if I think this is possible, but I already know from reading his body language—utter silence—that it's not going to happen, so I'm trying to figure out how to get out without making whatever is already bad here, worse. I put my soap back on the little marble shelf.

He says, "I'm giving the opening address."

Now he's washing his armpits, his chest, and I'm just standing here, naked, flat-footed.

He says, "I can't very well show up ten minutes late for that," which wasn't necessary. I wouldn't have asked him to be late to his own speech if I'd remembered. Even though I'm pretty sure they spend at least an hour before the opening address drinking coffee, getting people registered, shaking each others' hands, slapping each other on the back.

"Okay," I say.

"You understand, don't you." It's not a question.

I say, "Yeah," and this is a big thing for him, this speech, and knowing him, he wants to get there before everybody else and do a sound check, so it's not the time to say, —But do *you* understand?

For one thing, if he said, Understand what? I wouldn't know where to start.

I lift my face and purse my lips and he bends for a quick kiss, and I open the shower door and get out. I didn't step under the water, but I'm wet, and I dry myself off with a towel as big as a single-bed sheet. I wrap the towel around me and go back into the bedroom.

Once, in Atlanta, I tried to have that conversation. I started off saying that something was missing, and Lawrence pointed out that he's never denied me anything, I can have everything I want. I said I wasn't talking about things, and I couldn't believe he didn't know that. I ended up telling him I wished he'd just hit me, I wished he'd hit me so hard it broke the skin and left a scar. He walked out of the room, and I sat on the bed, having no idea why I'd said that.

After a while, I heard myself think, —Because if he hit you, it would be his fault, and you could leave and make your life better, and when things got hard, you could look at the scar and know you did the right thing.

Then I thought, —But this is not his fault, and leaving wouldn't fix it. If anything, it would just make everything worse.

I look at Lawrence's notes again. I don't understand p-branes. They're units of energy that for some reason have stretched themselves out into huge membranes, invisible to us, that can span all of spacetime. They have something to do with the possibility that our universe has not four dimensions, three of space and one of time, but eleven, some of them curled in on themselves like knots, and when spacetime gets so tangled that it tears open, the branes patch it up. That's probably not accurate, but I think it's close. I can't make sense of it and have no idea what branes might have to do with the omega point, which I thought he'd given up on. His interests go in waves: Sometimes he thinks constantly about the Big Bang, the beginning, but right now he seems to be focused on the end.

He comes out of the bathroom wearing his boxers, and I'm

still just wrapped in my towel, and he says, "Ellen"—that's all he says, but his tone of voice implies, Don't tell me you're not dressed because you still want to have sex after I *told* you I'm giving the opening address.

I look at him blankly and he goes to the closet.

I let my towel drop to the floor and put on a robe.

When he comes back out, wearing his dress pants and shirt and tying his tie, I'm watching Andrew Morton on TV, who's explaining that Diana cooperated with his biography because she was sick of living a lie: "She was willing to risk everything for the truth. She wanted more than anything to present her story to the world and subsequently take control of her life and create the possibility for true love."

I think, —Plus, she was really mad at Prince Charles for sleeping with Camilla Parker-Bowles, and she wanted to make sure people saw him as the villain and her as the victim in that picture before his people got any further in their attempt to paint him as the long-suffering wronged husband and her as the promiscuous loon.

Then I hope she didn't hear me think that, which, apparently, she didn't.

Lawrence says, "Are you okay?" He's looking in the mirror, making a knot at his throat.

"Yeah. Why?"

"You're taking this Diana thing pretty hard. It surprises me."

I don't know what I'm doing to make him say that. I haven't been crying. I'm just watching TV. I turn it off.

Lawrence says, "I never realized you had such strong feelings about her."

"I didn't. Or I didn't know I did. I really don't think I did. I think it's sad that she's dead, but . . ."

I look at him, expecting him to tell me of course it's sad she's dead, but he doesn't say anything. He just looks back at me, and where usually I feel like I can't force him to look at me and really see me, now I want him to stop. There's something in his eyes that gives me the feeling he's suddenly seeing me from Mart's point of view and he doesn't like what he sees.

He says, "Okay."

I say, "I've read one book about her, but only because she supposedly collaborated on it, and I bought a few *People* magazines when she was on the cover. That hardly qualifies me as a Diana fanatic."

"Right."

Finally he gathers his notes and papers and whatever else he keeps in his briefcase and puts on his jacket.

"I'll meet you here at seven," he says.

I say okay.

Then he gives me a quick kiss and leaves.

I turn the TV back on with the remote and curl up on his side of the bed. A psychologist is worrying about how Diana's death will affect William and Harry. She predicts it will be harder on Harry because of his age. He's likely to suffer from depression later in life. Though William is already known to hate the paparazzi, so it doesn't bode well for him, either. There's a montage of pictures of Diana with the two of them, culminating in the one where she drops to her knees with her arms outstretched to them and they run to her embrace, only this time they're doing it in slow motion with violins playing in the background.

I turn it off and pull the covers over me and I feel a heaviness almost like sleep settling over me, and I close my eyes and Diana comes to me again.

My boys will be all right. It will be difficult for them at times, but I made sure they grew up knowing every day of their lives that they were loved—I loved them to bits—which will be a great source of strength to them. When I was alive, my grandmother looked after me in the spirit world, though I haven't heard from her since I died, but I'll find a way to look after them. How could a little thing like death separate you from those you love with all your soul?

Maybe that's what I'm meant to sort out now, something about love, because that's where the memories keep circling, around the people I loved. I loved my husband. I loved James Hewitt. Most people thought that was a mistake, but I did, and that carried me through a very difficult time, kept me from doing myself in prematurely. I loved Hasnat Khan, wanted to marry him, but he wouldn't because I wasn't Muslim and I couldn't convert. I considered it, read a book about it, read lots and lots, kept stacks of them by my bed, called it my knowledge corner. I said, "Does it have to be public? Doesn't it matter what's in my heart?" Yes, it has to be public. So no, it doesn't matter what's in my heart. At the end of the day, I was the mother of the future king of England, the future head of the Church of England, and no matter how I felt about the monarchy's relationship to the church, the gross hypocrisy of it all from day one to now, I couldn't do that to my son. Broke my heart. I don't regret it, though.

I can't regret a single act of love. In one sense, I think, who you love defines who you are, but in another, love turns you inside-out, makes you willing to become someone you're not, though in the process you become a bigger person than you were. I was always trying to become whoever I thought the people I loved wanted me to be, and of course your children want you to be the whole world, but there's a sense in which whatever you are, is *the whole world. They just want you to love them, and they understand that love is everything there is. Where with adults—men, but also the media—they have an idea of you, and that's what they see when they look at you, and that's what they think they love. I once heard someone say I fell in love with the idea of Prince Charles more than Prince Charles himself, but that was all I* had *to fall in love with. He wasn't there. We were together thirteen times before the wedding. And he never tried to be the person I was in love with. When I loved somebody, I tried desperately to be the person they thought they loved, even if that meant lying, hiding, pretending, sometimes literally wearing a disguise.*

Hasnat didn't want to date a princess, wanted everything to be very normal. So I'd dress up as Frances Spencer with a bubble-cut, dirty-blond wig and some very boring outfit, not likely to turn a single head, and I'd leave the palace in the boot of my butler's car to meet him. We'd go out for a curry or a fish and chips. I felt so desperately happy, curled up there in the dark, feeling the hum of the motor on my legs. We'd go into a garage and the lid would pop open and I'd feel like I was jumping out of a cake. It was like that—exhilarating and humiliating at the same time.

And I loved Dodi, in my way. I loved being able to be myself with him. Not the Princess of Wales. Not Frances Spencer or anybody I wasn't. Just Diana. We listened over and over on the boat to a George Michael CD, Older. *The song about fame, "Star People," had a refrain that said, "How much is enough?" and I remember thinking that was my problem in a nutshell—this endless, bottomless sense that it's never enough. That is, when it's not too much. One or the other, though. A bit like going through life as Goldilocks, only there's no Baby Bear. Nothing is ever just right. Or almost nothing. A soft chair, a comfortable bed, a warm bowl of porridge. The smell of your child, sleeping.*

We danced all over the deck of the boat. The nights were so amazingly full of stars and we were just dancing right through them, floating through the galaxies. That's how it felt. Everyone should dance under the nighttime sky from the sea before they die. I loved to dance. Lots of happy memories. No point in being bitter.

It feels like the room is spinning, or she's spinning around inside me, and then things slowly wind down to a silent halt.

I open my eyes. There's nobody in the room, of course.

I look at the clock. It's almost ten. Maybe I fell asleep—I seem to have lost about an hour—but I didn't dream Diana.

I get up. I'm still listening for her, but I think she's gone again.

I finish my bottle of water, take off my robe, put back on my clothes and jewelry. Then I get the picture of Diana out of its envelope in my suitcase and write Max's information from the back on a piece of Ritz notepad paper. It's legible, but it barely looks like my writing, which is usually neat and careful and feminine, but my hand is trembling, and this comes to me less like a decision than a realization: The reason I hid the photograph in the closet is that I don't want Lawrence to know I met Max. I could easily have told him I ran into one of the photographers from yesterday at the scene of the crash and I was thinking of calling him to see if he had a studio because wouldn't that be interesting to see, and Lawrence would have been noncommittal. But I kept it a secret because I wanted to go to Max's studio and ask him to let me see his work, thinking maybe he'd lead me into his darkroom and we'd look at the pictures of Diana he took yesterday outside the hotel, maybe we'd develop them together, the darkest parts appearing first and the lighter details slowly filling themselves in like a mystery solving itself while we watched, and as her face emerged on the paper, hours before she died, we'd both feel sad for her and a little fragile, and our shoulders would touch and then our arms and our hands and somehow we'd end up making love.

And later, when Lawrence came back to the hotel and said how was your day, he wouldn't be asking how my visit with the photographer went, so I wouldn't have to decide between lying and telling the truth, even to myself. I'd just say, ever so casually, —Fine.

I take my little map book out of my purse and I look up Max's street in the index and turn to his page and move one finger down and one finger across until they touch at his square on the grid. I'm imagining moving the tips of my fingers over his skin.

Then I think, —I'm not really going to do this. It's just another fantasy.

—Maybe I'll go see his studio, but that's it.

Then I find his street, which is not far from the church of St-Germain-des-Prés, which is right next to Les Deux Magots, where Lawrence and I had lunch yesterday and which I might well have gone to for lunch today anyway. It's also one block over from rue Princesse, which, even though I don't believe in signs, seems like a good one.

I put Max's address in the map book and put the map back in my purse.

I go into the bathroom and watch myself brush my teeth in the mirror.

I spit and rinse. Then I push my fingers through my hair and meet my own eyes in the mirror.

I think of meeting Max's eyes, then watching him look at my breasts, cup them in his hands.

It's been a long time since Lawrence looked at me that way. I don't want to think about *how* long, because I'm not sure he ever has. For one thing, when we first got together, his wife had just died — of breast cancer.

On our first date, we met for coffee when I got off work from the children's bookstore where he'd come in to shop for Alec, and he had no idea what Alec's reading level was, and he wasn't wearing a wedding ring, from which I assumed he was recently divorced—though, as it turned out, he never had worn one, still doesn't—and I figured his not knowing his son's reading level was typical of why the marriage hadn't worked, so the only reasons I was wasting my time with him were that I was desperately lonely and he seemed so fragile, I couldn't say no. So I ordered a small decaf, and as soon as we sat down with our cups, he thanked me again for the book suggestions, he was sure his son would love them, and I said I hoped so, and he told me his wife had died four months ago and he still hadn't gotten the hang of being a single parent.

I said, "I'm so sorry."

I wanted to comfort him, or at least let him know I had some idea what he was going through. I wanted to comfort his son. And I suddenly wanted somebody to comfort me.

I said, "My father died when I was a child."

—And my mother left me with my grandmother, promising me she'd find me another father and come back and get me and everything would be fine, and she did find herself another husband and she did come back and get me, but Big John was never anything like a father to me, and everything was not fine, no matter how hard we all tried to pretend it was.

"Oh, well then you know something of how it is for my son," he said.

"Yes."

Then a pause.

Then, "How is it?"

I'd never believed people who said they knew in one specific moment that they were going to marry somebody, but I did. I was a senior in college, and three weeks earlier, I'd broken up with my boyfriend of five years, the guy I'd followed to Emory and who everybody including me had always assumed I was going to marry, and my mother was calling me in my dorm room every night, not wasting any words on how I'd just thrown away the rest of my life and I should call him up and get down on my knees if I had to and beg him to take me back, because otherwise, my college years would have been a waste, I'd never be near that many eligible men again in my life, and how many boys my age were already set to go into the family business, buy a house right out of college, didn't I know how many girls get out of school with no husband, no job, no way to meet men, and simply *flounder,* and don't think she and Big John were going to furnish an apartment for me and pay my rent because they weren't, so what was I thinking?

My ex-boyfriend was already dating someone else, which was why I'd broken up with him, but I began to see that my mother had a point. I was an English major with not so much as a summer camp-counseling job on my résumé. I didn't even *have* a résumé. So I'd taken the position at the bookstore a few days before to get some job experience, and when I'd added up what my income would have been if I'd graduated from college and started working at the store full-time, I'd had the same tightening in my chest that I used to feel as a child playing cards when I got the Old Maid. It wasn't just that she was alone — unloved — where all the other cards had mates. Her eyes were buggy, her hair was a mess, her skin was covered in dots that were either freckles or zits, her clothes were torn, and she was missing a tooth: She was unlovable. My mother had told me more than once that she'd just barely missed becoming an Old Maid when she met Big John. It was not much of a leap, therefore, for me to conclude it a fate that could befall anybody. Any girl.

And there was Lawrence with a job and a house and a motherless child, not to mention a Nobel Prize. And he needed me. What more could I ask?

I turn on the faucet—the handle is a gold wing, and the water arcs into the sink out of the mouth of a gold swan. I turn it back off.

I think, —Plus, I loved him. It wasn't that mercenary. I had real affection for him, and I knew I could love him and his son. I just no longer believed, as I had for most of my life, that love was enough. I'd loved my ex-boyfriend, and look where that got me.

I think, —I'm not going to see Max.

—Of course I'm not.

—I'll go shopping, have a nice lunch in a café, see Notre Dame.

Then I think, —If we ever redo the guest bathroom, I want a gold swan faucet.

I slip the photograph of Diana back into its envelope and put the envelope in the suitcase, and the suitcase in the closet, then grab my room key and my purse.

I go downstairs and out the revolving door and a bellman asks me if I need a taxi, but I suddenly don't want to get in a car, so I say, "Non, merci."

He tells me to have a nice day, and I wish him a bonne journée.

I WALK PAST THE JEWELRY STORES THAT LINE THE PLACE Vendôme, past millions and millions of dollars' worth of diamonds. I look in the windows and pretend I'm looking for a piece of jewelry for myself as I make my way around the square to Repossi, where Dodi picked up a $200,000 diamond ring for Diana yesterday afternoon. There's a wreath on the door—lilies—and it's closed.

I can't find anything I like. Everything's huge and artless, soulless.

I keep going.

When I get to the rue de Rivoli, I buy a special-edition British newspaper about Diana, then sit down at a sidewalk table to have a cup of coffee while I read. French police are questioning the seven photographers they've already arrested. Their film has been confiscated, viewed for evidence, and destroyed. Whoever else was in the tunnel—and they know there are more—is required by law to turn themselves in and turn over their film. Anybody who knows of a photographer who was there should call the police and report him.

People on the street are yelling at anybody with a professional-looking camera, calling them murderers, assassins.

—If I were Max, I wouldn't open my door for the next month.

—I'd leave town, maybe even leave the country.

—For all he knows, I'm obsessed with Diana, which is why I was at the tunnel at five o'clock in the morning, and I think he killed her and I'm a vigilante, which is why he didn't much want to talk to me. It's not outside the realm of possibility that some nut would try to kill a paparazzo to avenge her death. Stranger things have happened.

—I should let this go.

—For a hundred reasons, just leave him alone. Even if he doesn't think you're a vigilante, he's still in no mood to entertain a complete stranger. He barely spoke to you yesterday, so what are you thinking, anyway? Go shopping.

—Right.

I'm trying to get into the spirit of Plan B, which, I remind myself, used to be Plan A, so I look up Le Bon Marché in my map book, a department store that one of my guidebooks says was the first of its kind and the inspiration for a novel by Emile Zola, and I tell myself, —This is what I love about Paris: You can go to one place and get history, literary provenance, and Coco Chanel.

I feel a stirring in me that I'm hoping is Diana and I listen, but there's just silence, so I'm sitting here people-watching and replaying Diana's words in my head, trying to make sense of what's happening, when I see Mart. She doesn't see me. She's stopped in front of a window a few doors down, just gazing into it, smoking a cigarette.

Several things are wrong with this picture. One, most of the shops around here are either really expensive designer boutiques, which I don't think she cares about and which I know she can't afford on her salary, or tacky souvenir shops, so why is she skipping the conference to window-shop a few blocks from the hotel, because two, she's supposed to be at the conference, she's missing Lawrence's speech. She's dressed for it, in a conservative black suit, flat shoes, but she doesn't even appear to be headed there. She's not headed anywhere. And three, there's something about the way she's carrying herself: Where last night she was all straight-posture confidence, today she's less angular. She moves aimlessly to the next window. Last night, I would have guessed that she never did anything aimlessly, but now I get the feeling that she'd be looking at that window with the same amount of interest no matter whether the glass had miniature Eiffel Towers or couture clothes or raw meat, which in France, means whole dead animals, behind it. Also, she's smoking, which is only odd because she didn't last night, so either last night or today, she's not acting how she usually acts. I think something's troubling her, and I'm trying to decide whether to say anything to her or not, leaning toward not, because what makes me think Mart would want to confide in me, when she looks up and sees me and hesitates before she says, "Ellen?"

She's not completely sure it's me. She spent the whole evening with me last night, five hours, without ever really taking in what I look like.

I say, "Yes. How are you, Mart?"

She's walking toward me, and I stand up to shake her hand.

It's just possible that she has liquor on her breath. It's at least as easy to get a stiff drink at ten o'clock in the morning here as it is to get coffee. I could be wrong, though. Maybe it's her perfume, which is competing with the cigarette smoke, and losing.

She says, "I was hoping I would see you today," and now I'm not completely sure it's her. Or it is, of course, but it's not the same her as last night, and she looks at my table and says, "Did you have breakfast here?"

"No, I just stopped for coffee."

"Would you like to join me for an early lunch? Brunch?"

I can hardly think of a less pleasant way to spend an hour in Paris, but I say, "I would love to," and I don't know if I've said it because I'm morbidly curious about why in the world she would want to have lunch with me when not that many hours ago, I was pretty sure she didn't care whether she ever spoke to me again, or because I'm just not very good at saying no.

"Good," she says, "there's a nice café about a block from here, they make the best omelets. I know the chef."

"Okay," I say, and I leave some money in the little white dish that my check came in and she puts her cigarette out in my ashtray and we start heading toward Mart's friend's café.

I'm thinking, —Of course she knows the chef, if cafés even have chefs. What doesn't she know?

She's full of purpose again, walking so quickly I have to work to keep up with her.

"You're wondering why I'm not at the conference," she says as we speed-walk.

"A little," I say.

"Because it's full of arrogant pricks," she says. "It's . . . what do you say in English?"

"Arrogant pricks works."

"It's a good old boys' club."

"I'm sorry," I say.

In the daylight, she looks younger than she did last night. She could be thirty. She might even be in her late twenties, not that long out of graduate school and just beginning to figure out the politics, sexual and otherwise, of her profession, and more than likely, she has no female mentor to help her navigate.

Then she says, "Roger Tollman, do you know him?"

"I don't think so."

"Of course you don't. He's Canadian. He's not even . . . He's a third-rate physicist from a third-rate university, and we had a one-night stand two years ago. He's also a third-rate fuck, and now that he knows that I know that, he can't forgive me for it. I walk into the main conference ballroom this morning, and he comes up to me and I say, 'Hello, Roger,' and he says, 'So, you're fucking Eric Mandelstrom now. *And* publishing with him. Moving right up the ladder, eh?' I wish I'd seen that coming and had something to say, but I was dumbfounded. I simply said, 'I'm what?' He said, 'Oh, don't act shocked. I admire your ambition. Everybody does.' Then he lifted his coffee cup as if he were toasting me and walked away. My God. Roger is so far down the list of people you'd expect to be in the circle, in the loop, as you say. If he knows, everybody knows. It's practically a cliché that physicists are like children in that they retain their capacity for wonder, but if you ask me, their emotional growth also tends to be stunted. My idea is that most of them were misfits as children, and at whatever age they discovered physics, they stopped developing in any way other than intellectually. So it's like having five hundred sex-starved adolescent genius males for colleagues and being the one attractive woman."

We stop at a cross street.

"Some people would find that appealing."

Several cars rush past us.

"Not if what they wanted was the adult physicists' professional respect. If people like that see you as a sexual being, they can't see you as an intellectual one."

"No. Right. Sorry," I say.

She starts walking again before the light changes, which I don't like to do, but I hurry after her.

"And I just found out who won a major research grant I got turned down for. An idiot. A well-connected, male idiot. Networker. That grant could have made my career, would have changed the course of my life. But I said, 'Congratulations, Michel,' and he said, '*You* should have won,' but of course, he *could* say that, since he'd won it, so what he was actually doing was making it clear that he knew I'd applied for it and lost, information which should have remained confidential, so he's obviously chummy with the judge. At which point, I could have said, 'No, you deserved it more than I did,' an outright lie that I could not bring myself to tell, or I could have been as arrogant as he is and said, 'You're right,' and I refused to do either. So I left."

"Well, good for you," I say, which is a thing you pretty much never say to a person when things are actually going well for them.

"Assholes," she says.

When we get to the café, we take a table outside in the shade under an awning, and she speaks to the waiter in perfect French, though she ordered in English last night, and I think he tells her he'll be right with us before he leaves. Then she asks me if I'm hung over.

"Maybe that's what's wrong. I'm feeling a little funny. I didn't sleep much last night," I say.

"I've only got half my brain cells back up and running so far," she says, and another waiter comes up to her and asks her something in French, and she looks at me and says, "Hair of the dog, yes?"

It's eleven o'clock in the morning, and I can't drink this early or it will go straight to my head, especially after drinking so much last night, so I was going to ask for water, but what the hell.

I say, "Sure."

And she orders a bottle of white wine. I'm back to wondering if she's already had a drink or two. She's not acting drunk, but I thought she was stone-cold sober last night.

We both order ham-and-cheese omelets, and the waiter leaves, and she looks across the street at nothing in particular, as far as I can tell, and she says, "I'm just going to have to go back to the conference and face down the looks, refuse to try to figure out who knows what and where they learned it. And I can do that."

"Of course you can," I say.

She looks at me as if I've just given her the stupidest advice she's ever heard. Then she says, "But what for?"

I say, stupidly, "What *for*?"

"Yes, what's it all for?" she says.

I don't have an answer for that.

She says, "I'm thirty years old. Most scientists do their best work in their twenties, and I've barely done anything of consequence, made no original contributions. I'm never going to be a great cosmologist. Even those with potential greatness are in a crapshoot. Imagine spending the next twenty, thirty, forty years of your life trying to prove string theory, knowing that if you do, you'll have found the Theory of Everything that eluded Einstein for as many decades, and you'll be remembered in perpetuity for making the greatest contribution to physics ever, but if you don't, and this is a much more likely scenario, you'll have wasted your life chasing that rainbow, and thirty years later, some twenty-six-year-old graduate student either beats you to the proof, or, even more likely, demonstrates conclusively that the whole theory is utterly wrong? Then what was your life for? Would it not have been better spent raising children, gathering flowers, working on your abs?"

"Your obs?" I say, because that's what I hear.

Our wine arrives, and the waiter begins uncorking it.

"Abdominal muscles," she says. "Making lots of money, for yourself or for charity, having lots of sex."

She's just described Princess Diana, though I'm not sure whether she's aware of that.

She holds out her left hand, palm up, as if it's half a scale, and it's got children, flowers, abs, money, and sex on it. Then she puts out her right palm, looks at it, and says, "Or working as a third-rate scientist in a third-rate university, trying to prove a theory that may be nothing more than an elaborate work of fiction"—she seesaws her hands—"and failing." And her left palm sinks to the table.

The waiter pours her a taste of wine, and she picks up her glass with her right hand and drinks it all.

"Très bon," she says to him, and he pours me a glass, then fills hers and leaves.

I take a sip. It's good wine, not very sweet, and it's cold on a hot day. I take another.

She says, too casually, "Eric wants to get married, but I would have to move to America. He wants to have children, and he doesn't have to say it out loud for me to know that if I say no, he'll find someone else."

"Wow," I say. Then, though it doesn't seem appropriate, given her glum expression, "Congratulations."

I hold up my glass, and we both drink.

"Thank you," she says, drinking more wine and sounding like she's accepting my condolences.

"You'd have smart children," I say.

"Even very smart children, I find boring."

I drink some more wine, then tell myself to slow down. Wine tends to loosen my tongue, and I don't want to hear myself telling her that if she really thinks she would find her own child boring, she shouldn't have kids, and I don't want to say anything I'll regret about Eric, who I don't actively dislike but who's not my favorite person in the world and who I wouldn't advise anybody in the world to marry but who is my husband's colleague. If she doesn't want to marry him, she shouldn't marry him, but don't put me in the middle of it.

She takes a long drink and says, "I owe you an apology."

Now I'm pretty sure this is not her first glass of the day.

"No you don't," I say, and I mean it.

"Yes, I was bitchy and condescending last night. I treated you the way I was treated this morning. And I'm sorry."

"Oh. Well, thank you," I say. "It's okay."

Then there's an awkward silence between us, and she gets her pack of cigarettes out of her purse and says, "Is it all right with you if I smoke?"

"Of course," I say. It's France.

"Would you like one?" she says.

I don't smoke often, but if I say no at this point, it will seem like I didn't really accept her apology, so I say, "Yeah," and she lights one for me and gives it to me and I take a long draw and hold it for a moment before I let it go, watching the shape of my breath until the smoke disappears.

The couple next to us stands up and leaves, and a waiter clears their table, and a Japanese couple sits down in their place.

Mart finishes her glass of wine, so I finish mine, too — they're small glasses — and she's pouring us each another when a man drives up on a big motorcycle and parks on the sidewalk next to our table. He's wearing khaki shorts and a khaki shirt, hiking boots, a panama hat with a tiny built-in fan, and what looks like a pair of binoculars hanging from his neck. He gets off the motorcycle, picks up the binoculars, and seems to look at us through the wrong end before he unscrews one of the lenses and takes a long drink. Then he starts photographing us, or pretending to, with a tape measure, every movement he makes slightly exaggerated, as if it's accompanied by silent music, like a mime. He's not looking at either of us except through the imaginary lens of the tape measure, but he seems aware of us as audience. He also seems harmless, but if he's crazy and he's acting out something having to do with Diana and the paparazzi, I'm slightly worried about where this is going.

He moves on down the sidewalk, taking fake photographs of all the patrons. Everybody here is pretending he's not there, which doesn't seem to bother him.

Mart's looking across the street again, and I notice a kiosk full of newspapers announcing in three-inch-high type: "DI EST MORTE! DI EST MORTE! DI EST MORTE!"

My glass isn't empty, but Mart tops it off.

Then she says, "I feel badly for what I said about Lady Di, too, now that she's dead. I wouldn't have expected to, but I do."

I'm trying to read her face.

I say, "I'm surprised by my reaction to her death, too."

"How so?"

I'm not going to say, —Well, for starters, I'm hearing her voice in my head. Not to mention, I'm slightly obsessing over a photographer who put a picture of her on the memorial at five o'clock this morning, and when you saw me, I was trying to talk myself out of going to his address, knocking on the door, and seeing if he wanted to have sex.

So I say, "Well, I guess it's a version of what you're going through. I mean, look at her. She spent so much of her adult life trying to figure out what she was doing on this planet, and I don't think she ever really felt like she found the answer. It just makes you think. You don't know how much time you have, and what am I doing with mine?"

I pour myself another glass of wine, which is like pouring another half a glass if they were regular-sized wineglasses, and one for Mart, and now we're almost out of wine, and a waiter brings our food and she asks him for another bottle. While he's setting the plates on our table, the motorcycle guy takes another drink from his binoculars and goes inside the café.

Then our waiter leaves, and we put out our cigarettes.

I'm trying to get her to explain, without knowing what she's explaining, why I'm hearing Diana's voice in my head, and I'm hoping to figure out if physics offers a way for Diana and me and even Mart to get to the places we need to go, wondering if we found a way to move a few millimeters in one direction or another and emerge in whole new lives, new universes, would we do it? Or would we choose comfort, stability, not having to start over and face the unknown?

I have no idea how to ask Mart any of that, but I figure I have to start somewhere, so I say, "I've been thinking about something you said last night, and I still don't get why, if there's a universe only millimeters away, we can't see it."

She says, "Because the only way we see anything is when photons come from the thing we're seeing to our eyes, but my theory is that our universe is surrounded by a gigantic brane that keeps photons and all open-ended strands of energy from getting out—or in, if there are any out there—because the ends of the string gets stuck to the membrane. It's also probable that some closed-loop strings like rubber bands, gravitons in particular, do escape because they don't have ends to get stuck, but we can't see them, of course."

"Of course."

I'm not going to tell her my theory—that when people die, spacetime rips open, creating a wormhole through which they travel to the next universe, and then the branes patch up the hole, but every so often, something goes wrong and they don't go through the wormhole when they get the chance, so they get stuck here—but I want to get her to tell me something that lets me believe it's true, or at least plausible. I take a big drink and say, "Do you think physics has anything to say about the afterlife?"

"No."

She pours what's left of the wine, which is not much, into her glass and sets the empty bottle on the corner of the table. She takes a sip. Then she's quiet.

I think maybe she's reconsidering her answer, which was rather hasty.

And I'm considering what she just said about gravitons, thinking, —Maybe some people have to tie up some emotional loose ends before they're ready to leave this universe, and when they do, the energy that is their soul closes its loop, so they don't even need a wormhole to get to the universe next door, they just pass through the membrane.

I say, "Don't you think it's possible that the universe we can't see is . . . well, not exactly heaven, but some sort of next life?"

"No."

She finishes off her glass, and I take another sip from mine. I've lost count of how many glasses I've had, but she's had more than I have. Though she seems to hold her alcohol better than I do.

I look at my omelet on the plate, then at her.

I should stop this conversation now—I know I'm not going to get what I want out of her—but I try again: "One thing about physics is that it makes a very strong case for reality being a thing whose complexity we can't fully grasp."

"True enough," she says.

I finish my glass of wine. "But then again," I say, "you have to keep trying, right?"

She says, "Of course." She's looking at her empty glass, not at me.

"Okay," I say. "So what if souls are like electrons?"

She looks around the restaurant, and I know what she's thinking: Where's that wine? I'm thinking the same thing.

Then she says, "I'm not following you."

"Well," I say, "an electron can move from one spot to another without ever being in the space between the two spots, right?"

"Right." She cuts herself a bite of omelet with the edge of her fork, puts it in her mouth.

"And it can be in two places at once, even two places that are miles apart, right?"

"Right," she says again, setting down her fork, chewing.

"And it exists as both a wave and a particle at once, and even though it can be collapsed into a particle that occupies a tiny pointlike space — or, two tiny pointlike spaces — every electron's wave function is spread throughout the universe, right?"

She sprinkles salt on her food and says, "Right."

Now she's just staring at her plate, as if a partially eaten omelet is more interesting to her than what I'm saying.

I say, "So maybe our souls have all those qualities, too. Maybe we exist throughout spacetime, but in any given lifetime, we sort of collapse into human-sized particles, and after we die, we go back to being waves."

I touch the base of my empty wineglass, and as if on cue, our new bottle arrives and the waiter gives us both new glasses and uncorks it and pours a taste for her. She drinks it and nods and he fills both our glasses and we drink.

She looks at the glass in her hand, thinking for a moment, then says, "The problem with asking what happens to our souls after we die, as I see it, is that from the cosmos's point of view, there *is* no afterlife because there's no death, only transformation of energy: E equals M C squared."

She takes another sip, then sets her glass down.

"Okay, don't call it your soul," I say. "Call it your energy. That's my point."

She picks up her fork again and glares at her plate in a way that makes her look like she's thinking, Is this what I ordered?

Then she says, "I don't have a reason to think that individual people have separate souls, energies—whatever you want to call them—but I do believe in what you could call an afterlife for the universe itself, if you want to insist on an afterlife."

"Now I'm not following *you*," I say. Then I take a bite of omelet, which is already cold.

The muscle in her forehead twitches. "When the universe stops expanding," she says, "it will probably begin to contract until it collapses into a superhole, at which point it's generally assumed that time will stop and the universe will end. But it seems to me that when the branes posited by string theory pass the event horizon, they *can't* be spaghettified into basically one-dimensional shapes because they have too many dimensions to start with. So I predict that when a ten- or eleven-dimension brane gets that severely stretched, or when several of them do at once, they'll open up, unfold, rip open, and begin repairing each other, realigning themselves and resulting, in effect, in a new dimension, or a new *set* of dimensions, and a whole new higher-dimensional universe will be created."

"Well, that's interesting," I say, though I actually think it's incomprehensible and profoundly boring, not to mention completely unrelated to what I asked her.

—And no, for the record, I did not *insist* on an afterlife.

I set down my fork and look for the waiter. If I could find him, I would ask for the check.

Meanwhile, she's not finished. She says, "In fact, it's possible that a version of this has already happened."

I look at her. I don't say anything. The waiter brings a basket of bread to another table, and I try to catch his eye, but he's pretending we're not here.

"Imagine a two-dimensional movie screen inside a three-dimensional movie theater," she says.

"Okay."

"Some cutting-edge physicists think that like the movie screen, our present, three-dimensional universe may exist within another, higher-dimensional universe which is outside our time-space but which contains everything that ever existed or will exist *in* time and space."

She pours us each more wine.

I say, "Well, if everything that ever existed in our universe still exists outside our timespace, that includes every*body* who ever existed, so how can you say we don't have afterlives?"

"That's not what I meant." She sighs. "At all."

She lights a cigarette and holds the pack out to me, offering me one.

Our waiter rushes past us. We seem to be invisible.

I shake my head. "I know, but—"

"Now that I hear myself say it out loud, I see that it's overwrought, way too speculative. I can't even imagine a way to translate the idea into math. This is why my career isn't going anywhere. I explained the idea to Eric, and he said, 'That's not science, it's poetry.' How can I marry a man who says such a thing? Even though he's right." She takes a long drag on her cigarette. Then she says something in German that I'm pretty sure is a cussword, or a string of them. Then she exhales two columns of smoke through her nostrils. I find myself liking her a little more.

"I don't know," I say, trying to help. "But I think you're on to something. Because what if our souls are in the movie-screen universe and the movie-theater universe at the same time? So when you die, it's like when you're watching a character in a movie and you suddenly realize, Oh, *that's* who that actress is. Except you're watching your own performance, and at some point it dawns on you—Oh, *that's* who I was—and you finally understand what your life meant, why you were here. But this you—the one that's recognizing you—is more than just the character you played during that movie, that lifetime. It's a superyou. Maybe we all play different roles throughout history, but while we're playing any given role, we're like the character on the screen—the actor knows he's playing the character, but the character doesn't know he's being played by the actor—so we're not accessing our whole being even if our superself has access to us, and it's learning from us, maybe even teaching us. Maybe that's what intuition is—your super-self saying to you the same thing you say to a character in a movie who's about to do something they shouldn't: Don't trust that man! Don't open that door! Don't go there! Know what I mean?"

"Not really."

She takes another drag on her cigarette, then rests it on the edge of the ashtray, still burning.

I think, —I don't know how this explains Diana, who doesn't seem to have figured out who she was at all, but I'm afraid I'm in the wrong movie, the wrong theater.

But that's not quite it.

I'm about to say, —I think I'm in the right movie, but I'm playing the wrong part.

But that's not it, either.

She doesn't say anything.

We both take another drink.

—I should probably stop drinking now. And talking. And I should eat something, but not this. Why didn't we get any bread?

But I try again: "I'm asking if it matters, after we die, how we lived. Does anything we do *matter*? Or is the whole universe and everything in it ultimately pointless?"

I'm not really asking Mart. I'm just trying to figure some things out.

—If I have sex with Max, will that matter?

But she answers, of course.

"If you want to ask whether the universe has a point, then you have to ask what kind of point there could possibly be that would make it *not* pointless, and right now, we understand so little about the universe that it would be premature to speculate. Maybe it's not the universe's purpose to have a purpose. Maybe it just *is*. And maybe it's presumptuous of us, not to mention anthropomorphic, to think that our individual lives have to be part of some grand universal scheme to matter at all. But I think, on a much smaller scale, if we matter to ourselves, then it matters to us how we live, so we create a purpose for ourselves. So, yes, it's possible to live a life that matters. Though it's also quite possible to live one that doesn't."

"Well, that's what I'm afraid of, that my life doesn't matter."

It's quiet for a long time. She fingers her pack of cigarettes, then pushes it about an inch away from where it was.

I have definitely had too much to drink. I wish I hadn't said that. Though it's true.

She takes her lit cigarette from the ashtray and taps off the ashes.

I think she agrees with me, though at least she has the grace not to say so. But then she says, "Isn't that what every thinking person fears?"

I want this conversation to be over. I want it never to have happened so I can have it for the first time with someone else. With Max, who's been shimmering just under the surface of my thoughts ever since I met him. This is not how this conversation would go if I were having it with Max. Max would believe in ghosts and in love lasting past death and in the human soul.

We both take another drink. I take another bite of my omelet, swallow it, and my stomach knots up. I put my fork down.

We've come to a place where neither of us has anything to say, and I tell myself not to rush to fill the silence, and this time I don't.

We finish our drinks, and she puts out her cigarette.

The motorcycle guy comes back outside. He's in a different mood now, quieter and sadder, as if the music in his head has stopped playing. He's not pretending to look through fake binoculars, not taking imaginary pictures. He gets on his motorcycle, looks straight at me, and says something to me, three or four sentences, in French. I have no idea what he's saying.

I open my hands to him: "Je ne parle pas français. Je suis désolée."

Then he says something else, to himself, I assume, starts the motorcycle, and drives away. I watch him merge into traffic on the boulevard St-Germain.

WE SPLIT THE CHECK, AND MART LEAVES HER PACK OF CIG-arettes on the table because she told Eric she quit. I take the matches as a souvenir. Then she takes a taxi to the conference, and I'm headed back to the hotel, where I plan to drink some water and sober up, maybe lie down for a while—I can't remember the last time I got drunk in the middle of the day—when Diana says, *I didn't understand most of what your friend was saying, found her a bit of a bore, actually, but one thing I've noticed is that there's no before and after anymore, no here or there—I can be in two places at once, at Balmoral and in the tunnel, for example—and I think perhaps that's possible because there is no time now. Or space. I don't mean I'm out of time, though I suppose I am. What I mean, though, is I'm outside of time. I just realized that. Just beginning to figure this out.*

I'm listening, but I'm also walking across the street to the newsstand to look at the Diana stories when she says, *Don't bother. The media never get anything right.*

So I pass the newsstand without stopping, and she keeps on: *Even my death—in America, it was still Saturday night, and the American media had me walking away from the car without a scratch. For a few hours, I think, they had me doing that, which was ironic, because it was true, in a way. I did. It was a tunnel, you know. Full of lights, which had their pull. I felt like a moth to them—the white camera lights flashing all over the place and then the blue police lights, spinning, and the red lights on the ambulance, pulsing like heartbeats. I could hear the sirens, those awful French sirens, screaming. And whatever they tell you about dying and the light at the end of the tunnel, well, it's funny, in a way, because it was dark at either end, and inside, the light was all around me, and for a while, I couldn't seem to move toward it or away from it. People kept arriving—cameramen and policemen and medics and tourists—everybody gawking. Except one man. I recognized him, though I couldn't remember where I'd known him, and he walked over to me—my eyes were closed, but I was watching him—and he seemed to be taking a photo like everyone else, but when he did, he covered me with a flash of light, and then I was inside the light, glowing, because it was also inside me, and I was lifted up out of the car by it. It was like being set free, let out of a cage. So I went over to Dodi—didn't walk, but sort of floated—still enveloped by this light, and he was gone, and then to the driver and the bodyguard, and the driver was gone, too, nothing left of him, and I stood there in the tunnel, between two columns, with the bodyguard.*

He said, "Are you okay, ma'am?"

I said, "I think so. Are you?"

He said, "I think I'm beat up a bit."

It was a terrible accident and he was in a bad way, but at least nothing was burning, I remember thinking that. The engine was smoking a bit, but even that was already fading rather than working itself up to catch fire. Otherwise, he wouldn't have lived, would have burned alive, which would have been a shame. Lovely man.

I stood there beside him watching more cameramen arrive and photograph the car, stroking his hand, telling him to forget. The pain his body was in, it wasn't worth remembering. No point, holding on to that. We were both very calm. So I told him he should get on back in the car because the medics were on their way. And he did. I knew he would live, and I told him so. Didn't stop to ask the same question about myself.

I wasn't sad about Dodi or the driver. Wasn't angry, either. I'd already left all that behind. Very much aware that they were not in pain or danger. None of us were in pain. I was wishing someone would cover their bodies, for privacy's sake. No privacy, even then.

I kept thinking of my boys, that I had to get to them, kiss them, hug them. Wanted desperately to leave, but couldn't yet. People were hovering over my body, hovering, hovering, touching, pressing, and I was just watching from my post by the column, and I had a feeling that the light that was still surrounding me was protecting me, making me invisible to them. Then I was at Balmoral—as I said, I was still there in the tunnel but also at Balmoral—walking down the longest hall, trying to get to Wills, just walking and walking and walking as if in a dream where the more you walk, the longer the hall gets, while back in the tunnel, I was watching all the people rushing around. Then I found myself wandering away, sort of floating in the ball of light, and then I was pulled back and the light stayed with me but it shrank tighter, like a filmy sort of membrane around me, perhaps a bit like the silk around the caterpillar inside a cocoon.

The car horn wouldn't stop blaring, I remember that, and people yelling my name as if it were a camera call or a walkabout. Diana, Diana, Diana. Di, Di, Di. Nobody having any idea where I was. Why don't you just leave her alone? So I came over to have a look at what they were gawking at and saw my own face, which I'd only ever seen backwards in the mirror or in two dimensions in photographs, so that was something, seeing my own three-dimensional face for the first time. Didn't quite know what to make of that.

Then I saw the man who'd covered me in light was leaving, and I watched him walk out of the tunnel and I thought, Am I supposed to follow him? So I did and I didn't. Confusing period. I was rushing through Paris at one point. And my body was in hospital briefly, which I watched for a while. I saw them tear off my clothes, cut me open, put their hands inside me, just total assault. Well, I'd had enough of that, so I left there, just floated for a bit, neither here nor there, and then I saw

the flowers and pictures of me going 'round what I was convinced was a
gigantic ice-cream cone, dipped in gold instead of chocolate, which struck
me as a bit odd. Touching, but odd, given what a favorite ice cream had
been during my bulimia. I saw it below me, as if I was in the air, and
it was finally quiet, which was a relief. All this fuss, I'm not quite sure
how to take it.

Then she stops, but I'm still roiling with her words—with
hers, but also Mart's and my own—and I can almost feel all
of our voices rushing through my blood as I'm replaying my
conversation with Mart in light of what Diana's just said, trying to make sense of it all, starting with reconciling Diana's experience in the tunnel with Mart's idea of the cosmic afterlife,
and I think, —Something that's outside of time and space at
the same time that it contains time and space sounds to me like
it's eternal and omnipresent, which sounds like God.

I think, —Maybe the multidimensional universe that contains our universe is God. So maybe, ultimately, Diana exists—
we all exist—in the mind of God. That would explain a few
things, like ESP and synchronicity and the collective unconscious and the belief in every culture throughout the ages that
there's life after death, not to mention ghosts.

—Except I'm not entirely sure I believe in God.

—But if our universe and everybody who ever was or is or
will be and everything that ever happened or is happening or
will happen does exist in the mind of God, it's not the God I
don't believe in.

I'm behind the Ritz on rue Cambon, the street where
Diana and Dodi left the hotel through a service exit and drove
away from the hotel, and I'm walking past a round church on
my way toward the Ritz front entrance when a memory rushes
through me: Once, at a little white clapboard church outside

Montgomery, Alabama, I sat in the front row next to the preacher's overweight wife on a hard wooden bench, watching my mother and Katie discuss Katie's very limited options in the pageant arena. Katie had curly red hair and buck teeth and seven big hand-painted freckles on each cheek. The children in the audience were laughing, and though I'd seen this routine many times before, I realized for the first time that they were laughing not with my mother, at her jokes, but at Katie. They were laughing at her for being ugly and still thinking she could be Little Miss Alabama, and they were doing it because that was exactly what my mother wanted them to do.

The air conditioning was on too high. My arms were covered in chill bumps.

My mother said from her podium, "Well, Katie, we can't all be beauty queens, but with God, the King of Kings, as our father, we can all be princes and princesses, and *that's* the title that matters for eternity."

Then, for the hundredth time, Katie prayed to receive Jesus as her personal savior, ending the prayer with "Thank you, Jesus, hallelujah." We weren't really hallelujah types, but my mother couldn't ventriloquize words with M, such as "Amen," without moving her lips, so she avoided them on Katie's behalf when she could. I thought there was an argument to be made that people shouldn't have been looking at her lips during the prayer anyway, but I didn't make it.

After hallelujah, my mother took off her tiara and placed it on Katie's wooden head, a reminder of the crown that awaited her in heaven.

On the way home, in the car, I said, "We're not really princesses."

Long silence. This was a new thing for me, disagreeing with my mother out loud.

My mother had always introduced me to the audience as Katie's little sister, but on this night, I'd suddenly, unwillingly, become the big sister. Katie was lying across the backseat behind my mother, taking up about half the seat. She would always be small enough to sit in my mother's lap. In the fall, I would go off to school every morning, alone, and they would stay home together. I realized in a way I couldn't articulate that part of Katie's charm was that she did not age. Another part was that she never had an independent thought, never disagreed with my mother—or when she did, it was because my mother wanted her to, so my mother could explain something to her and she could realize, out loud, that my mother was right and she'd been a fool to think otherwise. Then she'd say a three-syllable, "Oh," sort of like Lucy on *I Love Lucy*, which would always get a big laugh.

My mother said, "What makes you say a thing like that?"

"We have to grow up and die before we get our crowns," I said. "Cinderella didn't have to die. She just had to get married."

"Eventually she died."

"No she didn't. She lived happily ever after."

Another, longer silence. I was looking out the window, watching the wires sag in cartoon smiles between the telephone poles. Smile, smile, smile. My mother in front of a camera.

Then: "Cinderella wasn't real," my mother said.

I shrugged.

"But even so, Snow White and Sleeping Beauty both died," my mother said. "Then they were resurrected. By Christ figures! I just thought of that."

"No they didn't. She was *Sleeping* Beauty, not *Dead* Beauty."

"All right, yes, technically, they . . . well, I guess it was more like they went into comas. But when Christians die, we're not *really* dead, either."

"Well, we're not really alive," I said. I knew a little about death: I'd lost a grandfather and a cat.

"Yes we are," she said. Her voice was getting impatient. "We get resurrected. We're alive in heaven. It's just our bodies that die." She said it the way she would have said afternoons follow mornings, evening follows day.

I looked out the window again. More telephone poles. More fake smiles. Silent conversations rushing past us through the wires like prayers.

"Still," I said, "I'd rather be in a coma than dead. Even if I wasn't *really* dead."

My mother said, "Well, fortunately, that's not your choice to make."

I knew it was time to drop it, but for some reason, I couldn't.

"Plus," I said, "what good's being a princess in heaven if everybody else there is one, too? If everybody's a princess, nobody is."

She didn't answer me.

I said, "Like what if everybody was Miss Alabama?"

Reluctantly: "That's different."

"How?"

I'd stepped over a line and I knew it, but I didn't care. This was the kind of question Katie could get away with, though I couldn't. Katie could ask grown men—*preachers*—if they wanted to come up and see her after church, bring a bottle of communion wine, and of course they'd say they were married, and she'd say, wistfully, "All the best ones are," and my mother would explain how we're all brides of Christ and when we take communion, we're metaphorically drinking the blood of Christ, and Katie, who didn't know what a metaphor was, would say, "Well, that's disgusting!" and my mother would set her straight. Katie could tell women who wore big diamond rings that they'd had a great idea, wearing a flashlight on their hands, were they in a spy club?, and my mother would tell her about diamonds and how she was a diamond in the rough and how Jesus was a lamp unto her feet, and Katie would say, "You're telling me to think of Jesus as a flashlight? I'd rather have a big diamond!" She could ask skinny teenage boys if they had to run around in the shower just to get wet, if they disappeared when they turned sideways, then giggle and say she loved it when they blushed, which would just make them blush more. She would ask a member of the audience to come whisper his birthday in her ear and then say, "Onion sandwich for breakfast? Get this man a breath mint." She was a flirt with a mean streak— Tinkerbell with a machine gun, my father called her—and she could say anything to anybody. Then my mother would act shocked and make her apologize, which she would, reluctantly, while everybody laughed. Then she'd explain that we all have things we have to apologize for, we all fall short of the glory of God, which translated, to me, as, Nobody's good enough. Except, of course, my mother.

My mother took a breath. Swallowed. She didn't take her eyes off the road, not even for one second.

Then she said, a titch too brightly, "You *are* in a mood, aren't you?" and we lapsed into silence.

Usually, my father worked or stayed home with a TV dinner during our evangelical jaunts, but the next trip we took, my mother insisted that my father come with us, which I was certain she had done because she didn't want to be alone with me, and on the way home, my father died.

I was sunburned, and what I remember from the funeral is peeling the skin off my legs during the Lord's Prayer, saving the biggest pieces on my lap, and my mother putting her hand over mine to stop me. I was wearing black patent-leather Mary Janes with white lace-trimmed ankle socks, and when I heard my mother murmur, "Give us this day our daily bread," I noticed that flakes of my skin were caught in the lace like crumbs.

"And forgive us our debts as we forgive our debtors."

In retrospect, I think she meant, —Let's call it even, God.

"Lead us not into temptation."

—The deal's off.

"Deliver us from evil."

—Leave us alone.

"For thine is the kingdom."

—Take the crown.

"And the power."

—Take the fame.

"And the glory."

—Take the glamour.

"Forever."

—Keep it.

"Amen."

That was the last time I ever heard my mother pray.

THE NEXT SUNDAY, I GOT UP AND STARTED GETTING READY for church, and my mother came into my bedroom wearing her white cotton nightgown and carrying Katie. She said, "Don't put that on. We're not going."

"Why not?" I said.

"Because God let us down," my mother said.

"After all we did for Him," Katie squeaked.

And my mother walked out of the room.

I took off my Sunday dress and put my pajamas back on. I went into the kitchen, looking for my mother, who wasn't there. I went down the hall toward her bedroom. The door was mostly closed, and I peaked through the crack. She was sitting on the edge of the bed, her back to me, having a conversation with Katie. I couldn't make out what they were saying.

We stopped doing churches, but occasionally my mother would accept an invitation from a children's hospital or a women's prison, for which she rewrote her act. She kept the flirting and the insults, but she no longer consoled Katie's beauty-pageant woes by telling her that she could be one of God's princesses. She told her that there's somebody for everybody, and one day she would meet the man of her dreams and he would look at her and see a beauty queen.

Katie would say, "Will he need glasses?"

And my mother would tell her that he might be a fixer-upper, but she could do it.

Katie would say, "What's a fixer-upper?"

"It's a ship without a sail."

"What?"

And my mother would burst into song: "A man without a woman is like a ship without a sail, a boat without a rudder."

Then Katie would say, "A shirt without a tail?"

"Sort of," my mother would say. Then, singing: "A man without a woman is like a wreck upon the sand. But if there's one thing worse in the universe, that's a woman—"

Katie: "Oh, yes, a woman."

My mother: "I said a woman without a man."

The audience usually laughed, but my mother was dead serious.

I miss her. I want to talk to her. I want to hear her voice. For her, giving up on God didn't mean giving up on Heaven. If anything, she expanded it, made it easier to get in. I want to know she believes Diana is in Heaven now, happy, reunited with her grandparents and her father and her hamster and all her pets from her childhood and everybody she ever loved who died. And God. Why not?

WHEN I GET BACK TO THE ROOM, I GO STRAIGHT TO THE phone and punch in the code from our calling card and dial my mother's number. While I wait for the connection to go through, I turn on the TV with the sound off: Di with her babies, with her toddlers, her schoolboys, her teenagers.

My mother's phone rings, sounding like an alarm. I change the channel to a picture of the hospital on the southern edge of Paris where Diana's body lies and outside of which hundreds of mourners are gathering.

It rings again, and the fist in my chest tightens. She always answers on the second ring. I switch the channel again, this time to a Diana-and-her-hats montage: a green feathered beret, a brown velvet boater, something resembling a black and white swirled Frisbee that looks like it's ready to sail off her head.

The phone rings a third time, and I think, with a little puff of relief, that she's not home, they probably went to New Orleans for the weekend. Or the beach.

—Perfect.

—I just want to hear her voice on the answering machine. That's better, in some ways, than having a conversation.

—She'll answer—her voice will—and I'll say, very casually, Hi, it's Ellen. Just thinking of you. Hope all's well. Okay. Sorry I missed you. 'Bye.

—No.

—Hi, it's me. Lawrence and I are in France. Just thought I'd give you a call, in case you needed to reach me. We're at the Paris Ritz. We'll be here all week.

—Forget it.

I'm about to hang up when my mother answers: "Hello?"

"Hi," I say. "It's me."

Silence.

I'm sweating. Plus, I'm still feeling the effects of the wine. And the cigarettes.

I change the channel. BBC World is replaying a sequence I've already seen twice before—basically, what would have flashed before Diana's eyes if she'd drowned—and I move on to CNN's Good-Deed Di: Diana cradling a dying baby in her arms.

"Mama, it's Ellen," I make myself say.

A pause.

"I'm calling from France."

Diana touching a leper.

Then, "France," my mother says. "Now you're in France. I was in the garden. I would have let the machine pick up, but it's fried—power surge from a lightning storm—so I started running as soon as I heard the phone ringing because I didn't want to wake up Big John, and now I've tracked dirt all over the kitchen floor."

She's clearly not going to apologize to me for her long

silence, so I have two choices: apologize to her for mine, or pretend we never stopped speaking in the first place—this time.

"Sorry," I say. "About the dirt."

"It's my own fault," she says. "I'm spraying roses. I'm covered with poison."

"Well, do you want to go wash it off and I'll call you later?"

"No, I'm not finished spraying. I'd be covered in poison whether I were talking to you or not."

"Okay," I say.

"Where's Lawrence?"

"He's here, too."

Diana shaking hands with an elderly man in a hospital bed.

"Put him on."

I take a breath. Make a choice.

I could say, —Don't you want to talk to me?

But I don't want to hear the answer to that question, which is obvious, anyway.

I could say, —What is wrong with you, Mother?

But there is no answer to that one.

I say, "Well, he's not *here* here. I mean, he's at his conference." My voice sounds very calm, not at all like I could burst into tears.

Diana walking through a land-mine field, wearing a sign on her chest that says The Halo Trust.

"On a Sunday? Is it Sunday there?" my mother says.

"Yeah."

"And you're not there with him?"

"It's a physics conference."

"Well, good for him," my mother says. "Do you have any idea what time it is here?"

I say, "No, what time is it?"

"It's six thirty in the morning."

"Oh," I say. "Sorry. But you're already in the garden?"

"I have to garden at this hour if I don't want to die of heatstroke."

"How long have you been up?"

Diana listening intently to an old woman in a wheelchair.

"Hours," my mother says. "I don't sleep anymore."

I change the channel again. This station is doing Glamorous Di: Diana dancing at the White House with John Travolta.

I say, "Are you okay?"

Another pause.

My mother says accusingly, "What do you mean, am I okay?"

"Your insomnia?"

"I don't have insomnia. I just don't sleep."

I say, "I couldn't sleep last night, either. Finally I just got up and—"

"I'd *like* to sleep," my mother says. Interrupts. "I just don't. Einstein barely slept, either. I'm not claiming to be a genius. Just somebody who doesn't need much sleep. Not everybody does, you know."

I say, "Did you hear about Princess Diana?"

"How could I not?" she says. "It's everywhere here. All night long. That's why I finally had to go outside. There's only so much you can take. Is it everywhere there?"

"Yes."

"Well, of course it is, except it's in French," my mother says, "so you can't understand it."

"No, they have English channels, English newspapers. I saw her yesterday. In person."

"Where?" She doesn't believe me.

"Here. At the hotel. We're staying at the Ritz."

"She was just sitting around the lobby?"

—Don't tell her about the hair salon.

"Well, no. We were eating dinner in the restaurant."

"Oh, and she came in there for ten minutes? They said that on the news. And she didn't even eat."

"Yeah."

"Well, ten minutes is ten minutes."

—Drop it. You don't have to impress her.

"Actually, when we drove up, the paparazzi were there waiting for her, and they thought I was her."

"How could they think that?"

"Well, not for long, but when we were in the car."

"Have you had your hair redone and grown five inches and had plastic surgery since I saw you?"

"No, but we had tinted windows."

"Then they didn't think you were her, dear. They just thought your car was her car."

"Well, yeah. But still, it was interesting."

"You should hear what they're saying. They're already talking conspiracy theories on the Internet. Had you heard that?"

"No," I say.

"The Queen ordered it, Prince Philip, arms dealers, radical Muslims, British intelligence agents. The CIA, as if the CIA would have any reason in the world to want her dead. I don't believe it, any of it," my mother says. "And of course everybody wants to blame the paparazzi, too, and I'm not excusing rudeness, which they were, but there's a difference between being pushy and killing somebody. People are just desperate to believe it was murder because they don't want to believe in accidents because accidents can happen to anybody, whereas most of us aren't in danger of being assassinated. But she was just foolish. I mean, I don't want to sound judgmental, and I'm not saying it served her right, because of course it's a tragedy no matter what she was doing or who she was doing it with, but honestly, just from a practical point of view, what did she expect, racing around in a foreign country with a playboy in the middle of the night?"

Diana at dinner, flirting with Henry Kissinger.

I could say, —Well, Mother, I don't know what she expected. I'm just pretty sure it wasn't this.

But I hold my tongue.

That's the kind of statement that launched our trouble at Christmas. JonBenet Ramsey, the six-year-old beauty queen, had just been found murdered and possibly sexually assaulted in her basement, and the TV kept replaying images of her in a Vegas-style costume vamping on stage. In every picture they showed of her, her hair was dyed blond and curled and sprayed stiff and she was wearing full makeup — mascara, blush, lipstick, gloss. The police wouldn't say whether or not the millionaire parents were suspects, which meant they were, and my mother asked what kind of parent would do such a thing to their child, meaning they had to be innocent because no parent could, and I pointed out that plenty of parents harm their children and even if JonBenet's parents weren't guilty of murder, they were culpable of something, and my mother asked me if I meant this was what they should have expected, they enter their daughter in a beauty pageant, so they should have known she'd end up being brutally killed in their home, and I said I was only saying they obviously hadn't made protecting her innocence a high priority, and she pointed out that she did not do to me what JonBenet's mother did to her, and I said I didn't say she had, and we were off.

And alone, Diana alone, again and again, in the backseat of a car or in front of the Taj Mahal or on the street in her jogging clothes, literally running from the press.

My mother says, "You know I'm not Prince Charles' biggest fan, but one thing you have to say for him: This wouldn't have happened if she'd stayed married to him."

— Don't argue with her.

"That's true."

"Seriously, did she think she could do better than the future king of England?"

"Maybe she didn't want to be married at all. She was so unhappy in that marriage."

"She was just foolish. As soon as she got out of that marriage, or before, actually, long before, she was looking for the next man, each one worse than the one before. Did you hear she wasn't wearing her seat belt?"

"Yeah, and the bodyguard was, which is odd."

"Well, you know how I am about seat belts. You can be the Queen of Sheba, but you've still got to wear a seat belt. I mean, this certainly proves that."

I don't answer her.

Diana waving to a crowd, she on one side of a velvet barrier, everybody else on the other.

One of the network anchors teared up making the announcement, my mother informs me. There's nothing else on TV, they preempted Sunday-morning telechurch.

"You'd think she was Elvis," she says. "She slept with half the married men in England, you know. Not to speak ill of the dead, but really. Of course, Elvis was no saint, either, so there you go."

"Right," I say.

On TV, a little girl kneels in front of the gates at Kensington Palace to place a bouquet of flowers with the hundreds of other bouquets that have already been left there. Then she pauses, as if she's been told to wait for her cue before she stands up. I'm willing to believe that she really put the flowers there, once, but I have a feeling that what they're broadcasting is a reenactment.

After a pause, my mother says, "You want to hear a joke?"

"Okay."

"What's easier to lay than wall-to-wall carpet?"

"I don't know. What?"

"Princess Di! I heard it at the beauty parlor last week. It was funnier when she wasn't dead. Of course everything's always funnier at the beauty parlor. Have you ever noticed that?"

"No."

"Why is that? Do you think it's the chemicals?"

"I don't know."

"It's not really that funny now, is it?"

"It was funny. Thanks for telling me."

"You didn't laugh."

"Well, maybe it wasn't ha-ha funny. But it was funny."

"It was a joke. If jokes aren't ha-ha funny, they're not funny."

"It wasn't the joke. It's me. I don't feel like laughing."

"I know. That's why I tried to *make* you laugh."

"I'm trying to figure things out," I say.

"Figure what out?"

"Everything. How I feel."

"Well, good luck. I've never had *any*thing all figured out," my mother says. "For a while there, I thought I did, but looking back, that's when I was the farthest from it. I don't know. Now I think the day you have everything all figured out is the day you die."

"You figure it out and then you die? That's the New Gospel according to My Mother?"

"No. You die, and *then* you figure it out. Life is what happens before that."

"You think Diana has it all figured out now?"

"Well, I hope so, bless her heart. You know, speaking of her heart, did you know they literally tore off her clothes, sawed open her chest while she was still alive, sucked out the loose blood with a vacuum cleaner–type thing, and massaged her heart with their bare hands?"

"I hadn't heard that."

"Surely they tried those . . . what do you call them? Those shock paddles first. I mean, it's France, not the Third World. But can you imagine? People splitting your chest apart and squeezing your heart? That would give me nightmares, wouldn't it give you nightmares?"

"Probably."

"It would, believe me. I mean, they always say that people who have open-heart surgery have nightmares after, but somehow I didn't really think about it until now, or if I did, I thought it was about almost dying or about being hooked up to machines that breathe for you and pump your blood for you, like you're part robot. Dead and not-dead at the same time, you know?"

"Yeah."

"But there's more to it than that. I mean, I've always felt

like there was a little part of me that was all mine, because women especially, we can be *entered,* we can even be *inhabited* when we're pregnant, because seriously, it's like having an alien inside you, no offense. Anyway, what was I saying?"

"I have no idea."

"That I've always believed that everybody needs to have a part of themselves that no one else can ever touch, and I guess I've thought of that place as my heart. And now ... I don't know. Makes you think, though, doesn't it?"

"Yeah."

—You're right, Mother. Nobody can touch your heart.

"Isn't that the final irony—after all the money she spent on massages and beauty treatments and psychics and psychologists and remember the colonic irrigations—and then she dies while having her heart massaged?"

"Yeah. Mother, this is a transatlantic call. I should probably cut it short."

"Right, Ellen, dear, don't waste your money on me. I'm not saying anything worth listening to anyway."

"I didn't say that, Mama."

"I didn't *mean* anything. I'm agreeing with you. I have to go pee anyway. I'm serious about too much coffee. I think I've had three cups already."

"Okay."

"You be careful now. Watch out for those Frenchmen. Macy Roberts—do you know her?"

"I don't think so."

"Well, you should, she's darling. Her daughter's the journalist? Won some award?"

—When's the last time you won an award, Ellen? Oh, that's right. Never.

"Next time you're in town—of course I'll be dead by then—but I'd introduce you if you ever did come. You should introduce yourself at my funeral."

"Mama, please . . ."

"You'll love her. But anyway, she went to France last month and she says Frenchmen would just as soon go to bed with you as look at you. If you're asking them for directions, nobody speaks English, but if they're trying to get you into bed, they're fluent as natives. And she's sixty years old! Well preserved, but still. Claims she's never had work done, which I don't believe for three seconds, I just can't figure out *when* she did it because I've played bridge with her every Wednesday for the past twelve years. Maybe she didn't really go to France, had a little touch-up instead. But she claims all you have to say is, I'm meeting my husband in five minutes, and they run the other direction. That's the French for you."

I say, "Okay. Thanks for the tip."

"Thank Macy."

Part of me wants to tell her I love her, but the last time I did, there was a tiny pause after I said it, a pause long enough to make me wonder—hope—the phone line had gone dead. Then she said, "Well, I love you too, honey," though something in her voice made me think she was thinking, What a strange thing to say.

So I say, "Okay."

Then she says, "Stay out of tunnels."

"Okay."

"Say hey to Lawrence."

I say, "Okay. 'Bye." And hang up the phone.

I think, —Why is it that nothing I do is ever good enough

for you? Watch this: I'll have an affair with Max. I'll be talking to you on the phone and while you're disapproving of me for some little stupid thing like being in France, I'll be thinking, no, I'm not as bad as you think I am, I'm worse! Or better. I'm loving somebody. I'm loving a total stranger, which is more than you ever did for anybody but yourself.

To which my mother would say, —Having sex with a stranger is not love. It's the opposite of love.

I'm still sort of watching Diana—smiling, presenting a huge polo trophy to the man who later wrote a book about the affair they were having at the time—when I begin to picture myself, a version of myself I barely recognize, naked, in Max's bed.

—Why does this happen every time I talk to my mother? She makes me crazy, turns me inside out, and I can't even say what it is she says that does it, but I don't want to have an affair. The whole idea of it—wanting to sleep with some stranger because of your mother? That's sick. And it's wrong. I don't want to sleep with him. This isn't even about sex.

I'm walking around the room, from the bed to the window to the desk to the closet and back to the bed. I pick up the phone.

—Why do you do this, Mother? Why can't you just be nice and loving? Why can't you say, Have a good time in Paris, without it sounding like a guilt trip?

Then I put it back down.

—Stop it. I don't want to argue with my mother, not on the phone and not in my head. Why is that so difficult? Why can't I just have a normal, pleasant conversation with her without getting myself tied up in knots?

Then Diana: *No pleasing my mother, either.*

I stop pacing.

I think, —Right. There's no pleasing her. Stop fighting.

And Diana again:

She thought I was destroying my marriage on purpose. She was one to talk. I couldn't explain to her that it wasn't a way out. It was, how am I going to survive? It was a way of trying to find something. Maybe on one level it was a way of trying to make myself feel desirable in a way I didn't in my marriage, but on another, it was a way of trying to make myself understand that something much more painful and mysterious had already happened in the marriage, some failure of the heart. So being intimate with another man was a way of saying, The fairy story is over. It was me trying to make real what was already true.

I go to the closet and get out the picture of Diana giving the finger to Max Kafka and look at it. I turn it over and look at his phone number.

I think, —I don't want to destroy my marriage. I don't want to hurt Lawrence.

Of course you don't.

—I just want to find a way to be in it differently—in my marriage, but also in my body, in my life.

I never intended to hurt anybody, not even my husband. So you reach for someone who wants to help you, someone you think is good and kind and discreet, someplace you feel alive, and next thing you know, I'd be at the palace or at Balmoral or wherever I had to be, doing my engagements, but in my head, I'm counting the hours until the next time I see the man I've fallen in love with. I've got a whole imaginary life where we're out in the countryside, in Devon, and I'm a housewife, and we have a cozy little cottage and I do all my own ironing and cleaning and nobody bothers us and we live a happy, simple life. James and I used to read issues of Country Life *together and pick out dream houses. I knew on some level that it couldn't really happen, but pretending, hoping, it made everything else bearable.*

It was complex, why it worked for me, how it worked, but part of it was my need to be touched. I thirsted for it, wasn't able to simply go without it, so important, and my husband was not a tactile person. Nothing in that department. But another part of it was his mother. I loved her. And she loved me. I didn't think of her as a surrogate mother. She was the polar opposite of my mother. But she wasn't just a friend, either. We could talk for hours about nothing, and laugh. We didn't have a history. There was nothing to remember, nothing to forget. Nothing to forgive. With your own mother, there's always that, on both sides.

The same was true of him, in a way. No obligations. No past, no real future, despite what we liked to tell ourselves. So everything, every moment, was a gift, and you had to be there for it, in the present. You created something that was all your own, that had no real life outside of the one you made for it, and part of you just wanted to believe you could live in this bubble, but part of you wondered how long it would take the media to find out and how they'd distort it when they did.

It was not a question of if, but of when and how. They distorted everything.

After a while, you've read so many lies about yourself, and told so many lies, which you started out doing to protect the truth, but you get to a place where you've lied so much and for so long, you can't start telling the truth or you'll be exposed as a liar. By which time, you don't even know what's true anymore. You've played so many roles, you don't know who you are. That's what I'm trying to do now, figure out who I am.

And I think, —There's a sense in which I'm trying to figure out something about who I am as well, but I don't want to pick out a dream house with Max. I don't want to meet his mother. I don't want to make love to him. I don't even want to have sex with him. I just want him to rip off my clothes and tear me open and reach inside my body and grab me by the heart and fuck me.

I TAKE THE PICTURE BACK TO THE BED AND SIT DOWN NEXT to the phone. I take a breath. I look at the minibar. I can still feel the wine from lunch, just a soft buzz, and I'm not going to open another bottle, but if somebody handed me a glass of wine right now and said, Drink this and then call him, I would do it.

I look at the picture again. She's wearing sunglasses. Two dark, perfectly round lenses. It's light, but there are no shadows. It must have been a cloudy day, and she wore the glasses along with the cap to discourage photographers. The photograph is taken from a little bit of an angle, as if Max is crouched in front of her, maybe across the street from her. There's no one else in the picture. It's a sidewalk, but obviously not a crowded one. She seems to be walking toward a car. I can't make out what kind of car it is, it's just a bumper. Or, she was walking until she stopped to give him the finger, but now she's facing him directly. But there's part of a car, and behind it, mostly blocked by it, is the red, curved corner of what looks to me like the top of a London phone booth.

I turn it over.

Above Max's name, in italics, are the words "Reproduction interdite sans l'accord du photographe." Then in boldface, his name. Then in smaller block print, his address and phone number. It's all on a white sticker, more or less in the center of the white paper, more or less straight. Crooked, actually. It gives me courage, the crookedness. He doesn't take himself that seriously, it says. No appointment necessary.

I think, —I have to do this—I have to do *something*—so I

won't wonder for the rest of my life what would have happened if I had, so I'll just dial the number, and if he doesn't answer the phone, he certainly wouldn't have answered the door if I'd gone there, and he probably won't answer the phone—he's probably not even in town anymore—so here goes nothing.

Then I exhale and dial.

But he answers on the first ring. Or, *somebody* does and says, "Oui?"

I'm not ready. My heart's going a mile a minute and my brain is working in slow motion. We. No, oui. Oui. Yes.

I say, "Oh, hi, um, oui, yes, hello, I'm the American woman you photographed in front of the Ritz yesterday afternoon?"

"Yes?"

Two hundred people photographed me yesterday, and they probably photographed other women besides me, as well—anybody who drove up. I can't tell from the word *yes* if this person is French or American.

"So I was wondering."

—What the hell?

"I'm at Les Deux Magots. Well, I'm not *there*. I'm at the Ritz, where I'm staying, but you knew that. But I'm on my way to Les Deux Magots, which I know is near you, or your studio, and would you like to meet me for coffee?"

He says, "Oh," and I can't read his tone—I can't read anything about him—but my heartbeat has slowed down and now the pounding against my chest is so hard—bam, bam, bam—that it feels like somebody's in there, trying to escape.

I'm starting to think it's him.

"I'm sorry," I say. "It's okay if you don't. I just . . . I was so interested in your work, and I thought . . ."

"My work."

—He's American. He's also suspicious. Who wouldn't be?

"Your photography. I'm sorry. Is this Max Kafka?"

Pause.

Then, warily, "Yes."

"Right, well, good. See, when Princess Diana . . ."

"I have nothing to do with her. No pictures, no negatives. Nothing."

"No no no. I'm not . . . I'm sorry. It's . . . Well, with Princess Diana's death, and you had been at the hotel and you were there that morning . . ."

"No I wasn't. You have me mistaken for someone else. I can't help you."

"Wait. I might, I know. Be mistaken, I mean. That's what I'm trying to figure out, and I'm sorry if I am, but I think I walked over to the flame from the tunnel with you, and I was . . ."

"I wasn't there. I was at the hotel that afternoon—though I don't have any pictures—and then I left and went home. I was at home, alone, all night. I was not in the tunnel."

"No. I meant yesterday morning, when they were towing the car. I got your name off the back of the picture you put down by the flame. Or somebody put it there—maybe it wasn't you, and if not, I'm really sorry for bothering you—but that picture, it really got to me, and I picked it up after you left, just to look at it, and sort of ended up keeping it. That's how I got your number."

He doesn't say a word.

It *is* him—I'm 99 percent sure it is—but he doesn't want to see me.

"Okay, I'm sorry. Sorry to bother you, sorry I took your

photograph. I didn't . . . This was incredibly insensitive of me. I can only imagine how you must feel, with everyone so mad at the paparazzi. So I just want you to know, for what it's worth, that I wasn't thinking of you that way. That's not why I called. My timing is just . . . couldn't be worse. Anyway, I'm sorry. I feel terrible."

—How many times did I just apologize?

He says, "It's okay."

"Well, you take care of yourself."

"Yes. Thank you. You, too."

He doesn't hang up right away, so I say, "Will you just tell me this much? Am I talking to the right person? Are you the one who was there this morning, at the flame?"

"I was there. But a lot of people were."

—It's him.

"Okay, I just have to say one thing. It's what I felt when we were there and you called the other photographers vultures, and now the newspapers are calling them assassins, and you seemed so . . . well, *good*. And sad. And I was sad, too. That's the thing that made me call you."

There's a long silence.

Then I say, "Or, part of what made me call you."

And he's still silent. I'm not even sure he's still *there*.

I say, "Well, okay. Thanks again."

—This irritating habit I have, thanking people for nothing when I feel uncomfortable.

And I'm about to hang up when he says, "Where did you say you are?"

—Oh!

And my heart, which had calmed down, starts jumping around in my chest.

I manage to say, "I'm here at the Ritz, but I'll be at Les Deux Magots, in . . . how long does it take? I'll get a cab. Twenty minutes? Ten?"

He says, "I'm on my mobile. I'm here, next door, in front of the church, on my way to an appointment, but I have a half hour. Counting the twenty minutes it's going to take you to get here. So I don't know if that's worth it to you. For ten minutes."

"Oh, no, it is."

"I don't want to sit outside, though."

"You mean with me?"

"Yes. Isn't that what you . . ."

"No, yes. *Yes.* You want to sit inside?"

"Yes."

"Okay, that's fine. It's a hot day, anyway. I mean, it would be fine either way. But inside's fine. So I'll meet you inside as soon as I can get there."

"Okay," he says.

And I say, "Okay, 'bye," and hang up and I rush to the mirror and pull my fingers through my hair but my hands are cold and quivering, even though I'm sweating, so my hair sort of sticks to my fingers, and I fish through my toiletry bag and run a brush through my hair and put on lipstick and check my teeth and then I decide to brush my teeth because I've got cigarette breath and then I put on lipstick again and grab my purse and the room key and go.

As I'm getting out of the taxi, I hear church bells ringing, though not particularly melodiously, and I walk toward the door of Les Deux Magots, past sidewalk tables full of tourists, mostly couples, busily consulting their guidebooks, trying to figure out where to go next. All around me, people are holding intense conversations in languages not my own.

I go inside and look around the room and my eyes are adjusting to the relative darkness, but I don't see him, and I don't feel surprised or even disappointed.

—Right. He was just trying to get rid of me, treating me like a stalker, may as well have given me the finger. What a complete idiot I am.

But then there he is.

He's already sitting down at a table on a mahogany-red leather banquette in a corner, and when he sees me see him, he smiles and slides over and stands up, and I have that feeling you get right before you jump off a boat or a pier into water so deep and so dark that you can't see the bottom, and I take a step toward him.

He's showered and shaved since yesterday. The little cut on his forehead looks much better, which means he's a fast healer. I like that. He's wearing a clean shirt. It's not what I would call stylish—it's a striped shirt, cream with vertical tan stripes— but I don't know what French style is. It's not rumpled. I'd taken him for a rumpled-shirt kind of person. He looks different, better, but it's definitely him, and the thought that flashes through my head is, —He looks completely normal.

I don't know what I mean by that.

I'm walking over to him, and it feels like a very long walk, like in dreams where you keep walking and walking but you barely move forward, and when I finally get to him, I shake his hand and say, "Hi."

He says, "Hi," back.

It's a regular handshake, quick, the way you do when you meet a person you barely know and you're not that interested in, not even as warm or as long as when we first shook hands outside the Ritz. He motions to a chair for me and we sit down across from each other at a little wooden table.

It all seems very normal—elegant and even exotic just for being in Paris, but also like the kind of thing that happens every day, everywhere, two people meeting for coffee— though at least for me, it's not normal at all.

Max says, "I didn't think I would see you again."

—Which means you thought about whether you would? I can barely breathe, but I say, "I'm glad it worked out." Now he's supposed to say, Me, too.

But he doesn't, so I say, "I didn't expect it, either. I didn't think you would answer your phone, and I didn't even really think I would call."

And I want him to say, I'm glad you did, but he doesn't, so I say, "Wasn't even sure I could figure out *how* to call, but it's pretty much the same as in America. You just pick up the receiver and dial the number. But I'd never done it before. Here. Made a local call. Or asked a man I don't know to have coffee with me. Haven't even done *that* in America. So."

Pause.

—Please just say you're glad I called. Say something.

He's still on pause.

Then: "Anyway," I say, "I'm glad I did."

And then, because he's still not saying anything—he's not agreeing with me, but then again, not disagreeing with me—I say, "You're not mad I took the photograph?"

"No," he says.

I want him to say something more, anything more: I'm glad you took it, it's yours if you want it, I'm happy to see it in good hands, I've got other copies, it would have gotten rained on, anyway.

But he just says, "No."

He's looking at me like there's more he could say but he's not going to say it and like he's trying to figure me out.

I'm trying to figure him out, too.

—Why is he here? Why did he agree to come when he obviously doesn't feel like talking? When you agree to meet someone for coffee, aren't you also implicitly committing to have a conversation with them? And what is it about me that he's trying to figure out?

It makes me uncomfortable, him studying me this way. He's quiet, but it's a very intense kind of quiet, like he's got so much noise inside him that he *can't* say much or he'd have to scream it, but I can't stand the silence, so I say, "Good." And by now it's been so long since he said anything that I'm not sure he knows what I'm talking about—this is off to a very bad start, it's almost impossible to imagine going from this to him ripping my clothes off—but I say, "Good that you're not mad, I mean."

He says, "No," again, though this time he sounds sadder and slightly confused, as if he's not sure what he would be mad about if he were mad. It's impossible to imagine him ripping *any*body's clothes off.

I smile, sort of laugh. I nod, as if I agree with him, as if he's just said something for me to agree with.

Then he says, "What did you want to see me for?"

"Oh, I don't know," I say—which is true and not at all true

at the same time—"I didn't have a particular agenda, if that's what you mean. I was just . . . You were just so . . . interesting. And the photograph, of course, that intrigued me."

And he doesn't respond, doesn't move a muscle, doesn't take his eyes off me, so I say, "You must have quite a story."

"Is this an interview? Are you a reporter?" he says, suddenly pulling up straighter than he was, as if he's tensing every muscle in his neck.

"Oh, God, no. No, no, no."

Now I can't even look at him. I'm looking at my hands on the table—my wedding ring and my watch, my short fingernails. I run my fingers along the table's edge.

I say, "I don't . . . I'm not trying to get something out of you. I'm not really sure why I called. I just . . . *did*."

—And now I'm sorry I did. I went temporarily insane. Which happens—it's a legal defense. And to my credit, it's not like I killed anybody. Just made a complete and total fool of myself.

Finally he says, "I'm glad you did."

I'm out of breath, trying not to show it, so I take a shallow breath, exhale. Then I take a bigger breath because I'm in slight danger of passing out.

He says, "But there's not much to tell."

I say, "Oh there must be. I mean, I just wanted to know . . ."

—Don't ask about Diana giving him the finger, don't do it. And don't ask if he's heard her voice since she died.

"Well, obviously, you're American—or Canadian?—but you live here, which is interesting, living in exile, very Hemingwayesque, and well, I was wondering what you're doing here?"

"Living in exile is not as romantic as it used to be," he says. "Between phones and faxes and jets and . . . McDonald's, Disneyland, Madonna—you can't get away from America. It follows you around like a dog."

"Oh."

Then another quiet falls on us.

I say, "But you seem less American than I am, more French, though less French than the French, so maybe it's not exile, exactly, but you're *in* the culture but not *of* it, which is how they used to tell us to be in church, in the *world* but not of it. That was a definition of spirituality, which I never could figure out how to do."

And nothing. I get nothing from this guy.

I say, "So. Max Kafka. Was Franz Kafka, what, your great-grandfather, great-great?"

"I'm not a direct descendant. I think he's some sort of cousin, once or twice removed. I'm not into genealogy. We're all related. And we're all alone."

—Fuckit.

"What were you doing at the Ritz?" I say.

And when he hesitates, I say, "Well, I know, photographing Diana, so did you know her?" And he doesn't even move, so I rush on. "I mean, is that your job? Have you photographed her other places, like, for example, London"—he blinks—". . . and America and all over the world?"

He lets out a long breath, just barely shakes his head no. I don't think it's an answer to my question, as in, No, I haven't photographed her all over the world. More like, No, not this, please don't ask me about this.

I say, "Or do you just pretty much stay in Paris, you know, photographing . . . other stuff?"

"No," he says.

—No? No, what?

I'm starting not to like this guy. No, I *don't* like him. I'm certainly not going to fuck him.

I'm about to leave—I'll stand up and say, Well, thank you so much for your time, but I know you have another appointment—when, finally, he speaks. He says, "I mean, yes, I photographed her, some. But that's another life. It's over. It's not who I am anymore."

I could say, —Well, of course it's over: She's dead.

I could say, —It's who you were yesterday.

But I don't. Maybe I smirk or something, though I don't mean to, but he nods and says, "I took photographs—that was my profession—but when I saw the wreckage, I thought, This can't be true, and now those people are dead, and I don't even want to see the pictures I took. It's just a horrible memory. I can't stand it anymore. It's not who I want to be, not why I ever picked up a camera in the first place. It's certainly not who I want to talk about."

—Waitaminute. Did he just tell me he took pictures of Diana and Dodi in the tunnel? He said, "Those people." He said he took pictures he doesn't want to see, and now, meaning later, those people, as in the ones he took the photographs of, are dead.

I say, "Were you there?"

"Where?"

"In the tunnel, when she crashed."

"No. *God,* no. Of course not."

"I'm sorry. I shouldn't have asked that."

"Well, if you suspected it. I don't want you suspecting me. In this climate—"

"No, I don't, but even if I did, it still wasn't any of my business. I'm sorry."

"Technically, it *is* a matter of public business. There's an investigation. But I wasn't there."

"No, but if you had been, it would have been terribly rude of me. *I'm* not investigating anything. So I just wanted you to know that I thought I was picking up on something you said — I wasn't trying to *out* you — but when you said you didn't want to see the pictures you took, I thought . . ."

"I meant the ones I took that afternoon at the hotel. I regret having been there."

"Right. Of course. Of course you do."

"She was clearly distressed, even then."

"Right."

"I wish I'd left her alone. I wish we all had."

And now I'm the one who's not saying anything. I can't think of a single thing to say.

I say, "Sure."

I still don't want to make love with him, but I sort of want to touch him. He's looking at his hands on the table, and I think I would like to put my hand on top of his in a gesture of comfort, except my palms are sweaty. I just noticed that. I wipe them off on my pants.

We sit there in an awkward silence for a moment until a waiter comes up to us. Max orders a café au lait, s'il vous plaît, and I say, "Moi aussi."

The waiter leaves, and I'm trying to figure out whether I should introduce myself — by the way, I'm Ellen Baxter — or would that just call attention to the fact that we've still never actually met?

He looks at me — we're making progress, though progress toward *what,* I don't know.

I say, "So." Then I shake my head and open my hands to

him. I can't put words to what I mean by the gesture, but he seems to take something from it that he needs, or at least wants.

He says, "How long will you be in Paris?" And what he wants is to change the subject. Fine.

I say, "I leave Thursday."

"When did you come?"

"Yesterday morning."

He says, "That's not long enough."

"No. But how long would be long enough?"

"True. Where do you go from here?"

"Home. I have a son."

"How old is he?"

"Twenty."

He raises his eyebrows at me. "You had him when you were ten?"

I giggle. I actually giggle, and I'm not a giggler.

"He's my stepson. Sometimes I call him my son because *stepson* sounds so . . . well, that makes me a stepmother."

"You don't like being a stepmother?"

I say, "No. It's not that. It's . . . well, we all know what step-mothers are like. They're wicked, and they end up in a fiery pit. Are they wicked or evil?"

"Witches are wicked. Stepmothers are evil. But yes, unfortunately for you, they both end up in the pit."

I giggle again.

He says, "So, are you evil?"

"No!"

"Are you wicked?"

"Not where my stepson is concerned."

"And I take it he lives with you, so you have precious little opportunity to be wicked otherwise?"

"He's in college now, but yes," I say in mock sadness. "I've spent most of my married life acting like a solid citizen."

"And where do you carry out your civic duties?"

"Atlanta."

"Atlanta," he says in a tone of voice that says he might have guessed. Then he says, "Home of the Big Chicken."

"You know the Big Chicken?"

"Not well."

"But you've been to Atlanta?"

"I went last year, for the Olympics."

"Did you like it?"

"It's okay. Too much traffic. I like Paris better."

"Me, too."

"So why don't you stay longer? Your twenty-year-old wants you home?"

"No, he goes to a small liberal-arts college in Tennessee, it's about a three-hour drive from Atlanta, and he plays football, second-string offense. It's important to him, so we try to be there for the home games."

"I see."

Then silence. With that one little word—we—I've introduced the fact that there's a husband into the conversation. He knew that, he saw Lawrence with me outside the Ritz, but somehow my bringing him up here seems to have landed on Max—before now, we might have come to a tacit agreement to pretend Lawrence didn't exist, and there goes that—and this is not where I wanted this to go, but I also feel like I have to explain rather than just let it drop, partly because it *won't* just drop, so I say, "My husband . . . he loves his son, but he doesn't have . . . he doesn't always know how to show it. I mean, he's not much of a hugger, a toucher. I am, but he and his son aren't big talk-about-your-feeling types. So he has a list of things in his head that he feels like he has to do—*wants* to do—to be a good parent, and one of them is to go to his son's home football games, which are on Saturdays. And we missed last Saturday, the season opener. So he wants to be back for the next one. Which is Saturday."

Max looks at me, and I realize I've made Lawrence look inadequate, and I'm fighting with my own sense that he *is* inadequate in some ways, which is why or part of why Alec is the way he is and a big part of why I'm here. None of which I want to say out loud, so I say, "Can we not talk about my stepson anymore?"

"I would like very much not talking about him."

Pause.

Then Max says, "I just wish you were staying longer."

"Me, too," I say.

"I mean," he says, "for your sake."

"Right."

"So tell me what your life in Atlanta is like."

—Why is he asking me this? Does he want me to tell him I share his contempt for the Big Chicken, not to mention McDonald's and Madonna and Disneyland? Because I can't do it. I like America. I even like Disneyland and don't have a problem with McDonald's or Madonna or the Big Chicken. It's just a great big steel chicken—fifty or sixty feet high—outside a chicken restaurant. I realize it's no Eiffel Tower. But still.

—And while it's true that the French would never put a sixty-foot-high snail, for example, in front of a snail restaurant, snails aren't funny, and chickens are. And I realize the French have a different sense of humor than we do—the whole Jerry Lewis mystery—but snails aren't even funny by French standards, unless maybe you slip on one like it's a banana peel, which isn't relevant here. And for another thing, if you put up a fifty-foot-high snail in the shell, you'd block the restaurant—the Big Chicken is actually pretty thin, it's more of a big chicken face on top of a long, thin body, where snails don't even *have* faces—so if it didn't have its shell, it would look like a fifty-foot-high penis, which is not only not funny, not to mention inaccurate because snails don't stand up, but it's also not appetizing, not to mention a little scary.

—I should not be thinking about fifty-foot-high penises—or any penis—right now.

—So anyway, where were we? Life in Atlanta.

I say, "Well, there's not much to tell. My husband is a physicist at Georgia Tech. He's here for a physics convention. I'm a faculty wife. I do a little bit of charity work. I entertain some. We travel a lot."

I shrug: —That's pretty much it.

He says, "When you entertain, do you cook?"

"Sometimes. It depends."

"You're a good cook?"

"I don't know. I like to."

"I can't stand false modesty in a beautiful woman."

—You think I'm beautiful?

"I'm a good cook."

"I thought so. What else?"

"What do you mean?"

"What else do you do?"

—Nothing. I go shopping. I go out to lunch. I'm a Lady Who Lunches.

"Well, the football games, like I said."

—Surely there's more to my life than this. It sounds so

completely pointless. What am I leaving out? And if I'm not leaving anything out, what am I doing with my life?

He says, "But you don't like football."

"Not particularly."

"Do you go to Georgia Tech football games, too?"

"Occasionally. Only when we get invited to sit in the president's box, which is not a box at all. The first time I went, I was expecting something sort of . . . like a box. You know, a little bitty room."

He doesn't say anything, but he's listening, so for lack of a better idea, I keep going: "But it's a huge glass-enclosed space at the top of the stadium with tiered, cushioned seats in front to watch the game, and in the back, the whole back half, there's a buffet with really bad food—cold cuts with stale buns and little orange and yellow cheese cubes and huge bowls full of potato salad that sit out there the whole game—and by the third quarter, you just look at people walking up to the table and think, Stop! Don't eat that!"

Max laughs and says, "America," and part of me wants to argue with him, but he's right. Where else would this happen? Not even Canada.

Still, not to be disloyal, I say, "But it's for a good cause. It's basically fund-raising for the university."

"How?"

"Well, they invite big donors and potentially big donors, and at halftime, the president and the dean and all the people they're trying to schmooze stand around."

"It sounds very boring."

—It *is* boring. My life is utterly boring. I'm boring. But I don't want him to know that. I want him to think I'm . . . I'm not sure what I want him to think I am. But I know what I want him to think I'm not, and that's boring, or even tolerant of boredom.

I say, "It's godawful, and there's no alcohol—just Coke and Diet Coke."

He rolls his eyes as if to say, How American, again, but he's interested. He's listening to every word I say, enjoying it, I think. If he's trying to decide whether he likes me, I think he's leaning toward yes.

So I continue. "And everybody's wearing mustard gold, which is just not a color anybody should ever wear, especially not in large numbers, and most of the men have little scowling cartoon yellow jackets, our mascot, on their ties. Some of the women wear yellow-jacket earrings or necklaces."

"Do you wear mustard yellow?"

"No, I wear black, with gold jewelry. And no insects."

"Your secret rebellion."

"Yes. Though you're the first person to notice."

"So you're standing around, quietly rebelling, and?"

"Well, I like to observe people, and some of the donors want to meet the guy who won the Nobel Prize—others, of course, couldn't care less—but the dean will say, 'This is Dr. Lawrence Baxter and his lovely wife, Ellen.' "

—Now I've told Max my name.

"And the president always says, 'This is Professor Lawrence Baxter, our Nobel laureate, and his lovely wife,' to which I'm like, Thank you, sort of, and I stick out my hand and say, 'I'm Ellen,' or sometimes I don't even bother, because either way, nine and a half times out of ten, the person who wants to meet my husband because of the Nobel doesn't even acknowledge me. At all. Or maybe just barely. It's a strange phenomenon. No matter how the introduction went, they put out their hand to my husband and say it's *so* nice to meet him, and it's like I'm invisible."

"It makes you angry."

"It used to. And it used to hurt my feelings, being almost literally anonymous. It was actually kind of scary, in a way, to the extent that I accepted as true what was implicit there, that it didn't matter who I was, I was just the generic wife. Hislovelywife, all one word. I remember thinking once, during an introduction, that there was absolutely no difference between what was happening to me and what would have been happening to my husband's first lovely wife if she hadn't died — I even have her name, Mrs. Lawrence Baxter, we get mail that I don't know if it's for her or me — and I thought, If I'm living her life, who's living mine? But then . . . Have you ever heard that every cell in your body now wasn't part of you seven years ago?"

"Something like that."

"We lose about three million red blood cells every second, plus about two hundred thousand other cells of skin and bones and organs. Or, technically, we don't so much lose the cells as replace all the atoms in them. But somebody would be introduced to me and not shake my hand, look straight through me, and I could almost *feel* cells dying off. I'd be very much aware that I was changing out atoms, sort of re-creating myself on a subatomic level, which, of course, involved a little bit of falling apart."

"Not quite as solid a citizen as you seem?"

"Right. And then one day I'd just had enough, and I removed myself, emotionally, from the situation. Took a step back and watched. It's actually pretty interesting, what it says about human nature."

"What does it say?"

"Well, say you want to look at a photon . . ."

"But I don't. I'm happy looking at you."

—Good. This is good.

"But if you did, you'd never be able to see the whole thing. You would have to know something about photons beforehand and set up a situation where you could see the aspect of the photon that you wanted to see—its wave function or its particle function—and that would be all you saw. And I think most people go through their whole lives that way, not able to take in the whole picture, seeing only what they want to see, what they're prepared to see. So a lot of women go through life with the sense that all they are, in most people's minds, is their husband's wife, or sometimes their children's mother. And sometimes they internalize that so much that it becomes how they think of themselves. I mean, even Diana, the most famous woman in the world—who'd have cared about anything she ever did if she hadn't married Prince Charles? Even after her divorce, she couldn't escape it because she knew that whenever people looked at her, what they saw was a princess, which was still because of who she'd married instead of who she really was, except of course by that time, that *was* who she really was, or part of it, because after years and years of playing a role every day of your life, you can't help but start to become that character. But imagine being the most photographed woman in the world and being frustrated because nobody ever sees the whole picture of you."

"Do you wish people would look at you and see the whole picture? You don't have secrets?"

—Wait. Wait wait wait.

"No."

"No, you don't want them to see the whole picture, or no, you don't have secrets?"

"I don't know," I say. "Both, maybe? Or, neither. I don't know."

And then there's an awkward little silence, and then he says, "So your husband won a Nobel?"

And we've just turned a corner, closed a door.

I could have said, —Yes, I have secrets.

And I'm not sure what we would be saying right now, but I know we would not be talking about Lawrence's Nobel Prize. And maybe I should feel like I've done the right thing, but I don't, because it wasn't moral courage that made me do what I did. It was *lack* of courage.

I say, "I'm sorry. What?"

I want to back up. I want to say, —I'm not saying I don't have secrets, but they're secret, secrets aren't supposed to be part of the picture, even Diana had secrets.

Though the truth is, I don't have secrets, or at least not the kind I think he's asking about, and for what it's worth, I don't think Diana had many secrets for long.

He says, "Your husband won a Nobel?"

"Yes. In physics."

"What kind of physics?"

"It was for work he did on subatomic particles."

He nods. He's tired of asking me questions, tired of hearing about my boring life, and I can't even blame him. *I'm* bored with myself.

—Think of something interesting to say, something smart, something about secrets, something about you.

All I can come up with, though, is Lawrence's work, and I say, "After his first wife died, his interests shifted to the role chaos plays in the evolution of the universe, the relationship between subatomic reality and . . . well, everything else. Then he started looking for a Great Attractor that somehow pulls everything toward it over billions of years, as if time moves not so much away from the beginning but toward the end, the final destiny of the universe that philosophers have called an Omega Point and some people call God."

"So he's found God?"

"Not yet."

"But he's looking."

"Actually, he *was* looking. I don't think he still is."

"That's too bad," he says.

—I've made my husband sound pathetic.

"No, it's just how science works. You go down a road for a while, and it turns out to be a dead end"—much like this conversation—"so you try something else. Now he's working on a book . . ."

"Isn't everybody?"

". . . that will probably make him famous."

"A natural second choice."

"What?"

"Looking for God is always a little iffy," he says, "but anybody who wants fame badly enough can get it. And it serves some of the same purpose as finding God does. It makes your life feel bigger than it is."

"Are you being sardonic?"

"No, I'm being ironic."

"What's the difference?"

"I'm sorry. I do a lot of celebrity photography. It makes you cynical, which I don't want to be."

"*Now* you're being ironic."

"Why?"

"By implying that photographing celebrities has damaged you. I mean, if you don't want to be cynical, stop being cynical."

—I hate this person.

"You're right."

—I'm what?

I can't remember the last time Lawrence said I was right.

"I'm sorry," I say. "I shouldn't have said that."

"No, you're right. I'm going to stop being cynical. Right now."

"Are you serious?"

"Yes. So tell me. What's your husband's book about?"

"Well, *physics*. The structure of the universe."

"Okay. And I don't mean this cynically, but does he really think he can become famous by writing a book about physics?"

"Not celebrity-photography famous. But physics-book-author famous."

"Stephen Hawking."

"Stephen Hawking without the mystique of being a great mind trapped in a wheelchair-bound body. I mean, thank God. But. So I think it's more realistic to say Timothy Ferris—famous. Or Richard Feynman."

"I've never heard of either of them."

"So there you go. One man's fame . . ."

"Your husband sounds like an interesting man."

"He is."

—But I wish we could stop talking about him.

"Very intelligent."

"Yes."

"Ambitious."

"Yeah."

I'm looking into Max's eyes. I can't figure out if I like him or hate him.

I say, "Would you like to meet him?"

"No."

And I hesitate and smile and say, "Good."

And a half-second silence where we both let that land.

Then he says, "If he'd won the Nobel Peace Prize, maybe I would want to meet him. But physics, no."

He looks at me and smiles, and I smile back, and I like where we are, wherever that is.

"So this life that you have in Atlanta," he says, "does it make you happy?"

"What?"

And our coffee arrives, and the waiter is talking to Max in French and I can't understand them, and I'm sitting there holding, Are you happy? in my mouth, thinking, Why did I say, What? when I heard him perfectly clearly. I should jump in as soon as the waiter leaves and say, Yes, I'm happy. But the moment has passed and now I don't want to answer the question—it's too personal, for one thing, it's almost rude, it's the kind of thing a paparazzo would ask—and I'm about to change the subject and say, Anyway, I'm having a wonderful time in Paris, which is entirely untrue, or ask him for a restaurant recommendation—everybody who's ever stepped foot in Paris has a favorite restaurant here—when the waiter leaves and Max says it again: "Are you happy?"

"Oh, yes," I blurt out, "very happily married."

—Why did I say that? Why didn't I just say, Yes? Or, Reasonably happy, most of the time, and you? Or even, No.

But, "Good," he says. "Good for you."

And then it's quiet, and I think about mentioning that I take Prozac, which helps with the happiness thing, but I don't.

I lift my cup and say, "Cheers," which is stupid, toasting with coffee, but he touches his cup to mine as if he doesn't think it's stupid at all and we smile at each other and drink.

Then I open a packet of sugar and pour it in. Stir. I'm looking at my coffee, watching the foam swirl as I stir. I'm trying to keep my mouth shut, let him talk, but he doesn't, and I'm not good with silences.

There's no music in this restaurant. I just noticed that.

I say, "Why did you ask me that?"

"You told me, when you called, that you were sad."

"Well, yes, about Diana. Of course. But basically . . . you asked me about my life in Atlanta."

"And you're happy there?"

—Here's your chance. Say what you want. Do you still want it or not? Say, I'd be happier if you'd make love to me.

—I can't. I don't know how to seduce a man. And I don't want to seduce him. I never wanted to seduce him, and I didn't even want him to seduce me. I just wanted it to happen on its own.

I say, "Yeah."

"Good," he says. He doesn't believe me.

Then he says, "Do you have children of your own?"

"No."

And I've had enough, this is starting to feel intrusive—no, it's way past intrusive—and I'm not waiting for the next question: Why not?

People who can't get pregnant either really want to talk about every detail of their attempts, or they don't like to talk about it at all. By my third miscarriage, I'd fallen into the second category.

I say, "Do you?"

"No."

And I look at him, and I get this weird feeling—a rush almost like a shot of caffeine or tequila that goes all the way through my body and out the top of my head, sort of like what Emily Dickinson said good poetry does, though I've never gotten this from a poem.

I say, "Are *you* happy?"

And I understand why he asked it. It's a very intimate question. It's, —Tell me where you are, inside yourself.

It's not even that, because it comes with a disclaimer: You can treat this as a casual question, you don't have to open up if you don't want to. But you can. You're safe here. And if you want to talk, I want to listen. I want to know what you feel.

And I blew it. Twice. The first time, I said, "I'm happily married." Then I said, "Yeah." In other words, Back off. Which he did, graciously.

He says, "Not particularly."

"Why not?"

"I don't know. I regret not having children. I was married, twice, but . . . it didn't happen."

"It still could. You could meet someone today."

—Not today. This is today. The person you're meeting today is me.

"Or tomorrow," I say.

"No."

"Yes you could."

"Okay, maybe. But it's not so easy to fall in love with some-body you want to marry who's not already married, get mar-ried, get pregnant, have babies. Or, I could do it, but it's the sort of thing I do badly—family life. I like to be alone. I'm set in my ways. I eat in one or two restaurants by myself, the same two restaurants over and over, a Vietnamese restaurant and a French bistro. I have my own table there. It's very boring, but I'm a creature of habit, and it's not to my credit, but I like it that way."

—You like boring? I'm boring!

He says, "I've thought, in the past, it was better to photo-graph people than to fall in love with them. I do that well, and no one gets hurt."

He sighs, and I wait, and it's not like I thought he was going to fall in love with me, but somehow, him saying he doesn't want to fall in love sort of hurts my feelings.

Then he says, "*Usually* no one gets hurt."

And we've turned another corner: I'm trying to figure out if he could fall in love with me, or why he's so sure he doesn't want to, and he's talking about Diana. I bite my tongue. I lit-erally bite it.

He says, "The paparazzi didn't kill her. It was just a terrible accident. Very terrible. I've photographed land-mine victims in Bosnia, earthquake victims in India, war casualties in Kosovo. I photographed Desert Storm. But never traffic accidents. But that's all it was—a traffic accident."

He takes a sip of his coffee.

Then he says, "I've photographed a lot of suffering. I've made a lot of money off it."

He's shaking his head.

"Well," I say, "but it's important."

"Yes, suffering is news. You don't suffer, nobody wants to hear about it. Do you know the famous photograph of the guy being shot in the head in Vietnam?"

"No."

"Nobody said to the photographer, 'Why didn't you stop them from executing him?' His name was Eddie Adams, that photographer. He won several prizes for that picture. You can't tell a photographer who sees a tragedy not to take a picture of it." He shrugs. "You can't expect a vulture not to circle a carcass."

I wait for him to go on, but he doesn't.

So I say, "Why were you photographing Diana?"

"Money," he says. "I did it for the money," and his voice is full of scorn.

I don't say anything, but it seems like as good a reason as any to me.

—How American.

"A friend of mine," Max says, "he's not a friend, he's an acquaintance, really, but he's made over three million American dollars photographing Diana. He just bought a villa in Tuscany."

"Wow."

"Photographers all over the world . . . they made money off her. But they loved her. And she loved them. It was love-hate, on both sides. It was like a terrible marriage, in some ways. But there was a relationship there. It was unlike anything else, ever."

Finally he's talking, and I'm just letting him talk.

He says, "Before Saturday, though, it wasn't what I did. Almost never. A couple of times in London—I used to date a British woman, so I was there a lot, for a while. I don't think

I would have done it this time if she hadn't called a press conference in a leopard-print bathing suit . . . when was that? Earlier this summer. I wasn't paying attention at the time. I didn't
go to her, to the South of France, didn't even consider it. But
when she came to Paris, an editor from Germany called to tell
me and said she'll be at the Ritz and he'd pay good money for
a photograph of her with her boyfriend." He stops. He's sort
of imitating himself going from not caring to deciding to go
there, he closes his eyes and cocks his head when he changes
his mind—a very French gesture, to my eyes. Then he says,
"Did you see the photograph last week of the kiss on the
boat?"

"Yes."

"That photographer is now a millionaire. From that one
photograph. So I admit it was just greed. But I thought, 'If I
could get one really good picture, I'd be set for life.' I'm getting too old to go to war, climb through earthquake rubble. So
I went to the Ritz and waited for her like a stalker. Otherwise,
normally, I had a sense of myself as . . . that there were certain
things I wouldn't do. Once, I did go with her—and many
other photographers—to Nepal, but I went because I wanted
to photograph the country. It was so beautiful and there was
such a need for people to know what it was like. So I photographed her—we all did—with a child the villagers believed
was a living goddess, with lepers, with beggars, in front of the
most astonishing scenery. She touched them all, literally
touched them, and some of those people hadn't been touched
in years. *I* didn't want to touch them. But I photographed
poverty and sickness and incense burning like hope. I was very
proud of that one—a leper lighting a stick of incense, holding
the stick with this grossly diseased hand, some of his fingers

were missing, others looked like they were about to fall off, but the expression on his face, behind the smoke, was utterly blissful. It was haunting. I tried to sell it to a French magazine, but they didn't want it. I was freelancing for a German newspaper, sent them at least a hundred pictures, and the only photo they printed was one where she was wearing a see-through skirt."

He drinks his coffee, the whole cup. I think he's finished, though I don't want him to stop.

Then he says, "If Hemingway was right, that morality is what makes you feel bad after, then being a paparazzo is immoral, at least for me."

I finish my coffee and say, "What else?"

"What else what?"

"What else is immoral?"

He puts his cup down, looks at me — he hasn't been looking at me while he talked, he's been thinking out loud, almost, just gazing into the air — but now he looks at me.

He says, "Lying. Even if it's lying to myself about what I feel."

—What are you feeling?

"What else?"

There's a long pause where he looks straight at me, and I meet his gaze. Then he says, "Not so much. I'm not a puritan."

"No?" I say.

"No."

Then I say, "Do you think I'm a puritan?"

"I don't know what you are. I'm trying to figure you out."

I push my hair off my face, then I let my hand fall lightly to the table, where his hand rests. So we're just barely touching, two of my fingertips on two of his fingers, almost as if by accident. Our feet are already brushing against each other under the table, my foot against his leg. I'm not sure how that happened.

I say, "So am I."

He hesitates and smiles and says, "You're a happily married American woman."

—So you *did* hold that against me.

I don't say he's right. I don't say he's wrong. I don't say anything. But I take back my hand. I pick up my cup, but I'm out of coffee, so I put it back down.

"If you were French," he says, "it would be different. The French can't understand why Camilla Parker-Bowles is such a big deal. If Prince Charles were French, no one would care about her, including his wife. They would care that he was a prince—cut his head off for that—but the only thing scandalous about her would be that people would think he should have done better. Americans are more like the British than the French that way. They're more like the British than the British."

"Yeah, I know."

I shift in my seat, and my foot moves away from his leg.

"Did you care?" he says.

Yes.

"About Camilla?" I say.

"Yes."

"I didn't have strong feelings about her."

—Are we talking about Charles and Camilla or about us? Because it's not the same thing. What they have, whatever it is, is totally different because for one thing, Camilla was there long before Diana came into the picture, she helped choose Diana, so because of Camilla, the whole marriage was a deception and Diana was only there to be used and manipulated and the only way she wouldn't have gotten hurt was if she'd been willing to play the dummy to Camilla's ventriloquist act, which, to carry off, she'd have had to be as cynical about the marriage from the beginning as they were. And this is not even about my marriage, or not to that extent. It's certainly not at the center of my marriage—Lawrence will never even know about it—where Diana got dating advice from Camilla. So whatever it is between them, this is not that. This would never have been that. This was going to be one encounter—maybe two, but no more than that—one moment of beauty and sadness and mortality and comfort and unbridled passion. But now it's just gross. Camilla Parker-Bowles? Are you comparing me to Camilla Parker-Bowles, who, on top of everything else, is ugly? I think I do not like where this is going. No, I don't like where it's *gone*.

We're both out of coffee, and I look at my empty cup.

Then he says, "If I had my camera with me, I would photograph you right now."

"You would."

"The look on your face, at that moment—it's already gone—but it was stunning."

"Thank you."

—Sort of.

"Do you know what you were thinking?"

"Yes, I was—"

And I'm about to tell him because what have I got to lose, but he says, "Don't say it. Just remember it, so you can think it again tomorrow."

"What?"

"Can I photograph you here, tomorrow?"

—Can you what?

"I don't see why not, if you want to."

—Which means, if nothing else, I'll see him again. Which I'm not sure how I feel about completely, but part of me wants it—I want it between my legs, where you want sex, and I want it in my gut, where you want to do something you're afraid of, like walking into a cave that's so dark you can't see the walls or the ceiling or the floor or even your own hand in front of your face, and I want it on the back of my neck, where you feel a stranger looking at you just before you turn and he looks away. Where I don't want it is my brain, which says, objectively, that this is not a good idea.

He says, "Good."

I'm looking at him, but I don't say anything. As far as I know, there's no expression on my face.

He says, "It's not the only thing I want."

I'm not a hundred percent sure I understand his subtext, or if I understand it, I don't trust it. It's just wordplay, which is just *play,* so whatever I would be saying, if I said something, I don't know how he'd take it, so I don't say anything.

He says, "I need to go in a new direction with my photography. With my life. I don't want to make my living off the suffering of others anymore, which means, essentially, that I don't want to do photojournalism. Profiting off other people's suffering—that's another sin, I think. And I don't want to tell lies. Paparazzi photographs are not exactly lies, but by glorifying trivial moments in celebrities' lives, they trivialize the real lives of real people, which is a kind of lie. And celebrity portraits are utter lies because you're trying to create an image of perfection and pass it off as everyday life. I want to create something that matters, something that's true."

"Really." I'm not agreeing, I'm not disagreeing, I'm not questioning whether it's possible to take a picture that's true or whether it would matter if you did. I'm just tired of this, and tired of being on my own emotional roller coaster, where one minute I think I'm about to get up and go back to his apartment and rip off his clothes, and the next minute I can't stand him, this intrusive, self-righteous, self-important, anti-American, American paparazzo.

—With Diana's blood on his hands, if you believe almost everybody in the world, and I'm not sure why I've been trying so hard to defend him in my mind when it's actually pretty obvious that he doesn't have to have literally killed her to be guilty of having contributed to a culture that created a situation in which she was chased to her death.

He says, "A photograph is a record of a hundredth of a second, and yet sometimes you can see a person's entire lifetime there. Doing portraits makes you very mindful of the importance of every moment, makes you start living in a state of awareness."

"Sounds very Zen."

He says, "No. It's not true."

And I look at him like, What's not true? I have no idea what he's talking about.

He says, "It's . . . it's why an artist shouldn't talk about his work. You have to believe in it, you believe it's that important, but as soon as you say it, you hear yourself, sounding like a pretentious fool."

I say, "You don't sound like a fool to me," though as soon as I say it, I'm not sure it's true. And not sure it matters whether it's true.

He's looking at me again, but not like before. Now he's looking at me like I'm a potential photograph, and he states as if it's more a fact than a compliment, "You're very pretty, but it's a sad beauty—an interesting paradox, because you try so hard to make people think you're happy. Princess Diana had that quality, too. It was part of what made her so appealing, that she wanted so badly to be happy, tried so hard at it. I want to capture that in you."

"That's not how I see myself, trying hard to be happy."

"No," he says, "it couldn't be. If you saw yourself that way, you wouldn't *be* that way. But I see you that way."

"Well, define 'happy.' Do you think *any*body really is? Do you think there are people out there who just go through life without regrets? And I'm not saying I'm *not* happy, for the most part, but have you ever noticed that the people who smile *all the time* tend to be mentally retarded?"

He laughs. "Maybe. But the thing I'm calling sadness in you is more than regret. Probably neither of us has the whole picture."

He smiles. Then he looks at his watch. "I'm sorry. I lost track of the time. I have to go, I'm late. You're still at the Ritz?"

"Yes."

"Can I pick you up tomorrow, then, around one?"

I hesitate.

He says, "Or would you be more comfortable meeting me here?"

"No, you can pick me up. That would be nice. Thank you."

—Wait. Don't pick me up.

"Good. One o'clock. Wear something . . . what you're wearing right now is perfect. If you go shopping this afternoon, don't . . . I mean, tomorrow, wear something that's not French."

"Okay."

"I'm going to do it in black and white, so wear a dark top to contrast with your skin and hair. Would you mind just wearing this same thing?"

"No."

"I'm sorry. I can see in your face—I'm being rude, rushing off like this, you don't know whether to trust me."

"No . . ."

"The time got away from me. I have an appointment— not something I can cancel. I was on my way there when you called. That's all."

"Okay."

—On a Sunday?

"But one o'clock tomorrow is okay?"

We're standing up now, and I nod.

The waiter has set our bill on the table without my noticing it and Max pays it and I thank him and we walk out of the restaurant together and stop on the sidewalk and he takes my hand in both of his and says, "Tomorrow, then," and I say, "Yes," and he smiles at me quickly before he dashes across the street—the WALK light is blinking—and gets into a cab.

I CROSS A NARROW SIDE STREET AND PASS A CREPE STAND and the church of St-Germain-des-Prés and a man who's sitting on the sidewalk, his back against the wall of the church, making birds out of vegetables and expecting people to give him money—he's got a hat with some francs in it sitting out in front of a row of carrot swans—and part of me wants to stop and figure out how he does it, but I keep going. When I pass the church courtyard where children are playing, I realize I'm headed the wrong way, in the opposite direction of the hotel, but I keep going to the end of the block and cross the street before I change directions, not wanting to look as idiotic as I feel. Just before I get back to Les Deux Magots—but across the street from it now—I pass through a wave of people coming up from a Métro station before I come to a sculpture and stop. It's made of concrete sidewalk squares, on the sidewalk, mixed in with some steel ones, and they're buckling, as if they've been pushed up by an underground explosion, all the energy from the rushing subways and the spirits in the catacombs coming together and escaping, and water rushes up from a fountain inside, as if a water line has burst.

I think, —You can walk through Paris and not be much aware of the subways underneath you and not aware at all of the catacombs, but I think it would be impossible not to sense some kind of turmoil just beneath the surface.

I think Max would agree with me, though I'm not sure Lawrence would.

I start walking again, and I pass the Brasserie Lipp and a hotel and then a man going the other way who looks just like my father, and I turn to look at him again—I can't remember exactly what my father looked like—but he's gone. And now I'm just moving along the boulevard St-Germain by myself. No Diana. No Lawrence, of course. No Max. And I don't know what to think about any of that.

—Did I actually leave the hotel thinking I was going to invite myself to a complete stranger's apartment and have sex with him, and now I'm vaguely disappointed that I didn't? I've never shown up uninvited at the home of a person I know, much less had sex with them. What am I doing? I don't even recognize myself.

I've got a kind of eddying in my stomach that feels something like guilt or maybe fear, but I'm thinking, —I haven't done anything wrong. I'm not in danger. Maybe I made a mistake, saying he could pick me up. Maybe I shouldn't have said I'd see him again at all, but why not, when we've already established that we're not going to have sex— did we establish that? Yes, I'm happily married, we covered that. Twice. So we're just doing a photo shoot, and maybe it's a surprise for Lawrence, a present, having my portrait done in a Paris café, which is actually very clever of me, even romantic, perfectly innocent, when I see the kitchen of my dreams. My stomach tightens.

I love this kitchen. I've seen it, this exact kitchen, in ads in a dozen magazines—*House Beautiful, Architectural Digest, Southern Accents*—but here it is, live, with three walls and a huge store window like the fourth wall of a stage. I stop for a closer look, and it pulls me back into my real life, the one in Atlanta, where I've been wanting to redo our kitchen just like this one— creamy yellow cabinets, shiny black granite countertops, a built-in maple chopping block, hardwood floors, professional-grade stainless-steel appliances, a crystal chandelier. I pull on the door but it's locked, so I press my face against the glass and put my hands on the sides of my eyes like blinders to block out the glare.

I want this kitchen, every single detail of it. I want to wake up every morning and go drink my coffee in it, pouring my cream from a little copper pitcher. I want to sit at the granite counter and read cookbooks and plan parties, and when I get home from shopping, I want to put my groceries in the built-in Sub-Zero refrigerator. I want to cook gourmet dinners on the six-burner Viking stove. I want to have friends over, and we stand around the farmhouse sink with the brass-and-copper Herbeau faucet, drinking wine and laughing. I want to come into this kitchen at night when I can't sleep and turn the chandelier on, dimmed, and make myself some chamomile tea and pour it into a hand-painted mug I've taken from the free-standing pine cupboard and sit with my elbows resting on the smooth, polished granite in the midnight quiet until I feel my body start to let go of the day and I think I'm at peace.

Lawrence doesn't want to do it, doesn't want workers tromping through the house at all hours.

The last time we discussed it, I said, "It's not like you work at home. You'd be gone almost the whole time they were here."

He said, "But when I come home, I need to be able to think. I don't want to live in a war zone."

I said, "You don't live in a war zone. This is not a war zone."

He said, "You know what I mean."

I said, "Yeah. And you know what *I* mean."

I've still got my face pressed against the window, and while I argue with Lawrence in my head, I'm also taking careful mental notes of how the kitchen is accessorized—copper pots, copper molds, things made out of hammered copper that I wouldn't have any idea what to do with but I want them anyway, and in a corner that's not in the magazine photographs, a formal portrait of a dog. It's a haughty-looking cocker spaniel, and he's wearing navy dress blues with lots of medals pinned to his lapels. He's a hero.

I think I'll bring Lawrence back to see it. Maybe if he sees it, he'll understand better why I want it. He'll see how much prettier it is than what we have, which there's nothing wrong with, as he points out every time we discuss it, but there's nothing wonderful about it, as I point out every time it comes up, and he'll want it, too, not just capitulate to it.

Then I'll say, —We'll have to get a portrait of a dog.

And he'll say, —Don't most people who have portraits of dogs have dogs?

—It doesn't have to be our dog. It could be a fictional dog. I'm pretty sure that one's fictional.

—Portraits of total strangers, whether dogs or people— what's the point?

—Okay, we'll get a dog.

I stop. I'm still looking at the kitchen through the glass when I realize that at some point in my imaginary conversation, I've switched from having it with Lawrence to having it with Max. It's Max I'm getting the dog with. It's Max I'm redoing the kitchen with. Lawrence hates redecorating, won't discuss it. He doesn't like change—he's willing to turn established science on its head, but God forbid you should move the couch—where Max does, for all I know. Or at least he doesn't mind it. And of course, it's not even Max. It's an imaginary Max who doesn't criticize the Big Chicken, which you can spend your whole life in Atlanta without even seeing, by the way. So as soon as I've imagined an identity for myself other than Mrs. Lawrence Baxter, I've brought all the trappings of this one with me—the lovely home, the lovely kitchen, lovely meals, lovely parties. I've simply swapped being Lawrence's lovely wife for being Max's. So if that's what I want—and it *is* part of what I want, I think—then what am I doing?

I start walking again.

I pass a women's clothing boutique, a shop full of Asian dishware and chopsticks and woks, a stationery store, a bridal salon. I stop to look at the gowns. When Lawrence and I got married, I wore my mother's wedding dress. She married my father in the summer of 1958, two months after her year as Miss Alabama ended, and it was a fifties concoction with layers and layers of netting over a hoopskirt.

I think, —If I had it to do over again, I'd get my own dress. I'd do a lot of things differently.

I'm starting to feel hot and tired and thirsty, and when I see a little café down a side street with no sidewalk customers, I turn toward it. I take a seat and order a Diet Coke with ice and the waiter brings it right away. I thank him, and he goes back inside.

I'm watching an elderly couple move slowly along the sidewalk across the street. They're probably in their eighties, and I'm guessing they've been together for fifty or sixty years. They probably finish each other's sentences. As they walk, their bodies share one rhythm, as if they're holding hands, though they aren't. Their faces have begun to look alike from laughing in the same way at the same things — they have the same laugh lines. Their faces, but even their bodies — after sixty years together, they've shared billions of atoms. On a subatomic level, they've each been the other, they *are* the other.

I think, —I should want that with Lawrence. But I don't.

I can't stand it when he finishes my sentences.

They turn the corner, and the waiter brings me a little glass — a big shot-glass — full of a bright green liquid that looks like something out of *Alice in Wonderland*. I'm still the only customer here. I just barely shake my head to say I didn't order it, but he says, "C'est gratuit." And I would have gotten that in one second, but as soon as he sees that I don't know what he means, he says, "Free!" He bursts into a smile.

"Oh, merci, merci beaucoup!"

And I take it and sip it and it tastes like Scope, but I swallow and say, "Très bon. Merci." I think it's crème de menthe, which it's never occurred to me to drink. I've only ever used it to make Kentucky Derby brownies.

He nods and goes back inside and comes back with another green drink and asks to sit with me, which I pick up more from his gesture than from whatever he's actually saying, and I point with my hand to the chair facing me where he wants to sit and say, "Oui."

He's very handsome—black, curly hair, light green eyes, early forties. A big, boyish, mischievous smile. Most waiters in Paris are somewhat formal, stiff, and they usually wear white shirts, black pants, and little white aprons, but he's very relaxed, and he's just wearing normal clothes. I have a feeling he owns this café, and this is what he does when business is slow—flirt with female patrons.

He says, "You are English?"

"No, American."

"I thought you were English because you looked sad."

"Sad?"

"Because of Lady Di. I want to cheer you up."

"Thank you."

"But you are American."

"Yes, but I'm still sad about Lady Di." I pronounce it Lay Dee Dee.

"Me, too," he says.

He lifts his glass and says, "To Lady Di."

And I touch mine to his, and I say, "To Lady Di," and we drink.

"You like?" he says.

"Oui." I like oui for sounding like we.

"Good!"

He seems genuinely delighted to have pleased me. It's very sweet of him. And very French. It's hard to imagine a forty-something American being happy about buying me a green drink under any circumstances.

Then I say, "Merci."

I like merci, too. I like the implicit connection between gratitude and mercy.

"So, America," he says. "California?"

—Wait. Did he just use Diana's death as a pickup line? And I fell for it?

I say, "No, Georgia."

"Atlanta?"

"Yes."

"Ah! Atlanta! Olympics!"

"Yes, we had the Olympics."

"I watch on TV!"

"Moi aussi."

He says, "I like to swim."

"Moi aussi."

He puts his hands together as if in prayer, then lifts them over his head.

I say, "Dive? You like diving?"

"Yes! Dive!"

I don't think Diana is anywhere near here, but I think if she was, she would like this guy. I think she'd like him more than Max. Or Lawrence. I can see the appeal, but I think she had worse taste in men than I do. This is a man who, if he had an affair with Princess Diana, would probably end up selling his story to the tabloids. Though with me, he's harmless enough.

We've run out of shared language—we're in an awkward little silence—when he says again, "Yes, I like to dive."

I'm imagining his English-language lessons: I like to swim. I like to dive. Claude, the speaker on my French-language tapes, likes to swim and dive, not to mention snorkel and sail, but I think we've come to the end of this guy's tape. Claude, who has a little bit of a Walt Whitman complex, also likes to drive cars, ride in trains, fly in planes. He's an architect, an engineer, a doctor, a lawyer, a student, an accountant. He has male friends, female friends. He is twenty years old and thirty and forty and fifty.

I say, "I don't like to dive."

"No?"

"I'm afraid," I say, and he looks at me to say he doesn't understand, and I say, "Scared?"

He still doesn't get it. I can't think of the French word for fear, so I make a face like a person who's just seen a ghost.

"Oh! La peur. Vous avez peur?" He seems very sad for me.

"Oui. J'ai peur. Un peu." I hold up my thumb and index finger, as if to say I have a half-inch-high fear of diving.

I thought, —If you believe Mart, my fear of diving is as big as the next universe is near.

"Mais you like to swim?"

"Yes," I say, "I like to swim," and he nods eagerly as if he's happy for me about that, and I say, "Very much," though I'm not actually that crazy about swimming, at least not in the ocean, which is entirely too big for my taste, not to mention too full of sharks and jellyfish and undertows, and not in swimming pools unless they're heated and I'm absolutely certain no child has peed in them, though of course I have no way to tell him all that, and then I realize we're still talking about the Olympics: He just told me his favorite Olympic events are swimming and diving, and I agreed with him about swimming—I like to watch Olympic swimming—but then I told him I was afraid of Olympic diving. He must think I'm insane, but I don't have the French and he doesn't have the English for me to explain that I'm not afraid of *watching* Olympic diving, I'm just afraid to do it ever since I went off the high dive when I was ten. I was a guest at a country club, and my friend, who belonged there, could do swan dives and front flips and back flips, so I couldn't just *jump,* so I tried to spin my body like a top and landed on my stomach, which knocked the breath out of me, and the lifeguard had to come rescue me, after which I couldn't stop crying—gasping for air and weeping—while twenty kids and their mothers stared at me with a mixture of concern, delight, and contempt on their faces.

He nods again. My phobia of watching Olympic diving doesn't faze him. The French seem very tolerant of insanity, much more so than Americans are. I like them for that.

I nod back, and we finish our drinks. They're strong, and I feel mine hit the top of my brain with a little *ping!* and he offers me another. It's bizarrely tempting, the idea of sitting here all afternoon, getting tipsy drinking mouthwash with this sweet, handsome man, but I say, "Non, merci," and I try to sound sad, as if I *wish* I could stay and have another but I *can't.* I look at my watch. I say, "I'm meeting my husband in five minutes."

"Ah," he says and nods.

Then I ask for my check, and he says, "No! Is free!"

I say, "Diet Coke, too?"

"Yes! Yes! Free Diet Coke!"

"Merci beaucoup."

I stand up and shake his hand and thank him again and I *do* feel sad, though happier than I did when he first sat down. He kisses my fingers and says, "Your husband, he is lucky man. You are beautiful woman."

I say, "Merci beaucoup."

He says, "Au revoir," but he's looking at me with those big, green eyes like we could have had a damn good time together, and he might be right.

I thank him yet again and walk away.

I GO BACK TO THE BOULEVARD ST-GERMAIN AND KEEP walking.

I'm feeling better now. Mostly better and a little bit worse. A double shot of straight crème de menthe with a handsome Frenchman will do that to you.

I come to the river and cross the bridge to the place de la Concorde. The hotel is five or ten minutes to the right, and the Diana memorial is five or ten minutes to the left, and it's not even five o'clock, so I turn left.

As I walk, I'm looking for a florist's to buy Diana some flowers, though I'm also thinking of Max: —Maybe he's finished with his appointment and he'll be at the flame, too, pulled to it by whatever's pulling me.

—Or maybe not.

When I get there, I stand near the flame, right where I first met him, for a long time. Its base is covered, overflowing, with flowers now—flowers and cards and pictures of Diana, mostly postcards and newspaper and magazine cutouts, but also a Diana mask like from a Halloween costume, a couple of Queens of Hearts from decks of cards, and four or five really bad poems, most of them in English. It's unfortunate that

Princess Di rhymes with sigh, sky, why, I, lie, cry, and good-bye. This is not the first thing that has made me wonder how differently people would have responded if it had been Charles and Camilla who died. The only word I can think of, besides Arles, that rhymes with Charles is quarrels. Camilla, Godzilla.

After a while, a nun dressed in a black habit comes up beside me and kneels on the concrete. She lays a bouquet of wildflowers tied with a white ribbon next to a white rose and crosses herself. She's wearing white tennis shoes, and I look at the patterns like radio waves on the bottoms of the soles.

I think, —Calling God. God, can you hear me?

The fabric covering her head looks like a very ugly wedding veil, an anti-wedding veil. It's thick and synthetic—the stuff they used to make leisure suits of. It looks hot and uncomfortable and impossible to wrinkle. I imagine her hair underneath it, oily and flat and gray. I imagine that she likes being able to cover it up, likes not having to wear makeup or high heels or think about fashion. She prides herself on being practical. I think she's not technically a virgin—maybe she was raped by her father or uncle when she was a child, which had something to do with her decision to join the order—but she's never made love with anybody, and she prefers living a simple life that has nothing to do with glamour or fame or sex. She is, in some ways, Diana's opposite.

She stays a minute or two, praying, I assume, and I keep standing next to her quietly, watching her out of the corner of my eye. She has long, slender fingers, like Diana's only with age spots, and *she uses them to care for the sick and the dying.*

It's Diana. She's back: *She taught children for a while, when she was younger. That was a joy. She loved them, and they adored her. Sometimes she struggles with depression and self-doubt, but she tries to put a*

happy face on it. It's an ordinary life. What makes her ordinariness ex-
traordinary is the vow she took. She's the bride of Christ. But she sleeps
alone at night, and sometimes she aches so terribly, wanting to be held,
that she wishes she'd married an ordinary man, someone who loved her
in a way Christ didn't, couldn't. Next day she goes to confession and
can't explain what she's done that's wrong, albeit she can't stop feeling
that something about her is not right. This is, after all, what she signed
up for. As a very young woman. As a girl, really. She was nineteen. She
couldn't possibly have understood what she was getting herself into. All
she ever wanted was love.

And the nun crosses herself and stands up, and I'm thinking, —Wait! Should I tell her what just happened?

Excuse me. Excusez-moi. I have a message for you from
Princess Diana. J'ai un mot de Lady Di?

Right. For one thing, she's rather old, and I doubt she
speaks English and my French is so bad, I don't think I could
make her understand if I tried, and it's not even exactly a message, anyway, though maybe she'd see it as a miracle. If you're
willing to believe that dead saints can talk to people — and
plenty of people think they do, so who am I to say they
don't?—maybe non-saints can, too. Maybe Catholics acknowledge a phenomenon and call it sainthood that happens much
more often than that but the rest of us tend to keep our
mouths shut when it does. So maybe this nun is the only person I know—even though I don't technically *know* her—who
would understand what's happening.

The nun leaves without looking at anyone, without having
uttered a sound. I turn and watch her slowly make her way
across the street. She's slightly arthritic, I think. She walks as if
she's in constant pain. Or maybe she's one of those nuns who
puts rocks in her shoes to prove how much she loves God.

Which raises the very difficult question of what love is, if inflicting pain on oneself is what proves it.

It's Diana again. I hear her in my head, and I feel her in my body—my knees are wobbly and my hands and feet are cold—and I sit down, cross-legged, on the hot concrete in front of the flame where the nun was kneeling.

I used to believe I was a nun in a previous life. I thought I remembered putting rocks in my shoes to remind me of the suffering of Christ and therefore remind Christ of my devotion to Him, ripping my own back to shreds with a whip more than once.

I didn't do it for religious reasons this time. But it was the same impulse. I wanted my husband's love, couldn't bear feeling unloved, worst pain imaginable, and one morning, I was talking to him, and he wouldn't listen to me, wouldn't listen, wouldn't listen, and I picked up his penknife and stuck it in my chest. It was like screaming. You can't say why you've done it. You didn't think it through before, when and where and how you'd do it, what it would accomplish. You just felt as if you had no other way to let out the emotions inside you, and the next thing you know, it's done.

And he stood up and walked out of the room. No reaction whatsoever, just out he goes, and I'm left covered in blood, feeling deathly calm. Deathly, deathly calm.

It was a surface wound. I couldn't get it in any farther. It felt like sticking a butter knife into a rope. So I was in pain, but I wasn't in physical danger. My heart was just breaking.

But if it had made him stop and look at me, try to comfort me, tell me he loved me, it would have been worth it. Just to hear him say, "I see you're wounded. Are you in pain?" Would have happily put rocks in my shoes if that would have done it. So is that love?

I don't have an answer for her.

Diana's quiet now. I think she's waiting for an answer to her question.

So I say to her, —I don't know.

Then I say, —Are you in pain?

No, she says, *no more pain. I'm just trying to figure it all out. I'm a bit confused. I feel I should have moved on by now, so I thought if I came back here . . . Not sure what I was looking for, but it's not here.*

Then a flash goes off—a tourist taking a snapshot of the memorial—and Diana is gone. I don't hear her, I don't sense her presence, and I don't know if she suddenly got what she came here for and she's moved on, whatever that means, or if she just went somewhere else, looking for whatever she's looking for, or if she's hiding from the flash inside me, and I don't know if what I feel right now is about her being gone or if it's actually what *she's* feeling, she's just feeling it silently through me, or maybe it's empathy—people around me are weeping openly—but I'm suddenly filled with a terrible, aching loneliness, and I look across the bridge where I last saw Max disappear. He's not there, of course.

I ask her, —Why did you come to me here?

Silence.

—What do you want from me?

Nothing.

—What do you want?

Nothing at all.

And suddenly I'm not so sure I believe it was really Diana, not yesterday or today. I *don't* think dead saints talk to people. But maybe I identified with Diana more than I realized, and trying to keep her alive in my head is my way of trying not to confront my own mortality. Or maybe it's just a silly fantasy.

Maybe I'm just making the whole thing up because I want it to be true.

Except I'm not.

When I was little, after my father died, I would lie in my bed in the dark and silently ask God to love me. Then I would tell myself, I love you, I love you, I love you, and try to make myself believe it was the still, small voice of God. When I didn't believe it, I called myself a doubting Thomas and prayed that much harder: Please love me. I LOVE YOU, I LOVE YOU. And when I hear Diana's voice, I can't explain what it is, but I know it's not that.

Another flash goes off—I'm not sure where it's coming from—but it fills me with anxiety, and I want to get out of here.

I TAKE A BRISK WALK BACK TO THE HOTEL, STOPPING AT A souvenir shop full of Eiffel Tower magnets, Notre Dame snow domes, scarves of the French flag, "I ♥ Paris" T-shirts, and now, for a limited time only, special Diana-Is-Dead postcards. They don't actually say she's dead. They have her picture, and then below it, "1961–1997." I step in and buy one. Okay, I buy four—four different pictures. And a University of Paris sweatshirt for Alec. Black. Extra large.

When I get to my room, I shower, hand-wash my T-shirt and hang it in the bathtub to dry so I can wear it tomorrow after sweating all over Paris in it today, dress, and do my hair and makeup for dinner. Then I turn on the TV.

They're replaying her wedding. She's walking down the aisle accompanied by what sounds like a whole orchestra, the veil over her face making her look a little like a ghost. I change the channel to a replay of Diana's brother reading a statement.

He blames not only the paparazzi, but also the editors who bought and published their photographs. Everybody's blaming the paparazzi, though now they're also blaming the driver, who was speeding, and the bodyguard. Somebody points out that if Princess Diana hadn't felt her palace-appointed bodyguards were spying on her, reporting to Prince Charles, she wouldn't have fired them and they wouldn't have let this happen, so it's Charles's fault, which I also agree with. And Camilla's, without whom Diana would still be married to Charles and wouldn't have been in the tunnel in the first place. Although, someone else points out, if she'd been wearing a seat belt, she probably would have survived. So ultimately, it's her own fault.

I turn it off.

You could make an argument that if everybody who ever took a picture of her or bought those pictures of her has blood on his hands, then so does everybody who bought the newspapers, which kept the cycle going. Which would include me.

I feel guilty about something, but it's not that. I splurge on British tabloids when I'm in Europe, but I don't buy tabloids in America, and I do read *People* magazine sometimes, which bugs Lawrence, but I hardly think that implicates me for murder. So I pretty much believe in listening to your intuition, but you can't always believe you're guilty just because you feel that way. Survivor's guilt, for just one example. I've lived with that for most of my life because of my father, and maybe it's a version of what I'm feeling now. Given the chance, if I were single, and a billionaire fell in love with me and took me on a private cruise and then to Paris, and if that billionaire were Dodi, I'd have been the one in the car. I probably *was* in that same car earlier that day, went through the same tunnel. But I'm fine, and she's dead, and that's not my fault. That's common sense. Although common sense is no more trustworthy than intuition. Almost everything we perceive about reality through our senses and experiences is misleading at best. You look at the night sky, and you're seeing one star as it looked ten thousand years ago, one as it looked fifty thousand years ago, another a hundred thousand, so with any given star, you're seeing a moment that no longer exists, and when you look at the whole sky at once, you're seeing a moment that never existed. You look at a rock, and it looks perfectly still, but on a subatomic level, it's nothing but a loose gathering of roiling frenetic energy, and nobody, to my knowledge, can explain why it appears to be solid. There's no such thing as rock solid.

Maybe what I'm feeling guilty about is Max.

I sit down on the bed, and I'm suddenly in danger of bursting into tears.

It's exhaustion, just physical exhaustion.

How many hours did I spend on my feet today? How many miles did I walk?

My feet hurt, so I take off my shoes.

I'm not going to let myself cry.

Lawrence should be back any minute, and then we'll go to dinner. Dinner in Paris with my husband. My intelligent, softspoken husband who doesn't have strong feelings about the Big Chicken or McDonald's or Disneyland. May not even know who Madonna is but doesn't have an opinion about her if he does. Doesn't like to swim or dive or drink anything green. Speaks fluent English.

I get a bottle of Ritz champagne out of the minibar, averting my eyes from the price list. I open it and pour myself a glass, take a sip.

I sit back down on the edge of the bed.

I wish Diana would come to me now. She liked McDonald's and Disneyland. Or, Disney World, I think it was. Took her kids there, made them wait in line like regular people. I liked that about her.

I look down—I'm so tired, my head feels too heavy to keep holding it up—and I see my feet, which look like my mother's. They look exactly like my mother's. I'm wearing red toenail polish, a color called "I'm Not Really a Waitress," where I usually wear light pink, and my mother always paints her toenails red, which is probably why I don't. But I had them done the morning we left Atlanta, and the pedicurist talked me into red for Paris. I get my phone card out of my purse and call my mother, who answers on the first ring, before I have time to change my mind and hang up: "Hello?"

"Hi, Mother."

A tiny pause.

"It's Ellen." Your only child, the only person in the world who calls you Mother.

She says, "This must be my lucky day."

She's brilliant, in her own way. If I pointed out her sarcasm, she would say, —But I mean it. I do feel lucky.

I say, "Well, I just called because . . ." And I don't know why I called. I have no idea. I'm sitting all the way on the bed now, leaning against the pillows, my legs stretched out in front of me, looking at my feet. I say, "Do you realize I have your feet?"

"No, I didn't know that."

"Your exact feet. A person could see your feet and then mine, and not know whose were whose."

"Well, I didn't realize that. I haven't seen you barefoot in a long time."

"Yeah."

—Hang up now, before she says she hasn't seen you in a long time.

—Okay, so I'll talk to you later.

She says, "Is that why you called, to talk about feet?"

"No."

Silence.

"Ellen?"

"What?"

"What is it?"

"I don't know. I just, I think I need to know something."

"Okay," she says, though her voice is saying it's not okay. This is not how we do things: direct questions with the expectation of a direct answer.

I say, "When Daddy died . . ."

Then I stop. There *is* something I need to know, but I don't know what it is. Maybe, if I knew what it was, I wouldn't need to know it, but I don't, so I do.

She says, "Yes," with some irritation in her voice.

And I say the first thing that comes into my head: "Do you blame me?"

A fraction of a second delay, which might be the overseas phone lines but which is, I believe, her being appalled at my question. And then she doesn't say no. She says, "Why should I blame you? It wasn't *your* fault." Her voice is unnaturally high.

"I'm not saying you *should*. I'm just saying you . . . *asking* if you do."

"Honey, I would *never*. What kind of person would I be if I blamed you?"

—Human, I should say.

But I don't.

I say, "Then why are you so mad at me?"

"I'm *not* mad."

"Yes you are." My voice is calm, gentle, matter-of-fact. Tired.

"Well, I'm mad now. You all the sudden telling me I'm mad after all these years, *that* makes me mad. Have you thought I was mad at you for all these years and you haven't mentioned it until now?"

"No. At first I couldn't figure out what you were. Then I thought you were depressed. Now I think you're mad."

"Well, that's not even logical. I have no right to be mad at you."

"The human heart is not logical."

"Mine is."

This is true, to a certain extent.

I say, "The only reason you would reshape your heart into a thing of logic is that you were so mad, you couldn't let it function the way regular hearts do."

"Well, you've got an answer for everything, don't you? Fine, you want to believe I'm mad, then I'm mad. Now you tell me what I'm mad at you *for*."

"For walking away. For being the one that survived."

"*I* survived. Did you forget that? You're not the only one that survived, you know. If I were mad at you, I'd have to be mad at myself, too, to be fair."

"Nothing about any of this is fair, Mama. But for what it's worth, I think you *are* mad at yourself."

"Well, I can't win with you," she says.

"It's not about winning."

"Ellen, what do you want? I'm too old for this."

"Why were we driving in the middle of the night?"

—Had you had a fight? One of you got fed up with the vacation? With me?

"Because it was cooler. And, frankly, so you would sleep through the drive instead of asking are we there yet, are we there yet?"

My heart suddenly feels solid.

I say, "So it *was* my fault."

"That's not what I said. You need to blame somebody? Blame your father, who was at the wheel, blame God if you still believe in Him, blame bad luck and bad timing and Henry Ford and that goddamned bull and the stupid farmer who should have kept the stupid bull locked up or shouldn't have kept him at all, but don't blame yourself. You were just a *child*. Why are you asking me this?"

"I'm trying to understand you. You'd been married for, what, eight years, when he died? And you'd take any excuse you had to run around all over the state, leaving him at home, alone."

She says, "So it was *my* fault?"

"No. That's not what I'm saying.

"What *are* you saying?" she says.

"I just can't remember . . ."

Then I can't say it.

"What?" she says, angrily. "*What* can't you remember?"

"I can't remember knowing that you loved each other. Ever. I think most children know that about their parents, but I didn't. And especially when I look back at that last weekend, I remember having the feeling that you'd made him come with us—he didn't want to but he came because of me—and you were ignoring each other. Each of you would only talk to me, and I had a feeling like there were a whole bunch of things that weren't being said, *couldn't* be said, almost. I remember feeling weighed down by all those unspoken words and the effort it took to pretend I didn't hear them. Or didn't *not* hear them."

"Well, that is just . . . You're wrong. You're just completely wrong. I don't even know where to start. Of course you thought the world revolved around you. You were six years old. And no, given that the divorce rate is fifty percent and it's not like everybody who has kids and stays married does so because they're madly in love with each other, I seriously doubt that most children know their parents love each other, or if they think they do, they're mistaken, a lot of them. But your father loved me."

"Did you love him?"

"Of course."

"Do you love Big John?"

Pause. Exasperated sigh.

Then, "Well, *yes*. Ellen . . ."

"You don't sound sure."

"Of course I'm sure. Why are you asking this? What do you want from me? You want me to say I'm sorry?"

"No . . ."

"Because okay, I'm sorry. But I did the best I could."

"No, I want to understand what it means."

"What does *what* mean?"

"Um . . . love."

"Well, that's the biggest question I've heard all day. Are you okay?"

"Yes."

"Is Lawrence okay?"

"He's fine."

"Are you and Lawrence okay?"

"We're okay."

"Okay? Just okay?"

"We're fine."

"You just suddenly want to know what love means."

"I'd like to hear your thoughts on it."

"Well, it's a little early in the day for me to start preaching. I mean that literally. But I'll tell you one thing. I've been watching Diana stories on TV all day, and everybody keeps pointing out that when she left her marriage, she was so much happier, prettier, sexier, her life was so much better, but don't you go getting ideas from that. I mean, ever since she and Prince Charles separated, she never stopped trying to replace him with another man. And even she couldn't find anybody. Not anybody worth having. You reach a certain age, and it's slim pickings."

"What's your point?"

"You're thirty-six years old, Ellen. So I don't know if you're looking for greener pastures, but if you are, it's time to stop."

"I'm not looking for greener pastures, and I'm not asking for a sermon. I just want to know what you think. Not about marriage and certainly not about *my* marriage. About love."

A slight pause. Then she lets out a breath: "It seems like the older I get, the fewer answers I have. I can't come up on the spot with a definition of love. Maybe it's whatever you think it is. No, that would be sick—for some people, the things people do in the name of love. Love gets blamed for everything from child molestation to wife abuse to murder, and if you count love of God, you can throw in war and judgmentalism and all manner of cruelty. Maybe it's like pornography—you know it when you see it. Or when you feel it. No,

I've been fooled before. I do know it's not what I used to think it was. Maybe it changes as you get older. Or maybe I've just been let down by it so many times that I wouldn't recognize it now if it bit me."

She stops.

I say, "Have I let you down?"

Pause.

Long pause.

"Have I?"

"Oh, Jesus, Ellen. How'm I supposed to answer that?"

—You could say, No.

"I don't know."

"Every daughter lets her mother down. Just like every mother lets her daughter down. But you get over it. Maybe that's what love is."

"Getting over being let down?"

"Maybe not. I told you I couldn't come up with a definition."

"Okay, Mother, I have to go now. I'll talk to you later."

"Well, okay," she says, sounding put out. "I'm fine, by the way, thanks for asking. Good-bye." And she hangs up.

The line goes dead, and I say, "I'm fine, too."

I SHOULD CALL HER BACK. IF I DON'T CALL HER BACK RIGHT now, we'll end up going several more months, until we can pretend this conversation didn't happen, before we talk again, so I should just suck it up and call her and tell her I'm sorry for things I'm not sorry for—for bringing all that up, for whatever else she accuses me of—and ask her how she's doing, how are her roses, how are her friends, how's her arthritis.

But I don't.

I get out Max's picture of Diana. I'm thinking about the TV interview she did wearing all the black eyeliner—I saw a clip from it earlier today—and the interviewer asked her if she'd had an affair, which everybody already knew about since he'd written a book, and she said, "Yes. Yes, I adored him. But then I was very let down." In a way, it's the story of almost every important relationship of her life except her sons: Charles, all the men she had affairs with, the press, her mother.

I turn on the TV again. More Diana.

Some man in a studio complaining that people are starting to beatify a woman who, "Let's face it," he says, "was known to have slept with quite a lot of married men."

I pick up my champagne, and I'm thinking to the man on TV, Yeah, okay, but didn't Solomon, supposedly the wisest man on earth, have something like a thousand wives and six hundred concubines? I don't even get the logistics of that, much less the wisdom of it. And didn't almost every suppos- edly godly man in the entire Old Testament have at least one affair that we know of? Maybe not all of them, but a lot— Abraham and his wife's maid. One of them—I think it was Noah—and his daughter-in-law. David, who was called a man after God's own heart, and Bathsheba. And they all just got over it, like it wasn't a big deal, and they didn't even claim to love the women they slept with. Solomon had most of them murdered. David had Bathsheba's husband sent to battle, where he died. And now they're patriarchs of three major world religions. So I'm not saying beatify Diana, but give her a break.

And Diana, who I suddenly realize didn't leave when the nun left after all and has been listening in on my thoughts ever since, says, *I don't want to be a saint. I simply want to be remembered for who I was, because implicit in the saint* or *the trollop view, is that who I was — a flawed human being who tried to give love to people and fulfill her own needs as well — wasn't good enough. And I want to leave that behind.*

Once — I must have been four or five, this was before Mummy decided to leg it — I was in the nursery finger painting and my mother asked me what I was painting. I remember it being my mother, not a nanny. I remember looking at her blue wool skirt, at a seam in it where two pieces of fabric came together, thinking, "What do you want me to say?" I wasn't painting anything. I was just painting, *enjoying the way the paint felt on my fingers, the way my fingers felt sliding the paint over the paper. I liked watching what the colors did when they touched. I could see them touching each other, wanting to move into each other, right on the edges, but cautious, staying where they were. I could* feel *them, as if the blue were thinking, "Do I just keep on being Blue? Or do I let in Yellow, and then I'll never be Blue again, but maybe I'll be something better? Or maybe I'll always wish I were still Blue, and Yellow will always wish he was still Yellow and he'll blame me for his unhappiness, and I don't know, but I've got to decide now, before I dry." I could feel it on my skin, this empathy for Blue. Where do I stop? And a sense of urgency, of time passing.*

Then my mother asked me again what I was painting, and I couldn't explain, had no language for what I'd been experiencing, so I said, "It's a secret."

She said, "Is it an elephant?"

"No."

She said, "Is it a giraffe?"

I suddenly felt very embarrassed, for myself and for her. Realized I'd got it all wrong.

There were other children there that day. I don't remember who. It must have been a party. But I looked around at what the other children were doing, and they were drawing see-through houses and balloon-shaped trees and quarter-circle suns in the corners of the papers with yellow stripes for rays, and I thought, "What is wrong with me?"

I said, "Yes, it's a giraffe."

She was visibly relieved. "What a lovely giraffe!"

So I threw away the blue and yellow page, ripped it in two and balled it up while it was still wet, and started on a new painting, a square house with a girl — me — standing outside it, big red smile painted on her face.

It's always the same question — the wanting to connect, and the fear of it.

I spent most of my life trying to paint the picture people wanted to see. I could be blubbing my eyes out, and then I would get up and go do my engagements, whatever had to be done, smiling all the time. That was what the people wanted. And it was what I wanted and what Prince Charles and the Queen wanted. Everybody wanted the same picture. Just for different reasons, different ideas about what the picture meant. Different expectations about what would go on before and after the click of the camera. I always tried to do my best, but sooner or later, the media always twisted my efforts into something they weren't. I'd be trying to raise awareness about heart disease or land mines, comfort the sick, what have you, and I'd read an article criticizing my hair or my makeup or clothes or my mental health, and I'd think, "Okay, yes, I'm painting giraffes."

I don't think she's finished, but Lawrence opens the door and she vanishes.

Lawrence steps into the room and I jump off the bed as if I've been caught napping and turn off the TV and smile and say, "How was your day?"

"Good," he says. "Sorry I'm late."

"No problem," I say. "I just opened a bottle of champagne. Would you like a glass?"

He doesn't. He wants water, he's parched, and he goes into the bathroom to wash his hands.

I'm trying to clear my head. I open a bottle of water for him and pour it into a glass while he asks me over his shoulder how my day was.

I put the glass on the desk.

—How was my day? How was my day? What can I tell you about my day that we'd both want you to know?

I decide to skip over lunch with Mart and Les Deux Magots and Max and the crème-de-menthe guy and the flame and the nun and all the times I heard Diana's voice, and I'm left with "Fine."

Which is all he really wanted me to say. He comes out of the bathroom, gives me a quick kiss, and drinks the whole glass of water.

I say, "I bought a sweatshirt for Alec," slipping it out of its bag to show it to him.

He looks at it. I can read him—it's just a tiny breath he lets out, but he's not entirely thrilled.

"What?" I say.

"It was nice of you. Just don't get mad if he's not grateful."

"I won't."

"Good."

—We couldn't go to Paris and not bring him something, and you don't have time to buy him anything, where I do, so I'm stuck in a cycle where either I'm setting myself up for him to be ungrateful and me to resent that, or I'm being ungenerous. I can't win.

I hear myself, turning into my mother.

I drop the sweatshirt onto the bed.

"Let's go," Lawrence says.

AT DINNER, LAWRENCE IS PREOCCUPIED WITH WHATEVER happened at the conference today, and I'm thinking about Princess Diana and about Max, neither of whom I want to talk about.

I ask him how his speech went, and he says it went well.

He asks me if I bought anything today, and I say, "No, just that sweatshirt." Then, as an afterthought, "Most of the stores are closed here on Sunday."

"Oh, of course," he says.

I think about telling him about seeing the kitchen, but I don't want to raise the possibility of an argument. We talk about the food we're eating, which is very good, better than the Ritz. I tell him the chef is famous. He says Mart mentioned that. I don't ask what else Mart had to say. It's a long meal, full of long silences. Every so often, Lawrence gets out his little notepad and writes something down.

At one point, I say, "They offer cooking classes at the Ritz. Maybe I'll take one this week."

He says, "They give them in English?"

"No, probably not," I say.

When we finish dessert, our waiter asks if we want coffee. We both say no, and Lawrence asks for the check.

"I'm very tired," I say. I'm thinking I just want to go back to the room and go to bed.

But no, we're meeting Eric and Mart in the Bar Vendôme at the Ritz in an hour for a nightcap.

"I'm so exhausted," I say. "I barely slept last night."

"Just a quick toast. You can go on up, after, if you'd like. But they're getting engaged over dinner, and he wants us to be the first to congratulate them."

"They're getting engaged? You know that for a fact?"

"Yeah."

"What if she says no?"

"She won't."

"He's going to ask her to quit her job, leave her country, her family, her friends, move to California, and she's supposed to make a snap decision to give up all that to be married to Eric?"

"I assume they've discussed this before. He's just giving her the ring tonight."

"And that's what he expects? That she's already made up her mind to drop her whole life for him? And what? Join the UCLA Faculty Wives' Club?"

"I don't see Mart in a faculty wives' club."

"Me, either. That's my point. Can he get UCLA to give her a job?"

"I don't know. I'm sure he could."

"Yes you do know. He can't. Not in this economy when they know he's not going anywhere whether they give her the job or not. If she wants to teach, she'll have to do adjunct work and get paid beans, and if she wants to work in a lab, she'll never get her own lab, she'll have to spend the rest of her life being someone's assistant. Eric's assistant."

"Not necessarily."

"It's what happens in dual-scholar marriages. I've seen it a zillion times. If you haven't, it's because you haven't thought about your colleagues' wives. But one of them gets the real job, usually the man, and the other one does shit work for a few years, hoping they'll prove their worth and the university will give them a real job, and eventually, they either get fed up and quit, if they're lucky, or they continue to care about their work and believe in themselves and they get bitter that nobody else does, or they start believing the implicit message of their bottom-of-the-totem-pole status, that they're there because they don't deserve anything better, which becomes a self-fulfilling prophecy, and they start shutting down intellectually and creatively, which drives down their self-esteem, which keeps them from being able to produce anything publishable, and they start blaming their spouse, which is not altogether un-fair, though not really fair, either, because the spouse didn't create the system, but usually, the spouse isn't rising up against its inequalities, either, and in fact, the more successful the working spouse is, the more that person has invested in keep-ing things as hierarchical and unfair as they are, despite the harm it does to the person they supposedly love most in the world. So either they divorce, or the less-accomplished spouse decides she's got to find a way to live within the system, or without it, and she takes up a hobby like painting or photog-raphy or poetry, none of which she's particularly good at, and next thing you know, she's trying to create an identity for her-self, but it's somebody she's not, and her whole life becomes devoted to living this lie because the only way she can be happy is if she tells this lie to herself long enough and convinc-ingly enough that eventually, she believes it. Is that what Eric wants for Mart?"

Lawrence hesitates. He picks up his wineglass, which is empty. Puts it back down.

Then: "I don't know what the fuck he wants for her," Lawrence says. "He just wants to marry her."

And the waiter brings his credit-card receipt to him, and we get up to go.

So now we've got an hour to kill, and I've got strobe lights going off inside me, my emotions spinning in circles, and I suddenly want to see how big the hole at the center of our marriage is. I want to walk up to it, dive into it, and find out whether we get destroyed or sent into alternate universes or if, after a brief explosion, we end up starting over, new. I just have no idea how to do that.

We're walking down the sidewalk, and I say, "Come see the flame."

He looks at me. He doesn't even know what I'm talking about. He's been in the room with me when they showed it on TV at least ten times, but he wasn't paying attention.

I say, "Where she crashed, or, above there. It's not far from here."

He shrugs okay, and I pick up our pace.

We walk for several minutes without saying anything.

Then Lawrence says, "Is this about Mart or about you?"

"I don't know," I say.

We keep walking.

He says, "Nobody's stopping you from getting any job you want, you know."

"Not now, they're not."

"When did they ever?"

"Look, I know some people, lots of them, are able to rise above however they were raised and make better lives for themselves than their parents were able to give them. But I think those people realize at an early age that they don't want their parents' lives and they prepare themselves somehow. Or maybe they just have better imaginations than I ever did. But I didn't realize that I didn't want my mother's life until . . ."

"Until when? You don't have her life."

"I didn't think there was a better life than my mother had."

"You *have* a better life than she does. What do you not have that you want?"

I don't answer him. I can't. I don't know the answer, though I know there is one.

When we get there, it's quiet, though not as quiet as it was this morning, and there are still more flowers and cards. Somebody's left a red Beanie Baby dog. One card says, "Di + Dodi = 4ever." One says, "I love you, Diana." "Je t'aime, Lady Di." "We miss you, beautiful Di. You'll always watch over us from up in the sky."

I say, "It's so stupid."

He says, "What of several possibilities are you referring to?"

I look at him, and he's gazing down the river. He hasn't read one card.

I was going to ask him what it says about how things work on this planet that good people die and leave children behind, while mean old people with nothing to do but complain live to be a hundred. I was going to tell him how the fact that mean people generally live longer than nice ones just goes to show that everything's completely fucked up on this planet. But I realize that what strikes him as stupid here is not so much the cards and balloons and stuffed animals, which I admit are somewhat banal, as the people who left them here.

"I don't get it," I say.

"What?"

"How you can spend hours and hours and hours contemplating soulless galaxies, but this outpouring of real feeling in our own world, you're not even curious about?"

He says, "No, I'm not particularly interested in what you're calling real feeling for a woman whom more than ninety-nine percent of the people participating in this emotional flood never even met and whose actual accomplishments were . . . what? Nothing."

My emotions aren't spinning around anymore, which was at least a kind of order. I'm bouncing around inside myself, up and down and here and there and everywhere — emotional chaos.

But I say, very calmly, "For starters, all these people cared about her. I think if I came to the end of my life and this many people cared, I'd feel like I'd accomplished something."

"Well, one, you wouldn't know that. Last week, I don't think she'd have seen this coming. She was making a fool of herself and the world was laughing at her. But two, are you saying that fame — being *cared* about by throngs of people who don't even know you — is an accomplishment?"

"It's not the accomplishment. It's *evidence* of the accomplishment."

He doesn't actually roll his eyes — he doesn't move — but I sense that kind of flinching in him.

"Okay," I say, "*you* define accomplishment."

"It's an accomplishment to contribute some knowledge by which others can understand the universe more clearly, to make the world a better place."

"Is that one thing or two?"

Pause.

Then Lawrence says with a veneer of patience, "I think

contributing to humankind's understanding of the universe makes the world a better place."

"Better than touching a leper, holding a baby who had AIDS, sitting at the bedside of a person who was dying of cancer, making them laugh?"

"How are they even comparable?"

"You said Princess Diana's life didn't matter."

"No I didn't."

"Yes you did. You're saying that being a cosmologist matters, and I'm not arguing with that, but the number of actual, living people on this planet whose lives have been bettered in any tangible way by your discoveries, you have to admit, it's not a lot. It's not inconceivable that Diana directly touched the lives of more sick people, people who *did* actually meet her, than you have benefited with your work."

"It's a small number of people, but it's a large contribution to the world's body of knowledge, on which future scientists will build."

"But none of that undoes what she did. It's two different ways of valuing a life. She loved people, she touched them."

"She manipulated them."

"She went up against the establishment and survived."

"She created a fight because she was paranoid and blamed her husband for her own mental problems, and then she more or less won by destroying the public image of the man she picked the fight with. Nevertheless, if he hadn't been the future king of England and she hadn't married him, it wouldn't have mattered whether she'd picked the fight *or* won it. It had nothing to do with anything either of them accomplished."

"She started fighting when she realized her husband was just using her as a trophy wife and broodmare, and then she kept fighting for herself and a lot of other people who'd gotten bad deals out of life. I admire that."

"But that was the deal she made. Give me the crown, I'll be the trophy wife."

"When she was nineteen, when she couldn't possibly have understood what she was getting herself into. All she wanted was love."

"So she got more than she bargained for."

"Or less," I say.

"How many people do you know whose life at thirty-six is anything like what they bargained for at nineteen?"

"What are you saying? What I'm asking you is, what *could* she have done that *would* have mattered?"

Another brief pause.

Then Lawrence says, "Probably not much. She was an uneducated British aristocrat. How many people who fit that description . . ."

"Raised children?"

He says, "Sure." He says it, but he doesn't mean it.

I say, "Raising children doesn't matter?"

—*Now* you tell me this, when I just spent the last fifteen years of my life raising your child?

"Now *you're* picking a fight," he says. "What are *you* trying to win, here?"

"I don't know."

—But whatever it is, I'm not winning it.

I suddenly want to get away from all these flowers, which are starting to stink, and from the bad poetry and the balloons and the Beanie Babies, which *are* stupid, and I start walking and say, "Let's walk over the bridge," and he follows me. I stop in the middle, where Max stopped to light a cigarette this morning, and we're standing over the water and the Eiffel Tower is lit up beyond us — there are 1,216 days left in the millennium — and I say, "Please, Lawrence."

"*What?*"

I could bring up string theory at this point and tell him about the closed-loop strands of energy that escape the membrane that surrounds our universe and stretch that into a metaphor for myself, that I'm feeling trapped and I've got to tie up my own loose ends, but it doesn't help. For one thing, even if everything that's going on inside me was a matter of emotional loose ends that needed to be tied up before I could move on, the metaphor still doesn't tell me how to do that. And it's *not* loose ends. It's much bigger than that. And I don't exactly want to move on. I just don't want to stay here. I *can't* stay here. I've passed some sort of event horizon.

I think, —Now you could put your arms around me. Now you could say you're sorry Diana's death has raised some troubling questions for me. You're sorry we didn't make love this morning. You're sorry you have no clue what I'm trying to say, no idea what I need, you're just sorry. But you love me. Now you could tell me you love me.

I say, "Nothing. We should be getting back to the hotel now."

"Right."

It takes us a while to find a taxi, but when we get in the cab, Lawrence asks me what I'm thinking about. It's his way of apologizing without admitting he's done anything, which he hasn't, or left anything undone, which he has.

I say, "Schrödinger's cat." It's a hypothetical cat, a thought experiment familiar to all physicists, whose hypothetical life or death depends on the angle at which a certain subatomic wave collapses into a particle. Observation—consciousness—is what causes the wave to collapse, so until somebody looks at the cat, the subatomic element retains its dual nature as both wave and particle, so Schrödinger insists that the cat is both alive and dead, or neither not-alive nor not-dead. It's never made sense to me.

"What about it?" Lawrence says.

"I know how it feels."

The rest of the way back to the hotel, we don't say a word. Lawrence doesn't look at me.

I tell myself he knows something's wrong, very wrong, but he wants to discuss it in private, rather than in the presence of a taxi driver who probably doesn't speak English but who wouldn't care what we were saying if he did.

—Fine.

I'm doing the emotional equivalent of holding my breath.

When we pull up to the hotel, Lawrence pays the driver, we go inside, the receptionist gives Lawrence our key, and we walk into the bar without a word passing between us.

Eric and Mart are already drinking champagne, and as soon as we sit down, a waiter pours some for us and we all lift our glasses and Lawrence says, "To a wonderful life together," and we all drink.

"Show Ellen your ring, darling," Eric says.

And she does, she shows me her hand without meeting my eyes, and it's a huge diamond surrounded by several other big diamonds, and I say, "Wow. Congratulations." And then, "It's beautiful."

"It's from Cartier," she says, one of the jewelry stores that lines the place Vendôme.

"It's magnificent."

We toast the ring. Lawrence and I promise to come to the wedding, wherever it is. They haven't decided that yet. They haven't settled on a date yet, either. Mart says they have several things that need to be worked out first, and Eric says, "Details. Mere details."

I finish my glass and excuse myself, claiming exhaustion.

WHILE WE GET READY FOR BED, WE REMAIN SILENT. I FEEL like there's more distance between Lawrence and me than there's ever been, or maybe I'm just more aware of it than before. I think my own personal universe is expanding, and I'm wondering if it will just keep expanding and expanding until it's virtually empty, or if maybe one day, for reasons I can't anticipate right now, it will start contracting, and this will turn out to have been a natural part of the ebb and flow that is space-time itself. Or maybe it will keep on contracting, and eventually I'll implode.

I'm looking in the mirror, brushing my teeth, when it occurs to me that I don't know whether I'm going to stay married to Lawrence, and that thought flashes through me like heat, or light, and feels like it turns me inside out, like a negative.

I look in the mirror again, suddenly aware that I'm seeing my face backwards. I think of Diana's spirit, rising out of the wreckage, seeing her own face in the car for the first time instead of a mirror image or a photograph of it. I'm beginning to see myself in a whole new way, but I don't know what to make of it yet.

Lawrence is in the bedroom, emptying his pockets. He's got notes scribbled on receipts and matchbook covers and a page torn from a notebook with numbers written all over it, and he's putting them on the desk. I don't know what the numbers mean and I don't ask. I don't know, and I do. They're his way of trying to figure out the universe, which has something to do with figuring out himself.

It occurs to me that part of what I'm feeling right now is a glimpse of what it's like to be Lawrence: His mind is full of stars exploding and collapsing in on themselves, the whole universe expanding faster every second, all the stars in it moving farther and farther away from us, taking its secrets with them, and he's chasing after them, trying to find a way to make sense of them.

We're all trying to figure out the same thing, each in our own language.

And then we're in bed, side by side, and I look at Lawrence. I'm waiting for him to respond to what I said on the bridge, but he seems to be waiting, too.

—What are you waiting for?

—One. Two.

—Please. Just say something, anything.

—Three. Four.

—What the fuck is he waiting for?

—Five. Six.

I didn't know what I was counting when I started, but now I do. It's cells. Dying cells. I'm letting go of a part of myself.

Then he says, "Are you thinking you want to try fertility treatments again?"

—Seven million, eight million.

"No."

"Okay."

A long silence.

—Ten million.

—Twenty.

He's trying. I think he's trying to come up with something for me to do with the rest of my life that would matter.

But he can't.

Which I don't fault him for.

Neither can I.

He says, "You're very tired. You'll feel better in the morning."

I don't answer him.

He turns out the light and says, "Good night."

In the dark, I say, "Do you?"

"Do I what?"

"Want to have a baby?"

"No."

We lie here in the silence, and the universe keeps expanding, the galaxy keeps swirling around its black hole, and the earth keeps orbiting the sun as it spins on its own axis, so it feels as if we're sitting still, not moving a muscle, when in fact we're flying through space at immeasurable speed.

After a while, we're in a completely different place.

His breath takes on a slow and even cadence, and I close my eyes and think of Max.

I think, —I'm going to make love with him tomorrow. I'll take him inside me and wrap myself around him until all my boundaries disappear and I can't tell where I stop and the rest of the universe starts.

Then I think, —Or maybe that's exactly the reason not to. Maybe what I need to do is figure out exactly where I stop—who I am and who I'm not and who I want to become—and choosing not to make love with a man I barely know and don't even pretend to love is part of how to say something about myself to myself that's true.

—But one way or another, tomorrow, I'm going to do something that matters, even if the only person it matters to is me.

It occurs to me that at the Big Bang, the universe had no idea what it had set in motion—I think it's just making itself up as it goes along—which didn't make the Big Bang itself any less significant. Nor does the fact that nobody saw it happen.

I take a deep breath. Inspire, fill yourself up.

I exhale slowly until I empty myself out.

I do it again and again and again, and soon I'm sleeping like a rock.

THE NEXT AFTERNOON, I'M SITTING, VERY STILL, ON A small wooden chair in the book-lined living room of Max's walk-up apartment, fully clothed—I'm wearing the same black T-shirt I wore yesterday and a black linen skirt—facing the double glass doors to his tiny balcony and listening to the distant bustle of Paris below. He opens the doors, sets up a light on a tripod, and takes the ashtray off the small table next to me.

"Wait right here," he says and goes into the kitchen.

I'm not going anywhere. I try to read some of the titles of his books. About half are in English, half in French. Simenon, Flaubert, Hemingway.

When he comes back, he puts a glass of white wine on the table and says, "I want you to be sitting here, looking out the window and thinking about what you were thinking about yesterday at Les Deux Magots when I asked you to hold that thought, okay?"

"Okay."

I take a sip of wine.

He holds a light meter in front of me, then steps back and looks at me. "Do you remember what you were thinking?"

"Yes," I say.

I try to think about Charles and Camilla.

He puts the glass of wine in my hand, lifts the camera to his face, and says, "Now it's the end of the day, and you're relaxing with a glass of wine, it's a solitary moment, and you're gazing out your window, thinking something very private."

I think, —My window? Your window is my window?

He says, "Don't pay any attention to me."

I hear his camera: click-slide, click-slide.

So I try again to think about Prince Charles and Camilla Parker-Bowles.

Click-slide.

—And how yesterday, they mattered. They made me mad.

Click-slide.

—But today, they seem utterly irrelevant.

Click-slide.

"Ellen," Max says. It's the first time he's said my name.

"Yes?"

"Do you mind if I touch your hair?"

"No."

His fingertips barely brush my cheeks as he pushes my hair off my face, arranges it on my shoulders like a veil. It's the first time he's touched me all day. He took me to lunch at a little restaurant in the Bois de Boulogne, telling me, "It's very French, not for tourists," and I didn't say, But we're not French, because his point, I thought, made discreetly, was that it was discreet, so I said, "Perfect," and we talked about everything but what was on our minds. I didn't mention Lawrence or Mart or Eric. He didn't mention his jailed friends or the fact that everybody's blaming the paparazzi for Diana's death and at least one of them has received a death threat. Neither of us brought up the photo of Diana giving him the finger. We didn't even talk about Diana. Or sex. We talked about cubism, which neither of us like, and Clinton, who both of us like, and the people in the Heaven's Gate cult who killed themselves a few months ago so they could get on a spaceship that was supposed to be hidden in the tail of the Hale-Bopp comet, leaving behind their bodies, or containers, on their way to the "next level." We talked about what that level might be like, especially if you had to take an invisible spaceship to get to it—sparsely populated, for one thing. We laughed. He didn't touch me once. Our feet didn't even touch.

"Good," he says after moving my hair. "Now I can see your eyes. Good."

He's still just looking at me, like he's trying to figure out what else to fix.

I say, "What's wrong?"

"Can you try thinking about something else?"

"Sure."

"It's a fine line between what you seemed to feel yesterday and what I'm picking up—what the camera is picking up—today. One step past unfulfilled desire is frustration. I'm trying to get you back to desire. Can you get there?"

"Yeah. I'm sorry. I'm in a different place than I was yesterday."

Then he says, "Okay, don't try to get back there. Just think of something you want."

And he's aiming the camera at me, and so many things

rush through my body at once that I can't begin to name them, and he takes a picture.

Then he says, "One thing."

So I look at him and think, —You.

He takes another picture and another.

"Now," he says, "*want* it."

—I want you to rip off my clothes.

Click-slide, click-slide.

"Yes," he says, "that's good. Look right into the camera. Good."

—And tear me open.

"Good."

He's walking in a semicircle around me.

Click-slide, click-slide.

—And reach inside my body.

"Good."

Click-slide, click-slide.

—Grab me by the heart.

And he clicks and he circles and clicks and says, "Good. That's good."

Click-slide.

—And fuck me.

Click-slide.

"Very good."

Click-slide. Click-slide, click-slide, click-slide.

"Good."

Then he stops.

So I stop. I stay still on the surface, though just underneath my skin, I feel every string in my body vibrating so frantically I feel as if I'm about to levitate.

He says, "That was magnificent. You have a very steady gaze, very expressive eyes. Wonderful energy."

"Thank you."

He's rewinding the camera.

I say, "That was the whole roll? We're done?"

I'm trying to rewind myself.

"Yes. I think what I want is on there—we were both in the zone—but I'd like to try one other spot, just to be sure. Okay?"

He's putting in a new roll, looking around his own apartment as if he's never seen it before.

I say, "Sure." I take a deep breath and don't move a muscle.

I'm trying to slow the frenetic dance inside me, but my body is still humming with desire. I've never posed nude before, not even for Polaroids, but that seems not out of the realm of possibility now. Anything seems possible. Everything does.

And he's ready with the next roll, and he's looking around. "I'd really prefer to do this outside," he says, "but we're likely to be attacked out there today. I don't want to do it in front of the books. Maybe at the table. Do you write? A journal, poetry, letters? Anything?"

"A little."

"Yes, maybe at the table, writing."

He's neither surprised nor impressed to hear that I write. He expected it. I like that about him. It doesn't seem to have occurred to him to ask me to pose nude. I'm not sure how I feel about that.

"Or thinking about what to write," he says. The table is covered with books, and he's clearing them off the table, stacking them on the floor. "Try sitting here."

And I sit at the table, and he goes into the next room and he comes back with a sheet of white paper and a pen and puts them on the table in front of me. I pick up the pen.

"You're left-handed," he says.

"Yeah."

"So am I," and he's looking at me, talking to me through the camera lens. "We tend to die younger."

"We do?" I say, and he snaps my picture, and a flash goes off.

"That was a cheap trick," I say, and he snaps it again.

He says, "I didn't plan it. I'm not a planner. I'm an opportunist."

He walks across the room. "It's because we're clumsier."

"What is?"

He's not taking pictures now. He's just looking at me from every possible angle as he talks. "That we die younger. We live in a world made for right-handed people, so we get in more accidents. Stick shifts are made for right-handers—except in England. And scissors. Of course, stick shifts and scissors don't account for the whole difference. But . . . I like you being back-lit by the window, or sidelit, but I've got shadow problems. I'm going to have to move the light."

He puts down the camera and picks up the light, brings it closer to me, plugs it in, and I feel it warm on my skin. He raises it up, then slowly lowers it, looking at me the whole time. He puts a filter on the light and looks at me, studies me, or the photo I might become. He checks me with a light meter.

"When you write," he says, "do you drink coffee?"

"Sometimes. Not usually."

It occurs to me that Lawrence has never asked me anything about how I write.

—Don't think about Lawrence.

Max brings the wine from where I left it by the window, sets it next to me on the table, steps back, and looks at me.

Then, "I don't think I want you writing with wine. That's not . . ."

He doesn't finish his sentence, he just takes the wine away.

"Let's not give you a drink at all."

He takes a book off the floor and puts it on the table, then takes it off.

"No. Just pen and paper. It's just you and what you're writing. Very private moment. Would you write a few lines there? It doesn't matter what you write, it won't be readable. I just want something on the paper."

So I write my name and address.

"Good," he says, and he starts taking my picture.

I stop writing. I'm finished.

"Good," he says again. But then he stops, lowers the camera.

"You've stopped thinking," he says.

"Yes. Sorry."

"I want you to think about what you want to write. The thing you want to write most in the world."

Click-slide.

—I would like to finish the beauty-pageant story.

"Think about what you're afraid to write."

Click-slide, click-slide.

—The beauty-pageant story.

Click-slide.

—I'm afraid to write about my mother.

Click-slide.

—I'm afraid to write about myself.

Click-slide.

—My marriage.

Click-slide.

—I'm afraid to write about anything that matters.

Click-slide.

"Think about the thing you'll never write."

—The truth.

Click-slide.

"Now decide to write it."

I look at him.

Click-slide, click-slide.

He stops, puts down the camera, studies me.

"Wait right here," he says, and he goes into the next room
and comes back with another sheet of paper, swaps it out for
the one with my address on it.

He picks up the camera again.

"Just confront the blank piece of paper."

I look at it.

Click-slide.

"Listen to it."

I look at him.

He doesn't take a picture.

"Just try it," he says. "Listen to the story that wants to be
told."

And I look at the paper, and he's clicking and clicking, and
a hundred stories I will never tell are rushing through me at
once—the beauty pageant, but also my father and God and
Katie and my mother and Big John and Lawrence and Alec
and the Big Bang and even Princess Diana and Max, but thinking of any one of them, much less all of them at once, leaves

me feeling a screaming, dark void in the center of myself. I don't hear anything but that.

"Yes. Good."

Click-slide, click-slide.

"Now write the first word."

I look at the paper. It's utterly silent.

Click-slide.

"Write the first word that comes into your mind."

Nothing. I'm not thinking in words right now. I'm thinking in pictures—water turning to steam, rock turning to lava, explosions. It's a basic law of physics that certain systems, in response to heat or pressure, get to a point where their old order can't contain their energy, so they reinvent themselves and start following a new set of rules.

Click-slide.

I think of Diana: —Maybe that's all death is, too, a phase transition, but a transition to what?

Click-slide.

Still no word from the paper, though.

Click-slide.

Nothing.

I'm suddenly very aware of the light on my skin—on my face, my neck, my hair, my hands. It's hot, and I feel almost like it's spreading over me, seeping inside me, making me glow, and the din in my head begins to quiet. Then I realize it's not light. It's Diana.

Click-slide.

And I hear her voice: *my mother.*

Click-slide.

So I write it: my mother.

Click-slide, click-slide, click-slide.

"Wonderful," he says, and I hear the film winding itself into its spool inside the camera.

Then he says, "I think we're finished," and he takes out the film.

I take a deep breath. Something is finished. I just don't know what it is.

I say, "Good," though I'm not sure that's true.

"That was exhilarating," he says, putting the camera on the table.

I stand up because he's standing. "Part of it was," I say. "Part of it — staring down the blank page — that was terrifying," and we walk to the open balcony doors. We're both looking out, not paying attention to what's there.

He says, "Well, then you're very brave."

"No, I don't mean terrifying. That's overstating it. But it was scary."

"You didn't look afraid," he says, and I don't tell him that I'm good at hiding my fear. He says, "You have a quiet confidence about you that has a touch of fierceness in it. Some people hate having their picture taken, you feel like you're violating them. But you're very natural."

"Thank you."

He says, "Yesterday, you asked me if I thought you were a puritan, and I didn't know. But you aren't."

I say, "No."

Then he turns to me and I turn my face to him. There's no camera between us.

His eyebrows are just a little bit scraggly, and I have an urge to reach up and smooth them out, but I don't do it.

There's a long silence where we're just looking at each

other, taking each other in. I hear some kind of truck outside, a loud engine, and a telephone ringing—not Max's—and somewhere in the distance, music.

I reach up and touch his forehead where he was cut on Saturday.

"You're healing quickly," I say.

"Yes. Before you know it I'll be . . ."

"What will you be?"

Our eyes meet, and he takes my wrist and pulls it so my fingertips move down his cheek until they come to rest on the corner of his jaw. I can feel his bones under his skin.

"I was going to say good as new," he says. "But who'd want to be good as new?"

"A puritan, maybe," I say.

He smiles at that and lets go of my wrist and I take back my hand.

He says, "Anyway. Thank you for posing for me."

"Thank you for photographing me."

"I'll send you copies, if you'd like."

"Yes. I wrote my address on the paper."

—Are we saying good-bye? We can't say good-bye. For one thing, he has to drive me back to the hotel. Though I could get a taxi. So this is it?

"What I'm trying to say," he says, "is thank you for trusting me. At a moment when I'm feeling like the villain in a very bad movie, and you not seeing me that way—it pulled me through a dark night. And your complete trust in me during the shoot—you never said, 'No, do it this way,' or, 'That won't work,' or, 'Not that angle.' Thank you for that."

"I do trust you," I say. "You can trust me, too."

"I know that," he says.

A tiny pause.

Then he says, "Would you like to go out on the balcony?"

—Not particularly.

"Okay."

We step outside. It's a warm afternoon. There's a huge delivery truck below us on the narrow street, blocking traffic.

He says, "Tell me what you're thinking."

"To tell you the truth," I say, "I was hoping this balcony holds up. I was thinking what if it fell."

"It won't," he says. "It's safe."

"I know, I'm sure it is. You just asked me what I was thinking, and that was the bit of paranoia that happened to be flitting through my brain at that moment."

"You're not uncomfortable, then."

"No."

Our bodies are so close they're almost touching. The man in the car right behind the delivery truck gets out, walks down to the truck, and throws up his arms. Somebody honks his horn. A breeze pulls at my throat, tugs on my hair. The truck driver emerges out of nowhere and the man who's gotten out of his car is saying in a very loud voice what he thinks of him, his arms going everywhere, and the driver's just trying to get back in his truck before the guy punches him, and he climbs in and closes the door with the man still yelling at him and starts up the truck and drives away. And now the guy who was yelling at the truck driver is the one who's blocking traffic, and he runs back to his car and gets in and drives away after the truck, and the little traffic jam that had gathered below us follows them both down the street and disperses.

Now the street is empty and it starts to rain and Max takes my hand and we step back, just inside the doors, almost on the threshold. It's pouring, the kind of late-afternoon summer thunderstorm that falls hard and fast out of nowhere and disappears just as fast, and we're looking out at the curtain of rain together when a gust of wind blows into us, misting our faces.

We stay that way, looking out at the rain, for a long time. We're just standing side by side, holding hands, not saying a word. I don't know what it means that we're holding hands or if it means anything. Maybe it just *is*. But I like it. I like feeling the way holding somebody's hand can make you feel—safe and not completely alone in the world.

Then he lets go of my hand, and I don't know what that means, either.

He walks over to the glass of wine he poured for me, for my photograph, earlier, picks it up.

"Do you mind?" he says.

"Of course not," I say, though I'm not certain what it is that I don't mind.

And he drinks it. He doesn't throw it back like a shot, doesn't chug it like a beer. He just drinks it, the whole thing, like a glass of water.

Then he says, "Come with me."

He takes my hand again, and we walk down his hall toward what has to be his bedroom. We're not saying a word, and I don't feel a need to fill the silence.

At the end of the short hall, he opens a door and flips on a light—a regular light, not a darkroom safelight—but it's a darkroom. The windows have been covered, the light sealed out, though I can still hear the rain. I let go of his hand and step in, and it smells just slightly vinegary, a combination of vinegar and nail-polish remover and sweat and glue and something syrupy sweet. I take another step in. We're in a corner of the room, and the wall along my right side is a counter with a sink in it, and above that, shelves full of bottles and boxes and tongs and a timer and canisters in several sizes. On the next wall, the one I'm facing, there's a photo enlarger and over it, a safelight, and next to that, more photography equipment. I don't mention that I took a photography class in college, but I barely remember what any of this is for. I feel just a little bit intimidated, and I move away from the equipment toward the bookshelf to the left of the door, and on the other side of the bookshelf is an alcove that's exactly the size of his bed. And there's his bed. No headboard. Just a comforter and pillows. It's a double bed.

My heart starts to thump, and on the other side of the room, Max unzips a plastic case where a single strip of negatives is hanging and unclips them and I realize the pounding in my chest is not about the bed. It's Diana, pacing, wanting to see what's on those negatives. I've assumed without even articulating it to myself—once I realized he didn't bring me in here because it's where the bed is, or not just because of that— that he was about to show me the photos he took yesterday of me in front of the Ritz, but she knows what's there—it's her—and she wants to see it. She's not saying anything, so I'm not sure how I know this, except that she's inside my body now, inside my mind, and I know she's desperate to see it.

Max puts the negatives on the table next to the enlarger, and I feel her pushing me forward. She wants me to pick up the negatives and look at them, but I'm not going to do it— she doesn't care what Max thinks, but I do—though I do take another step in. He's setting three trays in a neat row on the countertop—he's going to make prints, which I sense Diana is happy about, happy and anxious at the same time. My heart has slowed to something of a normal pace.

He's taking bottles off the shelves.

There's an office chair on rollers sort of out in the middle of the room, like it doesn't belong any particular place, and he says, "Have a seat," and it looks like chemicals have been spilled on it, but I sit.

I watch him pour a different bottle of fluid into each tray. Diana's watching, too. We watch him measure the temperatures of the fluids with what looks like a meat thermometer. He's being precise, very careful, almost tender with every piece of equipment he handles. I like watching him work, though I feel Diana, impatient, inside me, a squeezing in my heart.

—Wait, I tell her.

He goes to the enlarger, turns on its light, slides the negatives into it, and an image appears on the white surface below, and I come and stand next to him so I can see it—and so Diana can—but I can't make out anything like a picture. There's barely a detail in the whole photograph. The left side is almost solid black, and the right side is white with a black blotch. He's moving the negative carrier so the picture is larger, then smaller, in and out of focus, and it's almost like looking at an optical illusion, one of those pictures where if you stare long enough at the blotches, you suddenly see Jesus so clearly, it seems impossible that you didn't see him before. Except I'm in the before stage right now.

Max turns off the enlarger light and turns on the safelight and says to me, "Will you get that?" and he's nodding to the light switch.

I turn it off.

He opens a box and looks inside. It's full of paper, all different kinds and sizes, and he picks one — a single sheet, about eight by ten — and closes the box carefully before he lines up the paper on the enlarger.

I move closer to him and stand with him, slightly behind him, in the red glow, and he sets a timer and the enlarger light comes back on.

We don't say a word as we watch the seconds tick by, and after forty long, Diana-tapping-her-foot seconds, a bell rings and the enlarger light goes off and he puts the paper in the first tray, and slowly, shadows begin to appear and darken. I'm looking for a picture of Diana in front of the Ritz, the picture he was waiting to take when he met me, and he picks up a pair of tongs and moves the paper gently in the fluid and the shadows start to take on a shape, and there's an arm reaching out, but it's not hers, it's a man's right arm and he's wearing a white shirt, and he's reaching into the picture, there's his hand and then, suddenly, at the end of his hand, there's Diana face.

I feel her jump inside me at the sight, and then we're both looking at it together, and she says, *That was it.*

She's in profile, and her eyes are closed.

She says, *That was the moment I left my body.*

Her hair is perfect, shining. She looks beautiful.

I opened my eyes, very confused, and a man who was dressed in light — I thought he was an angel, though I see now he was just a man, and he was being photographed — but he said, "You're going to be all right." He was reaching for me, trying to help me, and I knew it was true, that everything was going to be all right, and then I was suddenly cocooned in a ball of light, lifted up out of the car, out of my body by that light, and then I was inside the light, looking out.

I can't see her mouth. Her shoulder, I think, is blocking her mouth, though there's no sense at all of her body, just solid black where it should be. And now I see a curved black car door—no, the door is open and I'm seeing the door frame, the white flash reflected off the shiny black paint. It's Diana in the tunnel, and the rest of the darkness in the picture is the black jacket she was wearing and the black leather interior of the car. It's Diana, dying.

Everybody was yelling my name—"Diana, Diana, Diana"—but I wasn't there, not in the place where they were yelling. I walked over to a column—or, I floated. I just went. I was still enveloped by the light, as if it was making me invisible. Nobody but the bodyguard seemed to be able to see me.

She doesn't appear to be bleeding or in distress. Her hair is perfect—our hairdresser must have sprayed her with as much shellac as he sprayed on me. If anything, she looks peaceful, but not dead peaceful. In another context, you'd think she was asleep.

The bodyguard was standing there, and we had a little chat. I was watching everything that was happening. Photographers kept arriving, more flashes, and I was slowly becoming aware that it had been a photographer's flash that had pulled me out of the car, and then I was watching the photographer who'd taken that picture and he turned around, looked straight at me. He saw me. Looked me in the eye, and I looked back and recognized him. Max Kafka. I remembered him from Nepal. I knew many of the paparazzi by name, but none of the other people that night. His was the only familiar face—besides my own—and I vaguely remembered having been quite cross with him at some point, but I'd shed all that. It doesn't matter now. I was glad to see him. It was a feeding frenzy over there in the car, but Max had his back to all that and I remembered his response to the suffering in Nepal—he found it difficult to look at—so I knew someone there was suffering, but had no idea it was me.

That was when I left. I found myself walking down the hall at Balmoral, looking for my sons, only it wasn't Balmoral—it was and it wasn't, like in dreams—and again, I wasn't walking, I was floating. It was dark, but there was a light at the end of the hall and I was moving toward it. And then there was another flash of light and I was back in the tunnel and Max was looking at me and I knew he'd just taken a picture of me standing in between the columns with the bodyguard, knew he'd taken it while I was in the corridor, though I didn't understand how he could have, and it seemed to me that this flash had brought me back from Balmoral in the same mysterious way the other one had lifted me out of the car. I was beginning to see that things had changed rather drastically. I could still feel the light surrounding me, almost as if I were inside a balloon, only instead of rubber, it was light, and light itself was— is—a very different thing. It can take many forms—you can breathe it, but it's also liquid, thick as paint, and it's alive, and when it makes a noise, it sounds like music. When I first rose up out of the car, I was immersed in a pool of light, but then, standing in between the columns, I felt it wasn't as much a pool I was floating in as some sort of liquid armor. I felt coated with it, protected by it. And then I became it.

Max lifts the print out of the first tray and puts it in the second.

I told the bodyguard he should get back in the car. I thought he'd be safer there because he didn't have the kind of light around him I did, he was barely lit at all, although I didn't tell him that. And Max started walking away—the police hadn't arrived, the medics hadn't—but he was headed out of the tunnel, he was leaving, and I didn't know what I was meant to do. I wasn't afraid—it was very peaceful—but I was confused. So I followed him. And he got on his scooter and I rode with him, just floated through the streets of Paris on the back of his scooter, and we rushed down the Champs-Élysées with cars zipping past us on either side, lights twinkling all around me, and I was telling him how bloody awful it was, how glad I felt to be out of that tunnel, out of that crowd, and I was laughing, so happy, and at first I thought he was laughing with me — we got away! — I was pressed against his back and I felt his breath jumping and then I realized he was weeping. He was driving his scooter down the Champs-Élysées, weeping, while all the cars rushed past us, he didn't speak a word, but I knew what he was feeling, and I tried to tell him, "No, I'm fine," but it was as if he couldn't hear me. And then we were in the place de la Concorde, and God, what a sad place, so many angry souls who can't let go, they're stuck in a celestial traffic jam, and I said, "Hurry," because I was afraid of getting stuck there with them, I felt them coming toward me, urging me to stay, and we hurried across the river into a much quieter part of the city, and I was holding on to him tight, thinking I've got to see that photograph. Somehow, I knew I wasn't leaving until I saw the photograph whose flash pulled me out of the car. That's how my life is. Was. Not is but not was. But it came to be a way of processing personal information for me — look at the photographs of myself the next morning in the papers, try to get some perspective on how I'd done. Always learning. Sometimes felt I hadn't finished a thing until I'd seen myself doing it the next morning in the papers. So. Very eager to see it.

Max transfers the print to the third tray.

He got off his scooter and rolled it inside a metal door, parked. Then we went up the stairs and inside. He developed the negatives right away, but he didn't make a print, and I wanted to see the print, I needed to. So I stayed. I stayed with him, but not only with him. Found I could be in two places at once. Could go from here to there without moving through the space between the two places. So I went to India, Africa, Bosnia, Ireland, America. London. Balmoral, of course, to my sons. But I was always here, too, waiting. And now, there I am, in the photo.

Then he picks it up with the tongs again and carries it to the sink, turns on the faucet, and lets water wash over it and her voice is still washing over me.

Only this time, there's more to it than whatever I was doing when I looked at myself in the papers. I went to Third World countries during my lifework—not technically primitive tribes, but primitive in every practical way—and I never came across the superstition they're said to have about photographs, that the camera steals the soul. In my experience, most people are quite eager to have their picture taken. If anything, it's almost as if they're hoping it will confer a soul on them. But something happened with this photograph that felt to me like it had something to do with my soul. Perhaps it was partly because of the way I still felt embraced by the light from that particular flash—I don't claim to understand it all—but I thought that photo held something of me, of my soul, so I couldn't go without seeing it. And there it is, and the extraordinary thing about it is how really quite ordinary it is. Not my best picture ever. Not my worst. It's just my old face, my former face, and I feel towards it something like what you feel when you look at your hair that's just been cut, and it's lying on the floor of the salon. It's not yours anymore. There was a time when you cared very much what it did, how it looked. But now it's just rubbish. Don't know what to make of that. And now I don't know what to do with myself. This is what I've been waiting for, thinking that once I saw the photo . . . I don't know. Expected some sort of revelation.

Max and I are standing side by side in the dark, watching the water run over the picture of Diana.

"Are you going to turn me in?" he says.

I say, "No," and Diana agrees.

"You could," he says.

"That couldn't be farther from my mind right now."

"You'd get fifteen minutes of fame, more than that."

"I'm not going to do it."

And Diana grows still, meditative, inside me, though she's not gone. I think she's just looking at the picture.

"Maybe I want you to," he says.

"Do you?"

"I don't think so. Maybe part of me wants you to. Maybe I'm looking for either punishment or absolution, neither of which I can give myself, so I put my fate in the hands of a stranger."

"That would be sort of puritanical, don't you think?"

"So it would."

A long pause.

Then he says, very softly, "I'm sorry I lied, saying I wasn't there."

"No, it's okay," I say. "I understand. I shouldn't have asked."

"I wasn't there when she crashed. None of us were. But we heard it—it was so loud, I felt it in my ribs—and we all knew it was her, everybody picked up their pace, and I was on a little scooter, so by the time I got there, several others were already photographing the scene. One of my friends was afraid of blood, so he stayed outside to call the police, and I left my scooter with him and ran in, feeling absolutely ecstatic. A doctor was already tending to her, and everybody was screaming at him, 'She's English, speak to her in English,' in French, of course, and I ran toward the car and stepped in close and heard him say, 'You're going to be all right,' and I thought that was absolutely true, I thought she would be fine, though the other three clearly weren't—pure gore—but I took that photograph, and then I stopped. It was a frenzied energy around me, but I suddenly felt like I was about to black out, like my blood had stopped pumping, my whole body, inside and out, just came to a complete standstill and I could have just collapsed into a little pile of salt. Then I felt sick to my stomach, several different emotions were washing over me in waves like nausea. So I started walking out of the tunnel to get some air, thinking, What am I doing? What have I become? When I got back on my scooter, I could barely start it, my legs were so wobbly. I trembled all the way home, feeling a terrible weight on my back, a heaviness that went all the way to my bones. I couldn't have helped her. I know nothing about medicine, first aid. All I could have done is get in the way, or stay out of it. So."

He leaves the water running, walks over to his bed, and sits on the edge of it, but he's not getting into bed. He's just sitting—I get the feeling that telling me this is making him wobbly again—and I sit down next to him. He's not looking at me as he talks. He's just staring out into the darkness of the room. I'm watching him in profile.

He says, "I got here, drank a brandy. Then I processed the negatives, but I couldn't bring myself to look at this one. I don't have a TV, but I turned on the radio and at that point there was no news, but I kept changing the channels, not hearing a word about her. So I turned it back off and drank another brandy. I thought, 'Maybe it's somehow not true.' I couldn't quite believe it was, but I couldn't believe it wasn't, either. This was maybe one o'clock in the morning, one thirty. I lay down on the bed, but I couldn't sleep. The phone kept ringing. At some point, I tried, half-sleeping, to convince myself the whole thing had been a dream, so I got up and turned on the radio, and I guess I had slept after all, because she was dead, and she wasn't declared dead until four o'clock. I changed the radio station, thinking they'd gotten it wrong. No, I knew it was right, but I changed the radio station over and over any-way—I don't know why—and it was the same thing every-where, 'The Princess of Wales and her companion, Dodi Fayed, are dead.' I walked around. I had no idea what to do. I remember walking around the apartment, saying, 'Oh my God, oh my God.' I opened the balcony doors, and it was completely silent out there, nobody knew what had happened, and I had this urge to yell, 'Wake up, turn on your radios.' At some point, I pulled out some pictures I'd taken of her and spread them out on the table like they were a storyboard and thought, 'No. This was not the trajectory at all.' So I went for a walk. I walked back to the site in the dark. I wasn't going there on purpose. I was just trying to walk something off and ended up there. The photograph you said you took—I don't even remember taking it with me, much less laying it on the . . . whatever that thing was. Several hours in there are a complete blur."

Then, with a sudden look of horror on his face, he turns to me and says, "Did I say I felt ecstatic?"

"Yes, but I understood what you meant."

He puts his face in his hands. "It wasn't ecstasy. It was something like . . . well, it was like being in a car crash, where every neuron in your brain is firing so fast, every cell in your body is so completely engaged in the moment that time seems to slow down and you start functioning on some entirely other level where you know the situation is beyond your control, you've already accepted whatever is about to happen even if it's your own death, and you're just above all those individual emotions—fear or happiness or . . . anything." Then he looks at me. "That *is* ecstasy, isn't it?"

"Yeah."

"But I didn't mean joyful ecstasy. There was no joy in it."

"No. Obviously."

He stands up, goes to check the photo.

"When I went home," he says, "I didn't call anybody. Ten minutes after the accident, a British paper paid about half a million American dollars for one photo of her—later, they pulled it, of course—but the editor who'd sent me to the Ritz that afternoon called me several times, all night and into the morning, leaving messages, offering more money than I've ever come close to making in a year. It was a tabloid called *Bild Zeitung,* and they ran a picture from the scene on their front page yesterday, but it wasn't mine. I don't know where they got it. I told him I didn't have anything, but he refused to believe me. Then he wanted me to injure myself so I could get into the hospital and when I was left alone, wander around until I found her dead body and photograph it. I said, 'You are out of your mind.' Later, he called wanting pictures of the wrecked car—said he'd pay more if there was blood—so I told him to go fuck himself. I wasn't going to do it, wouldn't have done it for all the marks in Germany. And yet, for that one picture I could go to jail. I could lose everything."

I go to him and touch him, just place my hand in the center of his back, Diana and I do. I say, "So what are you going to do?"

"I don't know. Any lawyer would say I should turn myself in—that's the law—but if I did it now, the media would spin it that I'd had an attack of conscience because I believed I deserved to be in jail, which they'd use to justify the imprisonment

of the men who are already there. I don't want to do that to myself, and it would be wrong to do it to them. So I'm thinking I
might just get out of Paris for a while, count on the ineptness
of the French bureaucracy and hope they drop the charges
against all photographers before they get around to finding me.
I've waited long enough so that if it comes to it, I can say I
wasn't trying to escape the law, I was just going to visit friends,
but any longer . . . the telephone could ring any minute."

"You should go soon."

"Yes."

"Like now."

He doesn't say anything right away.

—I'm an idiot. Why did I tell him to go now when that's
the last thing on earth I want?

He says, "Not now, not yet. Tonight."

I let my hand fall from his back.

He goes to the sink, lifts the photo out of the water with
a pair of tongs, and clips it to a string, and I go to it and look
at it and I feel Diana looking at it. I feel her, fragile, in my
chest, in my face, looking out through my eyes, and I feel her
in my arms, in my fingertips, and I turn to Max and he turns
to me and pulls me to him and I take him in my arms, Diana's
arms, and he picks me up and my legs wrap themselves around
him like I'm hanging on for dear life, and he kisses my throat
and I drop my head back so he can kiss me some more which
makes me dizzy and afraid of falling—I feel like I could fall
out of my body and Diana would just take over—so I hook
my feet behind him and press myself against him and hold him
tight while he carries me toward the bed, and my eyes are
closed, but I peek and he's just walking, but it feels like the
floor is rocking and we're spinning around the deck of a boat,

dancing through the stars, floating through the galaxy, and he sits us down on the edge of the bed, Diana and me, she's inside my chest and I'm straddling his lap, my skirt riding up my thighs, and his hands are moving over my skin and I feel something rush through me from my gut to my heart to my throat to my brain, I feel the blood being sucked out of me, and he touches my breasts through my clothes and I feel my chest open up, Diana's chest being cut open, a hand clenching her heart, and I feel like I'm floating up out of my body and I reach for him in the dark, I grab his arms and hold on tight, and then he kisses me, and he tastes sweet and warm and old and full of sadness, like an ocean, and we get up to take off our clothes though they seem almost to fall off on their own, and Diana pictures the medics who cut off her clothes, and she's thinking of Dodi taking off her clothes and Hasnat and Oliver and James, and then, with a pang of sadness, Charles, it's all rushing through her, through me, all the men who broke her heart, and Max and I are standing beside the bed now, naked, and he puts his hand high on the center of my chest, presses his palm gently there without touching my breasts, and his middle finger rests in the hollow of my throat, and I want him to slip that finger inside my other hollow place, all the places I'm hollow, and she wants it, too, though she says nothing, it's utterly quiet, and then I hear thunder. It's storming outside, but it feels safe and still and very private here, just Max and Diana and me in this room that's been sealed off from the rest of the world.

He sits on the bed and I start to move toward him, but he stops me.

He says, "Wait," and I stop breathing, and I think if I could collapse my being into a single particle now, I would.

I say, "What's wrong?"

He says, "Nothing," and I can't read the look on his face. I say, "Please don't do this."

He says, "I'm sorry. I thought you wanted to. I wouldn't have ..."

"No. I do. Want to. I mean, don't stop."

And he smiles at me and takes both my hands but doesn't pull me toward him. "I wasn't stopping," he says. "I just wanted to look at you. You're so beautiful."

He says each word separately—you're so beautiful—and he means it, and I feel those words go inside me and fall like rain. I feel them land all over my body at once, inside and out, like when you jump hard into deep water and you land but then you keep falling. It hurts, and part of what hurts is that I can't remember Lawrence telling me I'm beautiful, and part of what hurts is that I feel this huge empty hole deep inside me and I feel like I'm falling into it, collapsing in on myself, and I feel far away from Lawrence, far away from anywhere, separated from myself, and I'm trying to figure out how to get back to where I belong, and I feel those tiny words—you're so beautiful—sitting in the hole inside me but they don't begin to fill it up, in some ways they make it deeper, they just remind me that it's there. So I want Max to come inside me. I think maybe he'll fill me up or maybe he won't, but I don't care, I just want him there, and he's sitting on the edge of the bed, looking at me, and I move to him and straddle him again and I push him deep into my body and he pushes back and I'm pressing myself into him hard, if he could go all the way through me I would want him to, and it almost feels like he is, and we're moving faster and faster, and I close my eyes and let go of my body and I feel his hands moving over my skin and his voice moving underneath it and every neuron in my body is firing fast, every cell, every particle is dancing, every wave reaching out to the farthest corners of the universe, and I'm aware of my skin, as indefinite a boundary for my body as a shoreline is to an ocean, and I feel things breaking inside me, like waves on the beach, or a crash echoing in a tunnel.

And then time stops, everyday life gradually disappears like a picture fading, and I'm still myself, but not in a way I've recognized before, and I hear Diana: *This is what's it's like to die.*

When I open my eyes, I think Diana's gone—I feel like I'm completely inside my body, filling it up—and I start moving again with him, first slow and then hard, like I'm throwing myself at him, only every time I pull away, he pulls me back, and then he comes, he tells me he's coming, and he pulls me close to him and holds me tight, my breasts pressing against his chest as he breathes.

And then we stop. We stop moving, and our faces are touching, we're breathing each other's breath, and he says, "Do you feel it?" and I do, and I say, "It's like your heart is beating inside me."

Then we don't talk. We're both breathing hard and I stay pressed against him and we're holding each other so tight, I think he might bruise my arms and I want him to, so that later, I'll be able to prove to myself that this really happened. We're quiet and still, like we're afraid to move because we don't want it to end.

AFTER, HE SAYS, "YOU'RE A SCREAMER."

I say, "I've never screamed before in my life, I didn't even know what I was doing."

"Well, you're a fast learner."

Nothing's funny, but we're both laughing.

Then I slide off him and curl into his chest, and his arms make a circle around me like a halo, and he says, "I haven't felt this way in a long time."

There's sorrow in his voice, as if he's thinking about when he felt this way before and how it didn't last.

I say, "Neither have I."

I don't tell him I've never felt this way. I don't know if I was capable of it before now.

Then he asks me if I want to take a shower with him, but I need a moment to myself, and I say, "You go ahead."

He says, "Are you okay?"

I tell him I'm fine, and he looks at me as if he's thinking, You *are* fine, and I say, "Are you?"

"Yes."

He closes his eyes and takes a deep breath like he's taking me in, all the billions of my atoms that have died since I've been here are reconfiguring themselves, coming back to life in his body, and I breathe him in deep and I feel his cells turning into me. Then he opens his eyes and kisses me, a quick, soft kiss on the lips, as if we've been together for years.

He looks at me for a long time. Then he says, "If we leave soon, you'll get to the hotel before your husband gets back?"

"Yes."

"Are you sure?"

"Yes."

"Good. You should shower with your own soap, anyway."

And he leaves.

I wait until I hear the water running before I get up, pull on my clothes and go into the living room. I step out onto the balcony. It's stopped raining, and steam is rising up off the streets, like spirits rising from the dead.

After he showers, I go into the bathroom and close the door. While I wash my hands, I don't even look at myself in the mirror. I don't look at anything. I feel like I've taken in all I can take.

When I come out, he's dressed, and he's in the dark-room with the door open, standing by the enlarger. I go to him, and he hands me the last picture he took of me in front of the Ritz, when I turned to wave good-bye before I went inside. My arm is lifted, my face is red, my mouth is open, my hair is a mess.

"Oh, God!" I say, and I turn away from it.

"What? It's a good picture."

"No, it's awful. Is that what I looked like? It doesn't look like me."

I set it facedown on the counter, and he picks it up, turns it back over.

"Yes it does. Look at your face. Do you see what I was saying yesterday? About how you try to look happy?"

"No."

"You'd just stepped out of the car into a situation that often reduces women to tears and men to violence—I don't mean to sound sexist, but I've never seen it the other way around—but you've got perfect composure, and thirty seconds later, you're smiling for the camera."

"Oh. Right."

He hands it to me.

"Here. Take it."

"No."

"I've still got the negative. I'll make another copy for myself."

"I don't want it. I see what you saw now, and I don't want that."

"I'm sorry. But as I told you yesterday, I find that quality in you appealing."

I smile. "Thank you." And I'm doing it again—trying to look happy—and I stop smiling and I say, "But it's different now. I may go on trying to tell the lie that I'm fine, everything's fine, to other people—I don't know what I'm going to do—but I do know I'm not going to keep trying to believe it. I can't."

He puts the picture facedown—now it's a blank piece of paper—and looks at me.

He says, "I'm sorry if I've . . ." and I put my finger to his lips as if to say, Shh— whatever has happened to the way I see myself, I don't want him to take responsibility for it—and he kisses my finger.

Then he says, "I suppose that's a good thing, not lying to yourself."

"Maybe. Though I think it's how a lot of people get through the day."

Then he says, "You're going to be all right, you know."

I think of how he thought the same thing about Diana and how he was right, only not in the way he meant it at all.

I say, "I'll be fine," and I hear myself two very long nights ago telling Eric I'm fine in my Alabama drawl and Mart's comment about Zelda Fitzgerald: "What a waste of a life."

Now he's uncomfortable, I think—we both are—and he takes the string of negatives out of the enlarger, and I say, "Can I see them?"

"Sure," he says and hands them to me.

I hold them up to the light, and there's a frame after the

one of Diana in the car. It's two of the columns, overexposed, so it's mostly dark, which is light. Diana's not in it, but it's the picture she watched him take, the flash that brought her back.

I say, "Why did you take this?"

"I don't remember taking it," he says. "I was trembling, fumbling, but I wouldn't have taken it by accident. So I don't know."

Then he takes the whole strip of negatives and puts them through a shredder.

"Oh my God," I say. "Don't do that."

But it's done.

"I had to," he says.

"Right."

Then he picks up the photo of Diana in the tunnel, and I say, "You can't shred that."

"I can't be caught with it."

"Please."

He looks at me, and I don't know what's going through his mind, I don't know if Diana is whispering in his ear, I don't know if he's calculating its eventual market value or its immediate capacity to ruin his life. But then he puts it in a white envelope and says, "Take good care of her."

And he gives it to me.

"I will," I say. "I promise."

He's giving me a thing of infinite value with no price.

Which, it occurs to me, is also a definition of love.

Nothing I could do in response would be adequate or appropriate.

I say, "Merci."

He says, "Oui."

He takes my hand and we walk back into the living room, to the table where he put my name and address.

"I'll send you some prints sometime," he says. "I don't know when."

"Thank you," I say. "But not this one." And I put the picture he took of me in front of the Ritz, smiling for the camera, through the shredder.

He picks up the other piece of paper, the one with "my mother" written on it, and I'm ready for him to destroy that, too, but he says, "For now, take this, to remind yourself of what happened when you wrote those two words."

Diana came back when I wrote them, and not just back into the room, but she entered my body, my mind, and when I wrote "my mother" on the paper, the words meant her mother and mine and my memory-mother and my internalized mother and something much bigger than all that, or the beginning of something bigger, but he doesn't know any of that, so I don't know what he's talking about.

He says, "It was extraordinary. It was almost as if, before that moment, you had . . . light is what I work in, so the only way I know to describe it is, you had a darkness about you, and when you wrote that, you got lighter, brighter."

I don't say anything. I can't. What would I say?

"Maybe I just saw what I wanted to see. Anyway," he says, handing me the paper. "Take it. Next time you think of me, get it out and do what Hemingway said: Write one true sentence."

"Is that what you'll do when you think of me?"

"No, I'll probably just explode."

We sort of laugh at that.

We're looking at each other, out of words, and I get an

image of the two of us taking off on his scooter, driving down the Champs-Élysées with cars zipping past us on either side, laughing, my face pressed against his back, and then out of Paris and into the countryside, through the South of France and into Italy—no, Switzerland, the Swiss Alps—and we find a little room in a chalet and we register under assumed names: Mr. and Mrs. Price of Columbus, Ohio. Except I don't have my passport with me, so I revise the fantasy, putting us in the French Alps instead. As if that's the only factor that's unrealistic here.

WE DON'T SAY GOOD-BYE. HE OFFERS TO TAKE ME BACK TO the hotel, but he needs to get out of Paris, and I tell him I want to walk, alone. So he comes with me down the stairs outside his apartment and we kiss again when we get to the ground level, and he tells me how to get back to the boulevard St-Germain as we walk down a dark hall to the door that lets out onto the street.

Then we stop and I say, "Where are you going?"

"I don't know," he says.

I'm not going to see him again. That much is obvious.

I say, "Well, be careful."

"You, too," he says, and he opens the door and I step out into the bright of day and turn back to him and he kisses me for the last time, a long, slow drink of a kiss that sends something through me in waves.

Then I go, and the door closes behind me and I start walking.

I'm trying to convince myself that all I need is a little transition period, but I know I can't just go back to Lawrence and reenter my life right now, so I'm walking along the boulevard

St-Germain, thinking, —I just made love with a man I don't love, something I used to think was not possible, and it's ripping a hole in me, and not because I did it, but because I'm not going to do it again.

I can't even make sense of that.

I know what my mother would say, —What did you expect? You had sex with a complete stranger. That's not making love, it's the opposite of that. And now you're surprised that what you've created is emotional chaos?

And though I wasn't really talking to her, Diana responds: *It wasn't the opposite of love if what you were reaching for was love.*

—But I *wasn't* reaching for love.

Maybe it was love's mirror image. It's a complicated thing. Our first interview, we'd just gotten engaged, and the reporter asked if we were in love, and I said, "Of course," and Prince Charles said, "Whatever 'in love' means."

The reporter looked at me, stunned, and I looked away. I remember focusing on a cable on the floor—all kinds of cables and lights were strewn everywhere and I wasn't used to it, any of it—and I let my eyes follow a wire until it merged into a big tangle and disappeared. The reporter went on to the next question, and I made myself smile, laugh. We all just kept going.

After the interview, we didn't move. I suppose we were waiting for someone to take off our microphones, but I felt as if I literally couldn't move my legs. And also emotionally, I didn't know how I was going to go on from what he'd said. So we just sat there in silence, and the way I remember it, the interviewer, the cameramen, the palace people—nobody twitched a muscle. And Prince Charles, of course. Nobody said a word for the longest time and I thought to myself, "Stay here." That was all I would let myself think because I wanted so badly to disappear.

We never discussed it, after that. In all our years together, I never said to him, "So what do you think it means, 'in love'?" Spent the rest of my life trying to figure it out, though.

She stops, but I don't think she's finished.

I stop walking. I stand in front of a women's clothing store, looking in the window at a faceless mannequin, listening. A subway passes under me, and the ground trembles against the bottoms of my shoes.

I say, —So did you figure it out?

I look at my reflection in the glass.

She pauses, and I start walking again. Then she says, *I don't know. Maybe love is like your own face in that you can't ever really see it, you can only live inside it, look at the world through it. Maybe love is less a thing you figure out than something you do. Maybe it just is.*

It's heartless of me, but I'm irritated with her. She's been lying to herself for so long, throwing the word love around to the point where I don't know if she's capable of knowing the truth anymore, which might be why she's stuck here, if there's any reason at all. Because surely love wasn't what she had with Charles, who she left, with Dodi, who lied to her, with Hasnat, who wouldn't be seen in public with her unless she was wearing a disguise, with Oliver, with James, with all the married men she claims to have loved where, she said herself, nothing in the relationship was real. Surely she doesn't really believe that holding an AIDS baby in your arms for ten minutes, while being photographed, constitutes love. So she never figured it out while she was alive, and why should having had her heart ripped open in a car accident change that?

I know she can hear what I'm thinking, but she doesn't respond.

I keep walking until I see my dream kitchen, and I stop again. I feel the same clenching in my stomach as I did the last time I saw it, but for the opposite reason: I don't want it. I don't want the sink, the countertops, the refrigerator. I don't even see the appeal of the hammered-copper accessories I wanted so badly yesterday. I don't want to plan parties and put away groceries and serve dinner to Lawrence's friends. The me in that picture is like the dog in the portrait: It's a fiction, dressed up to look like something it could never possibly be. There's no *me* in that me.

I walk past the kitchen.

Diana's still not saying anything.

I pass a shop full of Asian cookery. Something I can't read is written on the window in Japanese.

I think, —Maybe there *is* no big revelation at the end. Maybe you just wait around until a wormhole opens up nearby and you step through it to the next universe and start over, and if you learned something in this life, you hope you get to take that with you, and if you didn't, you don't.

Then why am I still here?

—I don't know.

A long pause while I walk past a stationery store selling dozens of pens and every color ink and box after box, reams and reams, of blank paper.

Then, *Perhaps there's been a mistake.*

I don't know how to respond to that. I *do* think her death was a mistake.

We pass a bridal salon.

She's quiet, meditative. We both are. I think she's scared, and I don't blame her.

I come to the side street where the crème de menthe guy's café is, and I can almost taste the cold mint, feel its warm sting on my throat, and the smell of his hand when he gave me the glass—he smelled like bread baking, or maybe like sex—but I keep going.

I pass a bakery with a window full of pastries so beautiful they look like little works of art, then an art gallery full of ugly white cubes and spheres and cylinders.

Something seems to have gone terribly wrong.

I step onto the pont de la Concorde. A bateau is moving toward the bridge, and I walk to the middle and stop to look at the people on it. The top deck is almost solid red—it's a group of old people wearing identical red T-shirts, seated in row after row of tightly spaced chairs, watching Paris pass by. It makes me sad, all those tourists, lined up straight and packed in together. They're not going to let somebody else's death, even Diana's, change their itinerary, and why should they? It's because they're aware of their own imminent passing that they're here: They want to see Paris before they die. The bateau floats under the bridge.

I think, —Well, now you've seen it.

I start walking again, and if, in the beginning, I felt Diana near me, and later on, inside my mind and then, even later, in my body, now it feels like she's a weight on my back, and I'm carrying her, and she's heavy, every muscle in my body is aching, though I also think she's somehow directing my steps and I'm just going where she wants me to take her.

I come to the place de la Concorde at the end of the bridge, where traffic is stopped. It's a big, hot tangle, and it smells of car exhaust and bus fumes and stale piss and anxiety—people needing to be somewhere other than here. It's loud, and I can't quite identify all the sounds—car engines and bus engines and motorcycles, horns, water falling in the fountain, angry voices, and something else, too, a murmuring in my head. I can't hear Diana over all this, though I sense she wants to say something—I feel her pressing, hot, on my back—so I'm walking toward the park on the other side of the plaza, where it's less noisy, and soon I've stepped off the concrete sidewalk onto a gravel path, traded paved streets for green grass, though I can still hear the cars, still smell the city air. It's quieter, though, and a little cooler.

I sit down on a bench in the shade, and a pigeon flies away. There's a couple on the bench next to mine, making out, completely oblivious to everything but each other. A child runs into a group of pigeons and they scatter into the air, then come back together a few feet away. They peck at the ground, looking for crumbs that aren't there.

I think Diana's just watching it all, taking everything in. I'm feeling a nostalgia in her, a nostalgia for walking along a sidewalk in Knightsbridge on a day when the rain was so fine, she didn't see it until she felt the thrill of it on her face.

Whatever lies before her, I don't think she's ready for it.

She says, *Perhaps I'm not. I remember looking at the clock the night before the wedding—I hadn't slept a wink, and the fireworks were going off like gunshots, I could feel them exploding in my chest—and it was four in the morning, and the wedding was scheduled for eleven, and I didn't know what lay before me then, either, but I remember thinking I had seven hours left to be myself. Whereas this time, the feeling I've got seems less a matter of how much longer I'm going to be myself than, how much longer until I* become *myself, my truest self, the one I spent this whole life preparing to become?*

I say, —And who is your true self?

A pause. Then: *God, I don't know that, either. My God, I still don't know. I thought you were going to help me figure that out. I thought you were somehow my guide. And I thought something happened in that studio—including the lovemaking but not just that. When Max told you to write one true sentence, I thought somehow you were going to write the thing we both needed to hear.*

She's right that something happened. While I was making love with Max, I felt something in my body that could have been spacetime itself ripping open, and I thought I set some part of myself free, though now I can't figure out what part that was or where it went, and if I'm right about spacetime tearing open when people die and their souls taking a wormhole through it to another universe, she should have been able to go then, so maybe I'm just lying to myself.

Please try.

So I unzip my purse and get out a pen and the piece of paper with the words "my mother" on it. I close my eyes and listen.

It's quiet.

No, it's very noisy here—all the sounds from the traffic on the place de la Concorde and the Champs-Élysées, plus a dog barking, a baby crying, people talking, footsteps crunching on the gravel.

But when I look at the paper, it's silent.

I think, —My mother . . . *what*? It's impossible to finish that sentence. Like Diana, she's a mass of contradictions, and it's hard to say any single thing about her that's completely true.

I say to her, —I wrote it, but only after you thought it.

And she says, *No. I thought it—I agreed with you that it was the right place to start—after I saw what you'd written.*

The pressure on my back is so insistent now that it hurts, and I lean over, resting my forearms on my thighs. I'm looking at the dirt between my feet, at a tuft of grass. I pluck a blade: It's an elegant shape, symmetrical, tapering up to a rounded tip, and it's glossy and smooth, a perfect surface, and I think, —This blade of grass knows more about being what it is than Diana or I know about being who we are.

I turn it over and its underside is slightly furry, sandpapery, and I keep staring at it and staring until I begin to feel it as a group of cells and then a gathering of atoms and then a loose assemblage of protons and electrons and quarks and strings and loops and branes, no different from me on that level— grass and dirt and this bench and sound and light and laughter and memory and hope, vibrating like parts of a musical instrument the size and shape of the universe itself, and suddenly I see that just like light is both wave and particle and people are both bodies and souls, energy has a dual nature, too. You look at it one way, and it's mass times the speed of light, squared—it's *stuff*—but if you look at it another way, it's love. It's something Diana said before: Love is everything there is.

Then I blink and refocus and look at it again, and what I'm looking at is just a blade of grass.

—Yes, you're lying to yourself. For a moment there, you had yourself convinced that a blade of grass was love incarnate.

This is not Diana. It's just me.

I drop it back onto the ground.

A pigeon looks my way, takes a step toward me before turning around and walking in the other direction.

I'm very tired.

For a long time, Diana and I are both silent, though I've got memories tumbling through me: I'm in looking in the three-way mirror at three copies of myself in my pageant dress, and the gentle pressure along my spine as my mother zips it up makes me stand up straighter, taller, and when she puts her crown on my head, there are tears in her eyes and then in mine.

Then, *Oh, I see now,* Diana says.

—What?

My mother.

—What about her?

My mother and yours, they aren't so different, she says. *You have to start with your mother because that's where it all started. And you can't go on now, neither of us can, until we forgive them.*

I say, —But I'm not mad.

Of course you are. You tell yourself the lies you need to hear to survive, as I did. But you want to write your children's story for the same reason I did the Andrew Morton novel: revenge.

And now I realize, with a clarity that feels like it's a gift from Diana, what's missing from the beauty-pageant story. I've never understood that what the story is about, what it's missing, is that we were trying so hard to love each other. I kept focusing on what a bad job we did of it, so I never let myself believe that my mother gave me the makeover and entered me in the pageant as an act of love because it wasn't the expression of it I needed, but it was the best she could do. It was the thing she wished her mother had done for her. So she tried to speak love in her own language, and I heard her in mine, and it got lost in translation. And what I thought was the big lie we tried to convince ourselves of the night of the pageant—that the whole event had never happened—was not a lie at all. We were telling each other the biggest truth there is: I still love you.

So I finish the sentence, not with what comes after the words I've already written, about her, but with what comes *before* them, about me: I forgive my mother.

I don't know if it's true. But I'll try.

And Diana says, *Yes, I forgive my mother, too. And my step-*

mother. My brother. Fergie. The Queen. Charles, of course. Even Camilla. I blamed her for loads of things, but I'll grant her this: She loves my husband. And he loves her. I used to hate them both for that. But now I forgive them for it.

I want her to tell me a memory, another story, but she says, *I don't need to do that anymore, hash it all out. It's over now. I think I'm ready to move on.*

I say to Diana, —I want to move on, too. It's not true, though, that I was writing my story simply for revenge. And I don't think it was ever really a novel. Maybe I thought of it as fiction for children because I needed to explain something about my childhood to the child in me. But that's done now, and it doesn't fix what's wrong. In a way, it makes things worse, not having the illusion that I'm secretly writing a novel. Because I'm still the woman I was raised to be, and when you left your marriage, you didn't have a career, either, but you had your children, and you had money and fame, and you tried to do some good with it, which didn't solve your problems but it gave you something to do with your life. And I don't even have that.

She doesn't say anything. I think she sees my point, though.

I wad up the paper and stuff it back in my purse and stand up.

I start walking.

I still feel like I'm carrying her in some sense, and we move down the cours de la Reine—not the heart of the queen, but the *way* of the queen—and now I'm walking under a canopy of leaves beside the river toward the flame. I see five or six people in the several blocks ahead of me. We're all walking in the same direction. Everyone is silent. Most people are alone. One woman is carrying a mixed bouquet wrapped in see-through plastic. No one is rushing, no one is lingering. It's as if we're all on a strange pilgrimage, which, come to think of it, we are.

When I get to the pont de l'Alma underpass, I realize Diana and I are not going to the flame. We're going into the tunnel.

There's traffic, lots of it, but I'm not scared. I'm a little dizzy, but I wait for a gap in the rush of cars, and when I think no one's looking — there are cops everywhere — I climb over a temporary pedestrian barricade, and now I'm walking along the edge of the street where it curves and dips toward the tunnel. There's no sidewalk, barely any shoulder, and a car speeds past me so close I can feel the hot air moving, swirling around my legs. Then another car passes in the other lane and honks, and the horn echoes in my ears but it's a muted sound, as if it's very far away. I keep walking and walking — the road seems to stretch out before me, getting longer with each step — but finally I get to the tunnel entrance.

The last time I was here, the tunnel was floodlit, brighter than day, but this time, it's dark and empty and her Mercedes is gone, of course, but she's not, and I look down the street and there's another break in traffic and I cross over to the concrete median and stand between the first two columns, my heart barely beating, I'm so deathly calm. I hear a distant siren coming toward me from the other end so I step farther inside, closer to the second column, to hide — I press myself against it — and a police car whooshes past me through the tunnel in a blur and out the other end. The air is vibrating, or maybe it's just me, trembling, but I move to the next column and the next and the next, counting as I go, touching each column until I come to the thirteenth, the one they hit first, the one she stood next to just after she left her body, and I stop.

It's where I've thought she wanted me to go, but there's no

sense in her of having arrived. She's not ready to stop—we're in different places now—and there's a shift in her, as if she's looking forward, not back.

—Of course. This is it. I have to let her go now.

I take Max's photograph of her in the car out of its envelope.

—You look so peaceful, I say, and she says, *That's not me.*

—Right.

I think she wants me to do something, but I don't know what. I'm not even sure she knows what. We're both making this up as we go. I can't just leave the photograph here, though I think I'm trying to leave *her* here, and she says, *I can't move,* and I don't know if she's referring to the photograph—that she couldn't move when she was in the car—or herself now, or both, and there's no physics for this, it's just intuition. Or maybe desperation. Or that I know I have to destroy the photograph anyway, and this feels like the right time and space for it.

So I unzip my purse, fishing through my wallet, my lipstick, receipts, a pen, the piece of paper Max gave me, the keys to my house and my car, the Diana postcards I bought yesterday—there's almost no light in here—and finally my fingers find the matchbox and I close them around it. I take it out, zip my purse closed, and slide it over my shoulder. I open the box, choose a match. Then I strike it against the edge of the box, and just as it lights, a car whips past and blows it out. I get out another and try again and nothing happens and I try again, and this time the end of the match flares, and then the flame quickly shrinks to almost nothing, but I cup it with my hand, and it grows again and steadies. I'm holding it straight up, but it's burning quickly, moving down the match toward my fingers, so I hold it up to the picture, and a corner catches on fire, and I drop the match, and the edge of the picture melts to black while the paper curls over it and the flame begins to roll across it like a wave, destroying everything in its path, and she's watching as it makes its way toward her face, and she says, *My soul wasn't in that photograph. I see that now. I just couldn't go until I understood what happened in that car. I knew where we were headed. Dodi was going to propose, and I didn't know what I was going to say.* And the frame of the car door melts, the arm reaching in to her bubbles and lifts off the paper and splits open, and she says, *We were speeding away from the hotel and Dodi was yelling, "Faster, faster," and the bodyguard was arguing that we should slow down, but Dodi wasn't listening, so the bodyguard insisted we put on our seat belts.* And then the flame consumes her face—her white cheeks and her eyelashes, her shining hair—and starts in on the dark space that is her body, her black jacket against the black leather seat, and the ashes that were her last photograph are glowing and I think she's about to go and I'm watching the picture disappear as the fire moves across it, and Diana says, *The car made a turn, and I had my seat belt in my hand, I was about to slip it into the buckle, but then, in a fraction of a second, I saw a host of possible futures rolled out before me, and whether I was with Dodi or any number of other men, some essential thing was always missing. Even if I'd found the perfect man, it was too late, because nobody was going to be able to restore to me what I'd lost, not even me. Diana was long dead, and I was going to have to live with that, which was unbearable.*

Somewhere in me I've been holding on to Max, or to a fantasy where I'd meet somebody like him, only better, and start my life over, start myself over, and I'm looking at the rest of my own life with the same kind of clarity and letting go of Max while she says, *I still suspect there's been a mistake, but I'm the one who made it. I had the buckle in my hand, and I let go. I simply let it go. And so here I am.*

The picture is almost completely burned—it's mostly glowing embers now—and I have to drop it when the fire comes to the last corner, and her voice is fading, but I can still hear her: *Oh, listen. Do you hear that?*

—No.

Have you ever thought you heard someone call you from the next room, but nobody was there?

—Yes.

I've never given birth, but my part of what's happening feels like that, like my body is moving a human soul from one way of being to another, which is tearing me apart and making me whole, all in one strange moment, and Diana says, *Somebody was there, but it wasn't in the next room. It was right here. I'm hearing that voice, now, calling my name, and it sounds like music, like laughter, and the next room is a perpetually beautiful day.*

And a car rushes through the tunnel and the ashes from the photograph scatter in its wake and disappear and I feel her lift up out of me and pause the way you might stop to take a breath behind a curtain before you make your big entrance, and then for the tiniest fraction of a second I see a ghost of light, like what you see in front of you after a flash has gone off, and she's gone, but she's as close as the next universe, and the first thought that goes through my head is, —Wait! Wait for me.

I can just barely hear a car horn blaring toward me and I could take a small step into the street in front of it after her, and I want to, but I'm scared to, as well, and I close my eyes and in one fraction of a moment, I see everything I would see if I followed her into the street: I'm lifted out of the tunnel in a cocoon of light and my father calls my name and then I'm chasing fireflies in my grandmother's backyard, grabbing stars out of the night sky, holding them in my cupped hands, and I clench my teeth and try to talk without moving my lips while my mother says, Smile! and the camera flashes and I walk down the aisle at my candlelit wedding in my white dress, Dr. and Mrs. Lawrence Baxter, isn't she lovely, and I am lovely in a pair of glittered coat-hanger Christmas angel wings and a coat-hanger halo, so lovely as a ballerina, and I run through the yard in the rain while my mother calls, You'll get hit by lightning, is that what you want? and I open my mouth, yes, and drop my head back and spin until I fall on the ground and the rain tastes like sunlight on grass, my blood tastes like tears, and I light white candles on the dining-room table, I hear white noise, I see white headlights and white gold and a two-carat white diamond ring, and I hear, This is our Nobel laureate and hislovelywife, just lovely, and a door closing, a car door, and a bedroom door slamming shut, a glass shower door, shattering into a thousand pieces on the white tile floor, and I see a diamond watch on my wrist, the diamonds floating in its face like stars, spinning like galaxies, and I dance through galaxies, and my mother puts her tiara with rhinestones like stars on my head, and she says, Look in the mirror and imagine yourself, and I do.

And I see a car coming toward me, a pair of headlights, and I'm about to move into the light but my feet feel too heavy to move — they won't go forward — and I hear, *Don't!*

And the car passes, and I'm pressed against a pillar, as far away from the road as a person can be inside this tunnel.

I say, —Why the hell not?

But there's no answer, and another car comes and I try again, I take a step toward the street, and a horn blows so loud the air feels thick with its clatter and my arms won't move through it, I can barely breathe, and I can't get my feet to move off the median, and now the horn is ringing in my ears, and another car comes and goes and I do nothing but stand here and watch it pass, and then I'm crying hard, and I realize I have been for a while now. I'm letting something loose that's been pent up for ages, and I feel like I'm riding this thing in my body like a surfer on a wave, trying to keep from falling off.

I move back, away from the street, and a taxi passes with another car right behind it. I watch dozens of cars go by, maybe hundreds, until finally my body gives up and stops crying.

I'm empty now. I feel like I don't have a single teardrop left in my body, like the whole world could stop spinning around me and everybody I love could fall off the planet and I still wouldn't cry anymore. And I'm alone. Diana's gone, and she didn't come back to stop me—I see that now. I stopped myself, but not because I changed my mind. I stopped out of sheer animal fear of death.

I can't do this.

I get out the paper with the words "my mother" written on it and light a match to it, and it starts smoking and turning black and then bursts into flame, and I drop it onto the concrete and stand there watching until it's transformed itself into a crumpled wad of ashes.

I take a deep breath and exhale and press my spine against a cool pillar. I stay where I am, not moving a muscle, until there's a break in traffic, and I step out of the dark tunnel into a blindingly beautiful day.

WHEN I GET TO OUR ROOM AT THE RITZ, I OPEN A BOTTLE of chardonnay and pour myself a glass. I take two Percodans and wash them down with wine. Then I finish the glass and pour myself another. This one, I'll drink slowly.

I sit on the edge of the bed. I set the wine on the table,

next to the phone, and fold my hands together, as if in prayer. I hear something like static on a distant TV, and I close my eyes and see static. My head feels light and just a little fizzy and my whole body feels like I could lie down and sleep forever.

I open my eyes again, reach for my glass, and take a sip.

I sit here for a long time—I have no idea how long— eventually listening to somebody in the room next to ours, weeping. Or laughing. Or making love.

This is as far as I can see into my future: When my husband comes back, I'll still be sitting here. Maybe I'll have run a brush through my hair, put on fresh lipstick. Maybe not.

And even as I'm thinking this, I hear his key turning the lock, and the door opens, and he walks in and says, "Hi," and the door closes itself behind him.

I don't say anything.

He walks past me into the bathroom, setting his briefcase on the desk as he passes it.

His shoes are dusty. He smells of dust.

I don't follow him. I don't stand on the marble threshold, facing his back.

Instead, I take another sip of wine and set the glass back on the table.

I hear the water streaming from the faucet.

I hear him rinsing his hands, shutting off the tap.

Then, over his shoulder, he says, "How was your day?"

And I say, "Fine."